THE GLIMPSE

A Novel

After catching four unexpected glimpses of God,
Nick Conway realized he could no longer ignore him.

James C. Magruder

WESTBOW
P R E S S®
A DIVISION OF THOMAS NELSON
& ZONDERVAN

WestBow Press books may be ordered through booksellers or by contacting:

WestBow Press
A Division of Thomas Nelson & Zondervan
1663 Liberty Drive
Bloomington, IN 47403
www.westbowpress.com
1 (866) 928-1240

Because of the dynamic nature of the Internet, any web addresses or links contained in this book may have changed since publication and may no longer be valid. The views expressed in this work are solely those of the author and do not necessarily reflect the views of the publisher, and the publisher hereby disclaims any responsibility for them.

Any people depicted in stock imagery provided by Getty Images are models, and such images are being used for illustrative purposes only. Certain stock imagery © Getty Images.

ISBN: 978-1-9736-5027-0 (sc)
ISBN: 978-1-9736-5026-3 (hc)
ISBN: 978-1-9736-5028-7 (e)

Library of Congress Control Number: 2019900094

Print information available on the last page.

WestBow Press rev. date: 02/01/2019

DEDICATION

To Karen, my wife, my friend, and my continuous source of inspiration. This book was written, and is published, as a direct result of your enduring love and encouragement.

And to my parents, James and Rosemary Magruder, for being my Rock of Gibraltar and teaching me what a devoted marriage and a disciplined work ethic looks like.

ACKNOWLEDGEMENTS

Writing a novel is a daunting task with twists and turns, highs and lows, and starts and stops. Starting it was the easy part. Finishing it, the grueling part.

This novel is finished and in print today not because of the author, but because of the people who stood behind the author. I want to thank the people who inspired me, pushed me, and lifted me throughout this arduous journey: Karen, my wife, who contributed many fresh ideas and constant encouragement; David, my oldest son and his wife, Veronika, who challenged me to rewrite the original ending so it would be more enduring; Mark, my youngest son, and his wife Natalie who, by their lives, exemplify a "never give up" spirit. Thanks for pushing me forward.

To my siblings and their spouses for your steadfast love and reliable support: Kathii, Chris and Sue, Mary, Bob and Patti, Joanie and Ron. You were my first audience—and my continuing fan base.

To Jerry and Judi Tapp for challenging me to consider self-publishing this work to "get it out into the world" where it could have ministry value, and by God's grace, bring help or hope to readers.

To Jon and Kathy Beggs and Michelle and Jim Gross for being beta readers of this manuscript to help me find the flaws—and fix them.

My heartfelt thanks to Dr. Dave Dryer, my dear friend, who is practically my co-author. Thank you for ideas, insights, encouragement, and for believing in me, and this story, when I doubted myself. Your inspiration, friendship and creativity guided me down this long and winding path to publication. (We did it, Dave!)

CHAPTER 1

*When a relationship between a father and a son is dying,
must the son strive to keep it alive?*

*How does a son fill the hole in his heart when his father fails him?
And what, on earth, does he fill it with?*

Nick Conway mulled these questions early on a Saturday morning as snow fell outside his Chicago high-rise apartment. Steam curled from his coffee while he gazed out the window from the fifteenth floor and watched Lake Michigan churn ice cakes. He despised these near artic temperatures every February. He yearned for summer at his cottage in Lake Geneva, Wisconsin; there, on a balmy day, he could lose himself among the tourists, on the water, or in his thoughts as he strolled along the shore path with its spectacular views of homes that surrounded the lake.

Late yesterday Nick had been promoted to vice president and creative director at Morris, McGowan & Tate (MMT), a small advertising agency in downtown Chicago. On this frigid morning he let his mind wander to a place previously restricted: his past. He wondered if his father would be proud of his promotion. It was a fleeting thought. Who was he kidding? He would never talk to his father about this accomplishment. In fact, he would never talk to him about anything. As much as he wanted to, how could he? Especially since his father stole one thing from him even wealth couldn't replace: his childhood.

Nick reflected on the new account assignment that accompanied his promotion: Transitions Addiction Recovery Center. The client's goal was to help chemically dependent people recover their lives. Not exactly the kind of account Nick was passionate about.

For the past three years he had been creative director at MMT, and a good one. The agency had twenty-nine employees and forty-two million dollars in billings; chump change, compared to the big ad agencies in town, such as Leo Burnett, but Nick liked the small agency feel. Being the big fish in a small pond stroked his ego.

Transitions was an affiliate of Cook County General Healthcare System and, as the name implied, it was an opportunity to change; that is, if true change was really possible. Nick believed addiction recovery was nothing more than psychiatric services with temporary results neatly packaged in "feel-good" advertising. Underneath all of the superficial hope and glossy advertising, Nick was convinced Transitions Addiction Recovery Center was nothing more than a last-ditch effort for people who found themselves in the clutches of addiction.

Right or wrong, Nick felt "once an addict, always an addict" and "recovery" was just another politically correct warm and fuzzy word that advertising guys were paid to write. *After all,* he reasoned, *if addicts and alcoholics are always in a state of "recovery," then their lives really hadn't changed, had they?*

Nick knew, in the deep recesses of his heart, he wasn't always this cynical, but the age of innocence ended for him at age ten. Today, at thirty-nine, warm and compassionate were the last two words to describe this handsome, self-absorbed young advertising executive. Yet, if he could unwind the twisted path that had shaped his life, he might find his way back to what he could have been—what he should have been, if only he had a fair chance in childhood.

He poured himself another cup of coffee, took a sip, then checked for texts messages. He walked toward the windows of his apartment and staring far below, wondered if this promotion was really worth it. *Do I really want to immerse myself in* this *business? Addiction recovery services? Alcohol rehab? Please!*

CHAPTER

Monday morning came early, especially since Nick insisted on being at work at least an hour before his staff. He was finishing his third cup of coffee by the time they arrived. He grabbed the client briefs on the Transitions account and headed to the nine o'clock meeting with his creative team.

The team was small but talented. John Gesh, the account executive, was instrumental in landing the Transitions account. John was a bright, aggressive, and predictably arrogant guy. His competitive nature made him tough to get along with, but also a consummate salesman.

Allison Grant was Nick's art director. Creatively, she could marry words and pictures to make any ad sing. Right out of college they had worked together at Leo Burnett. At 37, Ally had long, rich, black hair, dark eyes, a warm smile and curves in all the right places. Resourceful, witty, and brutally honest, she wouldn't mince words if an ad concept wasn't fresh or a headline was dull, tired, or a cliché. Yet, she could trash an idea without trashing the person behind it.

Despite her frankness, she had a refreshing sense of humor and a warm sensitivity that drew people to her. Best of all, Ally was extremely passionate about things she believed in. If Ally bought into the client's commitment to addiction recovery, she would crank out compelling award-winning advertising.

A few years ago, Ally was the best thing that ever happened to Nick professionally and personally. Yet, like so many things in his life, he found a way to lose her.

Rounding out his creative team was Brett Stevens, a creative director and copywriter. Nick worked with Brett early in his career and envied his writing talent and his bright outlook on life. Before Brett married Karen, Nick secretly felt in competition with him. Brett's sandy blond hair, deep, penetrating blue eyes, beach boy good looks, and engaging personality captivated women.

Ally entered the conference room shortly after Nick. She stopped abruptly at the door when she noticed no one else was in the room.

"Hey, stranger," she said to break the awkward tension that flooded the room. "Congratulations on your promotion," she added with a stilted hesitation that made him question her sincerity, something he never did when they were a couple.

"Thanks." Nick looked up from his creative brief. When their eyes met Nick felt a sharp sting of regret. He hadn't worked with Ally during the three years he had been at MMT. They both had purposefully maneuvered their way around each other, finding convenient excuses to work on different accounts. Nick lived by a simple credo: it's much easier to ignore the past than to reconcile it—so he left more than one relationship in ruins.

Ally folded one leg under her as she sat in the swivel chair on the opposite end of the conference room table when Brett walked in.

"Sorry I'm late. Hey, congrats on your bump up, Nick." Brett extended his hand. He turned to Ally. "Hey, Ally."

"Good morning, everybody," John said, balancing his coffee

cup on top of four three-ring binders. "I've got the background on the Transitions account and updated creative briefs for everyone. Oh, by the way, nice promotion. The subtle cynical tone conveyed Nick's promotion was anything but earned.

"Thanks, John. You are largely responsible for it, you know. If you weren't bringing in so much new work, there wouldn't be opportunities for any of us."

"Oh, there still would be opportunities for *you*!" John asserted.

John may have intended the words to cut, and he felt their bite.

"Well, ah, let's get started," Nick said, clearing his throat. He stood and passed the meeting agenda to Brett. He took one and passed them to the others. John had posted charts and graphs from the client on the white boards and the smell of fresh coffee permeated the room.

"We have several goals today to launch this new account," Nick explained, "but our primary aim is to review the client brief and to meet Tom Sullivan, our client contact at Transitions. John has brought the background material, and Sam will stop in a few minutes to introduce us to Tom. John, will you get us started?"

"Let me start by walking you through the creative brief I e-mailed you late last week," John said. "As you can see, Transitions Addiction Recovery Center is a new service of Cook County General Healthcare System. Someday the Center would like to own a significant share of the addiction recovery services market."

Before John could continue, there was a light tap at the door, and Sam Morris walked in with the client.

"Good morning, everyone, I'd like you all to meet Tom Sullivan, vice president of marketing at Cook County General Healthcare," Sam announced. Tom was a bald, middle-aged man with a ring of red hair and kind, deep-set hazel eyes.

Nick invited Tom to have a seat while he introduced the team. Sam pulled up a chair next to him.

"We were just getting started but we've all read the creative brief and background. Now we'd like to hear directly from you since this Center was born from your personal vision. Why Transitions? Why now?"

Tom shuffled some papers in front of him. "Transitions was created based on the belief that the one thing ill people need most is hope. And not just the physically sick, but also the 'substance sick.' Nearly fourteen million Americans, or almost one in thirteen adults, abuse alcohol or is an alcoholic," Tom confided. "Alcohol and drug abuse are our nation's number one public health problems, and today more than 50 percent of men and women in America report that one or more of their close relatives has a drinking problem."

The moment these words left Tom's lips, Nick cringed and looked away. He wondered if anyone noticed his reaction.

"Tom, how much does alcohol abuse cost society economically?" Sam asked, interrupting Nick's train of thought.

Tom put the question to the team. "Anyone want to venture a guess?"

The team pondered the question as Nick glanced out the conference room window. As he feared, this discussion was beginning to make him squirm.

"Alcohol-related problems cost society about $185 billion per year," Tom answered. "Our mission at Transitions is simply to help people *transition* out of this addictive lifestyle and into full recovery. We hired your ad agency to help us communicate this mission to the Chicago community first. We want you to start by focusing our advertising on our alcohol recovery services."

When the meeting concluded, Nick realized he couldn't help but like this guy. He sincerely desired to make an impact in his corner of the world. Nevertheless, Nick felt there was a fine line between being sincere and being naïve.

When he walked back to his new office, he reminded himself that every business exists first and foremost to make money, not make a difference. So, despite Tom's warm demeanor and desire to help alcoholics, Nick wasn't buying it. One question plagued him: *Do I honestly believe in Tom and his let's-save-mankind mission, or have I just been suckered by a savvy salesman?*

CHAPTER

It was five o'clock on Friday afternoon, and Nick leaned back in his office chair, yawned and stretched toward the ceiling. *Man, I'm tired. The weekend is here—finally.*

It had been a long week. Since Monday he had directed two photo shoots, conceived a dozen ads with Ally, proofread and edited a ton of copy, and pitched some new business with John. And, of course, he immersed himself in getting to know the addiction recovery services offered by Transitions.

Nick loved the advertising business, but by the end of the week he had contributed more than his share to corporate America and the free enterprise system. He had taken enough work home that week to have worked a double shift. That's why he never brought work home on weekends. It was his personal policy to own these sacred two days. Even a workaholic knows where to draw the line.

As Nick poured over ad copy on his computer screen, Brett tapped on his door. It was slightly ajar, and he let himself in.

"Hey, Nick. Did you get the strategy brief and initial ad concepts I e-mailed you for the Transitions account?"

"Yeah, but I haven't reviewed them yet," he replied, never looking up from his monitor.

"No problem. Just let me know when you want to discuss them. I'd like to get your input before I finalize the headlines, generate rough body copy, and route my ideas to the team."

"I'll give you some feedback Monday morning, okay?"

"Monday is fine. Oh, by the way, thanks for inviting me to work on the Transitions account. I think it's going to be intriguing. Ally and I think our work could make a difference." Brett was considered one of the finest copywriters in the country. His portfolio included work on several national brands such as Nike, Microsoft, Sony and Coca-Cola and several health care facilities. After stints in Phoenix, Atlanta, Chicago and New York, Brett and his family came back to Chicago. The Midwest better suited him, Karen and their two young boys.

Nick stopped reading, turned abruptly and faced Brett, who had settled into one of his guest chairs. "You think you can make a difference? Really? To whom?"

"Who do you think?" Brett replied, putting his feet up on the coffee table and clasping his hands behind his head.

"Brett, you're starting to sound like Tom. You and Ally really think we're going to make a meaningful difference in the life of an alcoholic?"

"That's our objective, isn't it? Start them on the road to recovery and a better life by encouraging them to seek help at Transitions."

"Look, I know you're a religious man, and you want to believe the best in people—and I have always admired that—but the only difference we're going to make is the amount of money the client rakes in if we somehow inspire alcoholics to seek treatment at their facility."

"What are you saying?"

"All I am saying is Transitions is an account like any other account. And while it may have high ideals, its motives are the same—to make a buck! Our job is not to help Transitions change lives, it's to help them make money, and we do that by motivating alcoholics to get help."

"Yes, but once they get help, they have a good chance to beat their addictions and get their lives back."

"I don't want to burst your bubble, but you don't understand how hard it is to alter people who are already under the influence."

"Nick, you really surprise me sometimes," Brett said indignantly as he leaned forward to emphasize his point. "Are you really that uncompassionate?"

"Are you really that naïve?"

Brett shook his head, and Nick wondered what surprised him more—that he was so uncompassionate toward alcoholics or that someone this uncaring was asked to lead *this* account.

"Let's face it, Brett, despite what Tom told us, Transitions is in business to put its Addiction Recovery Center on the map and make money doing it—the Mayo Clinic of Addiction Recovery Centers, right? They're not in business to save people and change the world. Although that makes for good PR..."

Ally stepped in when he was in mid-sentence. It didn't take long before she interjected.

"What's the matter, Nick? You still believe that the profit motive drives everything and no one will ever contribute anything to this world if they can't make a buck doing it?"

"Thanks for the nice summary, Ally! Please tell me you don't think Transitions is in business for any other reason than to make money. Yes, they say they want to help people in the process, but their primary objective is to generate income, lots of it.

"And the minute this endeavor becomes unprofitable they will get out of this business. Face it, Transitions is nothing more than a separate profit center for Cook County General Healthcare System."

Ally rolled her eyes and then came back at Nick with both barrels. "Yes, helping people recover is how Transitions makes its money, and, yes, it's a business and separate profit center," she admitted. "But I believe there are *some* people in this world, like Tom Sullivan, who want to make a difference in this life despite the fact that they can also earn an honest living doing it. Do physicians choose a medical career for the sole purpose of becoming rich?"

"Yes, essentially," Nick said, fanning the flame that was about to set the room ablaze. Nick continued. "It's not just about the profit motive. What I really can't understand is why anyone, Tom included, would choose *this* career—addiction recovery! I mean, who would want to dedicate his life to helping alcoholics? Alcoholism is like a self-inflicted gunshot wound! Why would you want to help those kinds of people?"

The room fell silent. Nick's last four words hung in the air like humidity on a hot, sticky August afternoon: *those kinds of people.* Ally and Brett stared at him in disbelief. Suddenly, he felt like a bigot.

Nick wasn't quite sure why those words rolled out of his mouth, at least that way. His comment was anything but politically correct. But what troubled him most was he knew Brett and Ally could see through him.

There was something else behind his remark. Something deep and dark that had been carefully tucked in the recesses of his heart for a very long time. Before Nick could conjure up some excuse for his remark, Ally spoke.

"Nick, you haven't changed a bit. You're just as stubborn, opinionated and cynical as ever," she said, dragging their past into the room. She never accepted his excuses.

"Well, it's almost six and it's Friday," Brett said, changing the subject. "What's everybody doing this weekend?" His question could not diffuse the tension in the room.

"Nothing much," Ally said, turning her back to Nick and walking toward the window.

"I'm going to head to my lake house in Wisconsin," Nick offered, to keep the conversation from returning to his stupid remark.

"Lake Geneva is a great summer town—but in the winter? What can you do up there now?" Brett asked.

"There's plenty to do in winter. In fact, this weekend is the National Snow Sculpting Competition."

"So, you and a couple of guys build a snowman and snap a few pictures?" Brett said with a laugh.

"Very funny! It's actually a very big deal, Brett."

"Yeah, I know. I've seen some of those ice sculpture contests. Everybody gets a three-foot block of ice and a chainsaw, and they go crazy."

"Think bigger than that, Brett. This competition draws fifteen three-member teams from Alaska to Florida. Each team gets a block of snow, not ice, six feet wide by six feet long by ten feet high. They carve for three days. Almost thirty thousand people roll into town to watch this thing."

Ally cooled down and turned to face Nick. "Sounds like fun," she said. She relaxed her brow. "You really love Lake Geneva, don't you, Nick?"

"I do. And despite the fact I hate winter, I still enjoy the area year-round. There is always something to do. In addition to the snow sculpting, this weekend there is the Winter Carnival, a torch-light ski parade, fireworks, and helicopter tours of the area."

"I remember you talking about wanting to buy a lake house several years ago," Ally said, remembering one of the better days of their past together. "So, the lake house isn't just a great investment for you; it's a great escape for you."

"Exactly. I love to go there when I need to get out of the city and regain my sanity."

"Well, in that case, maybe you should make the trip daily," she quipped.

"Cheap shot."

"Are you sure you didn't buy the house just so you could make a big profit when you sell it someday? I mean, isn't that what life is all about, making a profit?" Ally glanced at Brett.

"Touché."

"Well, I'll let you guys go at it," Brett said, as he got up and walked toward the door. "I'm going to go home to see Karen and the kids. Have a great weekend. Don't get frostbite, Nick."

When Brett left the room Nick and Ally stood facing each other in silence. Although he didn't realize it, Brett had become a social cushion for Nick and Ally, providing emotional insulation between them. When Brett was in the room everything felt safe. When he left the room, both Nick and Ally felt the awkward vulnerability of a first date.

Suddenly, neither of them knew what to say. Nick had not been in a room alone with Ally for years. He expected her to leave, but she lingered.

To suppress the discomfort, she crossed her arms and walked to the window again. With her back to Nick, she gazed at a city of lights thirty-one floors below.

Nick had learned over the course of his life that there are moments you own and moments you must submit to. When you don't own the moment, it's best to remain silent. Never risk losing the moment by interrupting it.

This moment was owned by Ally. If he spoke too soon, he could influence or alter its outcome. The silence was unnerving, but he waited for her to speak first.

He wondered why she lingered. What was she thinking, feeling? There was so much she could say—and so much he needed to say. He held his breath and wondered if she would use this moment to redeem the past or condemn it. For three years he had left too much unsaid, undone, unraveled. He churned the loose change in his pocket. Ally slowly turned to face him. The moment would define itself with her next sentence. Her arms were firmly folded. She walked toward Nick, yet stared at the floor. Finally, she spoke.

"Nick," she said, avoiding his gaze. She struggled for the next words. "I hope you..."

Before she could finish her sentence, he felt a sudden rush of adrenaline. *She is going to tell me what a fool I am for what I said a few minutes ago. Can I bear that?* Yet, as abruptly as a thief snatches a purse,

13

Nick snatched the moment from her by interrupting and finishing her sentence.

"Ally, I hope you..." he paused ever so slightly, "...have a great weekend, too."

Their eyes met, Ally ran her hand through her shiny black hair to pull a strand behind her ear. "Yeah," she said, conceding the moment. "Have a nice weekend. See you Monday." Then she left the room.

Nick shut down his computer when Ally got in the elevator. He stared at the blank screen. *Why couldn't I have kept my mouth shut—at least for another thirty seconds? What did she really want to say before I cut her off?*

He got his coat out of the closet and grabbed his car keys on the back credenza. He waited for the elevator, realizing he had just stolen a moment that could have, in some small way, altered his life or at least his relationship with Ally. And he knew he might never get that moment back.

It was early Saturday morning as Nick made the ninety-minute trek from his Chicago high-rise apartment to the lake house. Lake Geneva was a quaint little town nestled in southeastern Wisconsin. It had a scenic drive once arriving in Wisconsin, especially on Highway 12 which ran along the city's eastern border.

Ally was right, the lake house was not just a good investment; it was an escape from just about everything that troubled Nick. At this stage of his life, he was clearly troubled. The daily deadlines of the advertising business were crushing; he agonized over the notion of restoring his relationship with his estranged father; he had never fully reconciled the death of his mother; he had sacrificed his relationship with Ally for the worst of reasons; and he was facing the prospect of spending his fortieth birthday this August alone.

A man measures his life against many landmarks but none as

daunting as his fortieth birthday. This midlife milestone is a brutal time as he measures his success not only against his fellow man, but worse, against the unforgiving expectations he had for himself. Job, home, wife, and family, boxes to check off. To leave any one empty was, well, to admit that one's life was empty in that area too.

Nick made his way into the city knowing parking would be a mess. The beauty of the lake and the surrounding area drew too many tourists, most of whom, to the chagrin of the locals, were from Illinois. Illinois money had snatched up much of the land, and every summer the tourists just south of the Wisconsin border dominated the lake, the beach and downtown. They were known as "flatlanders" and they were paid the big money Illinois offers anyone willing to work in a state overpopulated with potholes, tollways and people prone to road rage.

Nick couldn't tolerate flatlanders—even though he was a flatlander Monday through Friday. Perhaps it was because they reminded him of that long, lost relative who stops in for an unexpected visit but forgets to leave. Or, perhaps it was because they sauntered around as though they owned the place and treated the locals like tourists.

He couldn't blame them. They came for the same reasons he did: to lose themselves on a lake during the dog days of summer. Nick loved the anonymity he felt when he walked Main Street on a balmy summer day, licking an ice cream cone and casually slipping in and out of quaint coffee shops, apparel stores and art galleries. But today was far from summer with temperatures dipping to fifteen degrees.

He found a parking spot just off Main Street and turned his attention to grabbing a cup of hot chocolate at Kilwin's Ice Cream and Chocolate Shoppe. From there it was a short walk to Riviera Park on the lakefront where the teams were completing their snow sculptures.

Despite the temperature, it was a beautiful day. Nothing but blue sky and sunshine. Riviera Park was crawling with people, and Nick wormed his way through the crowd to gaze at the imaginative snow sculptures.

The steam from his hot chocolate warmed his face. He held the cup with both hands and sipped frequently as he meandered between ten-foot dinosaur, dragon, sea tortoise and ice castle sculptures.

The temperature plummeted by early afternoon, and the crowd thinned. He walked back to his BMW and headed to the lake house.

Nestled on the west side of the lake, the lake house was quaint and unassuming from the street. It featured a French Country elevation with a cultured stone gable as its centerpiece.

Nick pulled into the driveway, grabbed his duffel bag from the trunk and walked through the front door. The east side of the house was a wall of windows that faced the lake. The great room had a couch and loveseat that formed an "L" shape and sat adjacent to a gas fieldstone fireplace that ran from the floor to the ten-foot ceiling and featured a rustic oak mantel.

Sliding glass doors led to a cedar deck perched above a patio. The deck and patio offered a breathtaking view of the lake and an idyllic setting to read, write or work on a summer tan.

He visualized a summer view for a few minutes, then popped open a beer, cranked up the furnace and flipped on the gas fireplace to quell the chill in the air. He had plenty of groceries from last weekend, so he prepared for a relaxing afternoon and evening.

Beer in hand, he wandered into the great room, grabbed the multi-colored afghan from the ottoman in the corner and plopped onto the couch. He put his feet up on the coffee table and spread the afghan to cover his legs and feet. The afghan had a tattered edge on one side. He turned the tattered edge toward him and, as he always did, pulled it up so it would rest closest to his heart.

He took another sip of his beer and told himself, *this* is why he worked so hard. Yet, as he looked over the lake with glistening ice and snow capping its surface, he couldn't ignore the obvious. *I own all of this—and I have no one to share it with.*

The furnace hummed and the fireplace took the edge off the room. His mind wandered back to his conversation with Ally the previous night—or what should have been a conversation.

Perhaps he was kidding himself if he thought she would say anything remotely positive. After all, he must have come off as a chump last night.

There he was pontificating about the motives of Tom Sullivan and the Transitions staff. *All they care about is profits, not people. And who would want to dedicate their life to helping alcoholics? Alcoholism is like a self-inflicted gunshot wound. Why would you want to help those kinds of people?*

Nick couldn't believe he had said all that stuff, and to say it to his account team, of all people. He wondered if he came across as a raving lunatic or a hypocrite. *I'm sure they're wondering how I can manage the Transitions account if I have no faith in the client's addiction recovery services and no compassion for its patients.*

He played with some possibilities of what Ally was going to say: "Nick, I hope you...know you're a fool!" Or, "Nick, I hope you...know you should step down from this account." Or, worse, "I hope you...realize that working together again doesn't change a thing---and never will."

The afternoon gave way to evening and the sunset behind him cast an orange glow over the lake. He turned on the reading lamp and could feel his body winding down to relax from the long week. He debated getting up and making dinner. Hunger prevailed over comfort, and he eventually got off the couch.

With the dipping temperature, he knew it had to be a soup night. He heated a pot of tomato soup until it boiled and burned a grilled cheese sandwich. "Crispy, just the way I like it," he tried to convince himself. Not exactly a gourmet meal, but it was a menu that always brought a measure of comfort on a cold winter night.

The tomato soup started a chain reaction in his thought process. It made him think of his mother, who used to make him tomato soup whenever he was sick; his mother made him think of his father; and his father was inexorably linked to alcohol.

He slipped back into a comfortable position on the couch, put his feet up and pulled the tattered edge of the multi-colored afghan up to his neck. Then he peered into the darkness outside.

I'm tired of the excuses and the abuses of the alcoholic lifestyle. The truth is an alcoholic has no excuse. Yes, life is hard. So, get a grip. Don't wallow in your circumstances and expect alcohol to help you cope.

He paused in his customary mental tirade on alcoholism, and in the quietness of the lake house he pondered how much his father had alienated him.

As the night wore on, he relished the relaxation, but he felt conflicted. The more he tried to confront his feelings about his father, the more he found fault with himself.

Nick let his mind drift back to better times—when his mom was alive and he didn't have to deal with his father alone. He was eight and he had come home sick from school. In truth, he wasn't sick at all, maybe just homesick for his mother.

I loved being home alone with Mom. She had an easy smile; a joyful outlook and a radiance that made me feel better by just being in the same room with her. All I wanted that day was for her to wrap one arm around me, read me a story, and let me drift off to sleep on her shoulder.

Unfortunately, his father came home from work early after being laid off earlier that morning. Times were tough, and in tough times his father was always the first one let go—for obvious reasons.

Nick and his mother saw him coming up the front walk and knew he was drunk. He stumbled at the front door then fumbled for his keys. His mother usually kept the front door locked; so, she could observe his condition and have time to adjust accordingly.

"Nicky, let's go to your bedroom—quickly now," she said as she put her hand on his shoulder and pushed him toward his room. She swung open the closet door and shoved him in. Gripped by indecision, she turned toward the front door and listened for the click of the deadbolt. When the door creaked open, she heard him bellow her name. Suddenly, her indecision evaporated and she squeezed into the closet swiping at his clothes to separate them so they could hide behind them. She quietly closed the closet door and covered their feet with dirty clothes from the hamper.

"Rose," he roared, his voice getting louder as he approached my room. "Rose! Woman, where are you?" His words were slurred as he stood in the doorframe. Then silence.

Rose gently pulled Nick's head tight against her chest. He could hear her heart pounding and smell the sweet fragrance of her perfume. Her scent calmed him, but he wondered if his father could smell it too.

"Rose?" he said softly. Nick couldn't tell if it was a statement or a question. Did his father know they were in the closet?

Nick's heart raced. He grew numb. *He knows we're in the closet!* They both held their breath.

Sensing his fear, she gently stroked his hair. Her soft strokes slowed his pounding heart.

"Rose!" he shouted again, this time his voice projected away from them. Nick could see his father's bulky figure through the louvers in the closet door. He turned toward the hallway and lumbered down the corridor to the living room. She kissed the top of his head.

"Nicky, stay right here. Don't come out, no matter what you hear. Remember, your father doesn't know you're home from school."

"Where are you going, Mom?" he whispered, as he tightened his grip around her waist.

"Just stay right here until I come to get you," she instructed. Then she quietly slipped out of the room and hid in the front hall closet. Eventually, his father found her. Nick heard him open the front hall closet door and curse her like a man spurned. After her attempts to reason with him failed, Nick heard him vent his frustration and blame her for his job loss.

Nick wept quietly as he trembled in the closet. Peering through the louvers he saw their confrontation. She didn't back down and she lured him away from the bedroom closet. Nick crouched in the darkness and realized why she left the safety of the bedroom closet. She was protecting him. She knew he would eventually go through every closet, but once he found Rose, he wouldn't look for the boy.

Lost in his thoughts, Nick fast-forwarded to his mother's car accident two years later. He had kept the newspaper account under the glass on his desk in his home office for years. It was his way to help ensure that his anger would simmer forever and help him never to forgive his father. Today, the clipping resided somewhere in a musty box in the basement of the lake house. However, the newspaper article was eternally etched in his memory.

Last night Rose Conway, 40, was critically injured when the car she was driving was struck by a drunk driver on Rawley Road. Jack Randall, 47, reportedly left Tully's Tavern just after midnight, lost control of his pick-up truck on a sharp curve, crossing the center line and striking Conway head-on. Conway was reportedly on her way to Tully's to pick up her husband. Conway was taken to Cook County General Hospital where she is in critical condition. Randall was treated and released..."

Rose died a few days later. To this day, Nick has never read her obituary. He was not sure why. Perhaps to cope. Or, maybe it was his way of keeping her alive—at least in his memory.

Before Nick drifted off to sleep, he recalled Brett's question in his office yesterday, "Are you really that uncompassionate?" When it came to alcoholics like his father, Nick concluded that his answer was "yes."

CHAPTER 4

Nick awoke the next morning face down on the couch. He could feel the fabric pattern etched in his face. Groggy, he turned over on his back and squinted as the sun splashed through the windows. He looked at his watch.

It was 9:17. He couldn't believe he had slept straight through the night. It was another benefit of the lake house—total relaxation. He took a long stretch before he got up, turned off the gas fireplace he had inadvertently left on all night, and shuffled to the bathroom.

After a shower and shave he went to the front porch and picked up the Sunday paper. He brewed a fresh pot of coffee, scanned the paper for breakfast deals, and opted for Sunday brunch at the Grand Geneva Resort.

After browsing through the paper, he made the fifteen-minute drive. The Grand Geneva was an elegant resort. It not only had fine restaurants, a sports center and spa, it also had two championship golf courses. But Nick loved it for its natural beauty—rolling hills and spectacular scenic views.

In the summer he enjoyed having lunch outside on the café patio near the pool. The patio was set high above a golf course, a sprawling tree line and a spectacular man-made pond.

He waited only about fifteen minutes for the hostess to seat him at a window table overlooking the snow-covered golf course. The café was bustling. After his waitress introduced herself, he dispensed of the menu and ordered the Sunday brunch buffet and a large orange juice.

Famished, he got in line and started with a Denver Omelet, cooked the way he liked it. He added home fries, a few slices of bacon, and two sausages. He passed on the pancakes, waffles, bran flakes and toast, but grabbed a blueberry yogurt, bagel and cream cheese. When he sat, his waitress placed his orange juice on the table. He unfolded the green cloth napkin, spread it over his lap and began his feast. It was a beautiful Sunday morning and it was one of those days where his body felt as though it earned the breakfast. Everything tasted really good.

He sliced his bagel and noticed the party at the table directly in front of him. A man who appeared about his age sat with an elderly man whom he assumed was his father. The son's back was to him, and his father sat across from him. Nick could see the old man's face. He appeared to be in his late seventies. The old man's jowls flapped when he talked and reminded Nick of a bloodhound. He had thin white hair and wrinkles creased his forehead. His eyes were set deep and accentuated his long, pointed nose.

At first Nick could not hear their conversation, but the father's voice escalated as they talked. Nick spread cream cheese on his bagel and pretended not to listen.

"What time is it?" the old man asked.

"Eleven-fifteen," the son answered.

"When are we going to eat?"

"We're eating now, Dad."

"I'm not eating," the elder man replied as he chewed his food.

Nick glanced out the window and listened to this unusual conversation. In a feeble attempt to protect their privacy, Nick looked away but he could not rationalize the fact that he was eavesdropping. The old man's voice continued to escalate.

"When are we going to eat?"

"We're eating now, Dad," the son repeated.

The questions continued. The old man clearly had his own view of reality. Nick noticed the old timer had three collars. He was wearing a flannel pajama top under two shirts. The elderly man began to look around the room nervously and tapped his watch.

"What time is it now?" he asked, impatiently.

The son looked at his watch. "It is 11:20," he warmly explained as he cut his pancake.

"When are we going to eat?" he yelled.

Before the son could reply, the old man suddenly changed the subject.

"Where are we now?"

"We are having breakfast at the Grand Geneva Resort."

Fear suddenly swept over the old man's face. "Who are you, again?"

The son reached over the table and lovingly took his father by the hand. "I'm your son. Don't worry, you're safe with me."

The old man pointed at his son and cracked a relieved smile. "I have known you for a very long time, right?"

"Yes, you have."

"I really love you," the old man said, during a fleeting moment of comprehension.

"And I love you, Dad, more than you know."

The old man continued to repeat his questions and Nick was struck by the kindness in the son's voice. He seemed never to tire of answering the same questions over and over again. When the father became angrier, the son became more compassionate, speaking in gentle tones as if he was talking to a child.

As their conversation continued, Nick caught himself

staring now to see how this drama would unfold. The old timer's face telegraphed the direction his feelings were headed. He vacillated between anger and fear.

"Where are we now?" he asked sheepishly.

"We are at your favorite restaurant."

"Do you know how to get home? I don't know if I can find my way." Nick could hear the old man's tone shift from anger to anxiety.

"You live with Julie, the kids and me now, Dad. There is nothing to worry about."

"Will you take me home now?" the old man asked, with the innocence of a lost boy.

"Of course. Julie and the kids are in the gift shop, when they return, we can go home. Why don't you eat the rest of your eggs?"

The waitress broke Nick's concentration on the one-act play before him. "Would you like some more orange juice, sir?"

"Yes, thank you."

"Can I get you anything else this morning?"

"Just my bill."

She reached in her apron and pulled out the tab and set it on the table. "You can pay me when you're ready," she said, as she walked to the old man's table.

"Would you like some more juice here?"

"*No!* We're going home," he yelled and then he raised his hand to strike her. Instinctively, she reeled but his hand struck the pitcher, sending it crashing into his son's chest, drenching his sweater and pants. The pitcher landed on the table as juice cascaded over the edge. The son jumped to his feet and reached for his cloth napkin to blot his sweater and pants. Alarmed by the sudden confusion, the old man began to yell just as the son's wife and kids returned from the gift shop.

"Julie, honey, will you take Dad to the car for me? I need to clean this up and pay the bill."

"What happened this time?" she asked, exasperated.

"More of the same. Please help him to the car."

"Let's go home, Dad," Julie coaxed warmly.

"Come on, Grandpa," the kids chimed in as they helped him rise and slip on his coat.

The waitress grabbed several cloth napkins and started to mop up the mess.

"Let me help," the younger man said, and bent to assist her.

"I'll get more napkins," the waitress replied and headed to the kitchen.

Nick grabbed three napkins from the place settings on his table and offered his assistance.

"May I help?" Nick asked, as he squatted beside the man to help wipe up the spill. He could see the embarrassment in the man's face. Nick tossed the saturated napkins on the table. In the meantime, the waitress returned with several more.

"I think we got the worst of it," the man said. "Could I get my bill?"

"I'll be right back with that," the waitress said, and she disappeared to the kitchen again.

The man turned to Nick. "Thanks for your help."

"No problem." Nick paused not knowing what to say. "I'm sorry about your father."

"Alzheimer's," he said with a stone face. "It's a terrible disease. If it doesn't kill the patient, it will kill the caregivers."

"Must be tough," Nick said sympathetically. "I couldn't help but notice how you treated him while you were eating. How do you do it?"

"I try to put myself in his situation, I guess. Imagine what it's like to forget virtually everything."

"I can't imagine."

He looked at his waist and then dabbed his sweater and pants with another napkin. "Do you know what the hardest thing is?"

Caught by surprise, Nick answered with a simple, "No."

"It's realizing that he is afraid most of the time—and there is nothing I can do about it."

"What do you mean?"

"Alzheimer's patients live in fear much of the time because of what they no longer know. Think about it. They don't know who *they* are. They don't know who *you* are. And they don't know *where* they are. And if they don't know where they are, they feel lost. Imagine feeling lost *all* the time, even in your own home. And there is no way to console him because I'm a stranger, too!"

Nick could hear the pain and compassion in his voice but was helpless to encourage him. "He must have been a great father," he said, hoping it would comfort the man or help end the conversation.

The man smiled and said, "You would think so." Nick wondered what he meant and waited for him to offer more.

"Actually, in good health, he was a bit of a tyrant. Mom held the family together—and died doing it."

"I know what you mean."

"Oh, does your father have Alzheimer's, too?"

"No, he has a different disease, but let's just say it devastated the family, too." Nick's comment created a long pause as they continued to mop up the mess. Nick broke the silence with a question.

"If your dad was so tough on you, why are you so good to him?" *I can't believe I just asked a perfect stranger such a personal question.*

The man wiped the seat of his chair with the last napkin. "When he first got sick, I wasn't so good to him," he confessed. "I wanted to put him in a home and abandon him—to give him what he deserves. But one day my wife asked me a question that nagged me for months."

Nick waited for him to continue but he stopped short and grabbed the wet napkins on the floor and piled them on the table.

"If you don't mind me asking, what did she ask you?"

The man paused and then looked Nick in the eye before he answered. "Just because he wasn't a good father, does that mean you shouldn't be a good son?"

Nick felt the blunt force of his statement as the man turned to leave. It was personal. It was painful. And it scored a direct hit to his heart. Yet, he wondered if what he was feeling was compassion or guilt.

CHAPTER

Morning in the high-rise came early, too early, and the relaxing weekend at the lake house made rousing from bed on Monday a little bit like waking from the dead.

Nick was surprisingly late. It was 9:22 by the time he got in, and the office was already teeming with activity. Typically, Nick's coworkers would still be pouring another cup of coffee and catching up on weekend gossip, but today was different. John landed some new clients, and they would be in for ten o'clock briefing meetings with the creative teams. People were finalizing their presentations, putting on their game faces and tidying up the office.

Nick was late for a meeting he had scheduled for the Transitions account team. He quickly walked to his office, grabbed his creative briefs and Brett's headline concepts he never got a chance to read, then headed to the conference room.

When he walked in, Brett, John and Ally were waiting. Ally

was rocking back and forth in her swivel chair sipping her coffee while Brett posted rough layouts around the perimeter of the room. John was scanning the conference report from their last meeting.

"Sorry I'm late."

"No problem, we've got nothing else to do today," John snipped.

"You should have a personal policy about being late, especially for your own meetings," Ally chided.

Brett laughed. "Yeah, you seem to have a personal policy for everything else."

John felt compelled to throw in his two cents. "Have you ever noticed how Nick's personal policies always seem to benefit only him?"

"It's a strange phenomenon isn't it, Nick?" Ally teased.

"Okay, okay, you've made your point."

"I don't think he's going to be late for any more of his meetings," Brett added. "Nick, you didn't miss anything. We just talked about how we spent our weekend."

"Did you enjoy Lake Geneva?" Ally inquired. "Did the snowmen live up to your expectations?"

"Snow sculptures! And, yes, they did. In fact, my favorite, the dinosaur, won the competition."

"Well, if you're so good at picking winners, you can pick the winning headline for the Transitions account," John said, changing the subject.

"Great, let's see them."

"I wrote separate headlines to address both the alcoholic and the alcoholic's family," Brett explained. "Nick, did you get a chance to review them this weekend?"

"No, I never take work home on weekends."

"Oh, yeah. You have a personal policy against working weekends at home." Ally laughed. "Maybe *I* should create a personal policy to get out of work, too."

"Very funny." Nick retorted. "Let's see what you've got, Brett."

Brett pointed out Concept A and the layout Ally had created for his headlines.

"Concept A addresses the alcoholic. Research shows that people most likely to have a sustained recovery are those who admit they have a problem and are willing and motivated to seek help," Brett explained. "So, in Concept A we addressed this head-on with this headline: *The Difference Between Alcohol Addiction & Recovery is Admission.*"

Brett turned and faced Nick waiting for his reaction.

"So, what do you think, chief?" Ally inquired as she continued to rock in her chair.

Nick leaned back, stroked his chin and read it out loud. *The Difference Between Alcohol Addiction & Recovery is Admission.*

"I like it. I particularly like the double meaning."

"That works for me, too," John added. "If the alcoholic will admit to himself, he has a problem and then admit himself to Transitions Addiction Recovery Center, he has the best chance to recover."

Nick turned to Ally. "Talk to me about your layout."

"Well, as Brett mentioned, it is a very direct approach," she said. "The ad will feature a photo of a man with bloodshot eyes looking directly in a mirror. He clearly has a problem and realizes he must confront it, and the only way to confront it is to admit it."

"It's nice, Ally. I like it."

Nick always seemed to like Ally's work. Perhaps because it fueled his career. He quickly earned accolades for their early work together out of college on Kellogg's, Visa, and Hallmark accounts. More than once, Ally transformed Nick's early ads into award-winning creative work. She did the work, and he took the bows.

"But?" Ally said, raising her eyebrows and waiting for the other shoe to drop.

"But we need to be careful how we portray this guy. Let's not go over the top. He or she could be a very high-functioning alcoholic and look like you or me. He or she does not have to be the stereotypical, glassy-eyed alcoholic."

"Good point," Brett agreed. "We'll be careful how we portray him *and* her. We'll run separate ads, one featuring a male and one featuring a female alcoholic."

"What about your camera angle on this guy? Ally, were you thinking about shooting high, low, straight-on or close-up?"

"I thought we would shoot high. That will create a feeling of vulnerability and insecurity."

"I agree. What else have you got, Brett?"

Brett turned to the layouts again and explained Concept B.

"We continued our focus on the importance of an alcoholic admitting he has a problem in these next two samples. Using the same visual of the alcoholic facing himself in the mirror, the headline in Concept B reads: *Does Alcohol Addiction Have a New Face—Yours?*

"Wow." Nick said.

"Do you like it?" Ally asked curiously.

"Well," Nick said, pausing. "It's direct! Remember, we want to encourage this guy to admit he has a problem, not intimidate him or slap a guilt trip on him."

John pushed back. "Nick, I think alcoholics have to be addressed directly," he said, defending the creative approach.

"Yes, but I think this approach is too direct. Can we soften it a bit and have a more creative hook?"

"I think Brett nailed that in Concept C," Ally offered.

"Okay, let's see Concept C."

Brett continued. "Once again, Concept C features the visual of the alcoholic facing himself in the mirror. The headline reads: *The First Step to Overcoming Alcohol Addiction is to Look it in the I.*"

Nick leaned back in his chair, clasped his hands behind his head and pondered the headline.

"I really like Concept C, Nick," Ally interjected. "It works for me because of the play on words with the capital 'I.' We could even shorten this headline to read: *Look Alcohol Addiction in the I.* And this concept really supports our *admission* strategy."

"I think it works too," John agreed, "because it subtly forces the alcoholic to look at himself and take responsibility for his addiction."

Despite John's praise, Brett and Ally held their breath and waited for Nick's opinion. The room was quiet and Nick thoughtfully scanned all layouts. Finally, he spoke.

"I like Concept C. It has what is missing in Concept B. It is direct but not 'in your face.' And I love the creative hook. Brett, where are you going with the body copy for Concept C?"

"Well, we would play off of the 'I' in the headline. The body copy could start like this: *Do you see an alcoholic when you look in the mirror? If not, you may have a problem with your I-sight. The first step to overcoming alcohol addiction is to look it in the 'I.' By admitting I have an alcohol problem. I need help. I can't solve this alone...*

"From here the copy will segue to how Transitions Addiction Recovery Center can help," Brett concluded.

"Perfect," Nick replied enthusiastically. "Let's present only Concepts B and C to the client. After we successfully complete the alcoholism phase of the campaign, we can easily adapt Concept C for the other addictions treated at Transitions. For example, the headline could then read: *The First Step in Overcoming Drug Addiction is to Look it in the I.*"

There was a tap on the door, and Sam Morris stuck his head in. "Excuse me, Nick. I need to borrow John for awhile. Some new clients are in to see us. John, can you join me?"

John congratulated Brett and Ally for hitting a home run and excused himself.

"How are you coming on Phase Two campaign headlines aimed at loved ones of an alcoholic?" Nick asked.

"Brett roughed out some headline concepts, and I'm working on layouts now," Ally said. "They should be ready for our next meeting."

"Great! I guess we can adjourn."

"So, when are you going to tell us more about your weekend in Wisconsin's Winter Wonderland?" Ally taunted.

Brett started to take down the layouts and joined the fray. "Yeah, I'd like to hear more about that lake house."

"Okay, let's do lunch sometime," Nick retorted, knowing it might never be arranged.

"What's everybody doing for lunch today?" Brett countered as he stacked the layout boards.

"I'm open," Ally offered and turned to Nick.

Nick was caught off guard. He typically tried to distance himself from his co-workers, especially when they reported to him on key accounts. It was another of the personal policies he created after he had gotten burned. Nick never was very good at juggling friendships with direct reports. And then, of course, he hadn't had lunch with Ally for a few years. Yet, he wondered why she was willing to have lunch with him again.

"Fine, let's have lunch today," he agreed. "Let's meet in the lobby at 11:45. Ally, you pick the restaurant."

Ally picked Maurice's, a quaint little Italian cafe on Michigan Avenue, within walking distance from the ad agency.

They barely beat the lunch crowd and were seated immediately in the back room where it was quiet and conducive to conversation. Ally and Brett sat across from Nick. When their waitress arrived, they ordered soft drinks, breadsticks, and a pan pizza.

"I like the creative approach on the ads for Transitions. You guys did a great job," Nick offered.

"So then maybe *we'll* get the credit for it this time?" Ally said. Nick didn't know whether to engage or ignore her reference to his reputation. Thankfully, before he could react to her barb, Brett spoke.

"I think we can make a major impact with this campaign and genuinely help some people."

Brett spoke with deep conviction and a sincere hope to help others, and Nick found himself moved by his optimism—however naïve. Brett always carried himself professionally and was never shallow or flippant when rendering his opinion. In fact, he shared his opinion only when the topic was crucial, and he always spoke with a unique blend of confidence and compassion.

"Hey, this is not a business lunch, remember," Ally quickly interjected. "Tell us about your weekend in Lake Geneva, Nick."

"Well, what can I say? It was very relaxing. There's not much to tell. I enjoyed the snow sculpture competition on Saturday and the torch light parade and the winter fireworks on Sunday. I also savored kicking back at the lake house."

Ally persisted. "Tell me more about the lake house then."

Brett turned to Nick. "Just another bachelor pad, right?"

"Well, let's just say it's an upscale cabin with a great view. The east side is windows, floor to ceiling. So, you have a lake view from the great room, the kitchen and two of the three bedrooms."

"Does it have a deck?" Brett asked.

"Yup, it has an upper deck cantilevered over a stamped concrete patio, complete with a fire pit."

The waitress returned with their drinks and breadsticks. Ally grabbed a breadstick, burning her fingers, and passed them to Nick.

"Got a boat?" Brett inquired.

"I have a boat I store in Wisconsin. It's nothing fancy, an old sixteen-footer I use to tour the lake with friends or just to go fishing," he explained, as he folded his napkin over his lap.

"What else did you do this weekend?" Ally asked, as she bit into her breadstick.

Nick couldn't tell if Ally was interested in his life or just life in Lake Geneva, but he enjoyed her questions. When they dated, she knew he always wanted to own a lake house and she shared his love for the outdoors and the serenity of nature. Still, he wasn't quite sure how to interpret her probing.

"That's about it," he said. "It was a weekend to relax and reflect."

"Reflect?" Ally balked. "You? Reflect? What would *you* reflect on?"

Nick knew he had just invited them to step on sacred ground. And he didn't want to go there.

The waitress placed their steaming pan pizza in the center of the table. Ally transferred a slice to each of their plates.

"So, what were you reflecting on?" she persisted, knowing that broaching the subject was safe as long as Brett was there.

"Yeah, this should be good," Brett said with a smirk. "What in the world would Nick Conway *reflect* on?"

"Oh, you know, family, friends, and career."

This had to be generic enough to get him off the hook. Yet, Ally kept driving. "Any specifics?" she asked, as a long string of cheese stretched from her plate to her mouth.

Nick was cornered, and he didn't know what to say next. He certainly couldn't tell her how much he reflected on her. His only way out was to say he reflected on family. Maybe they would leave that alone.

"I had sort of a unique experience at breakfast yesterday, and it made me think about my dad, that's all," he said, desperately trying to dismiss the topic.

"A unique experience at breakfast? Really? What happened?" Brett asked, not knowing that he, too, was now treading on private territory.

Nick reached for another breadstick to stall but knew he was in too deep, and any fabrication at this point would be transparent. Avoidance wasn't working, so he elected simply to tell the truth.

"I had Sunday brunch yesterday at the Grand Geneva Resort. A father and son were having breakfast together at a table in front of me. The father had Alzheimer's. The son was about my age and was as patient as a saint..."

Nick went on to describe every detail of their conversation at breakfast, ending with the question the son's wife asked him. Ally and Brett hung on every word and never interrupted.

Just after Nick finished the story, the waitress returned, refreshed their drinks and left the bill.

Silence followed. Nick was not sure what they thought. Brett spoke first. "Nick, when the son told you yesterday that his father had Alzheimer's, you told him that your father had a different disease and it had a devastating effect on your family. If you don't mind me asking, what disease was that?"

The moment of truth had arrived for Nick, and he had walked right into it. *What was I thinking? I don't bear my soul to my co-workers! I have two policies against that!*

Nick tensed. He felt his stomach rise and fall. "He's...he's an alcoholic."

Ally and Brett looked at each other in disbelief. They didn't know what to say. Nick could see the wheels turning.

Now it all makes sense, they must be thinking. *Nick is the son of an alcoholic. No wonder he doesn't want to work on the Transitions account. No wonder he doesn't believe that Transitions can really help alcoholics and, besides, who would want to help "those kinds of people?" No wonder he is so angry, so frustrated, and so pessimistic about the effectiveness of addiction recovery treatment.*

"I'm sorry," Brett finally offered. "I didn't know."

Ally was stunned. She covered her mouth with her hand. Nick knew what she was going to say.

"You, you told me your father was dead," she stammered, looking him in the eye. "All of the time we dated, you told me he was dead—killed in a car accident with your mother. You were reared by an uncle you said. Do you even have an uncle, or did you lie about that too?"

There he was again, caught in a lie. "My parents had no siblings. But as far as I was concerned, my father *was* dead, Ally—at least to me. He was never there for me."

Lying was something Nick was good at, especially about his father. He'd had plenty of practice. Funny thing about lies, the more he could justify them, the easier they were to tell. And Nick had plenty of justification to lie about his father's embarrassing alcoholic behavior.

Suddenly, Nick wasn't sure what to do or say next. Ally was now reacting to their past, and Brett was wondering how this revelation might affect the future of their work on the Transitions account.

Brett broke the tension with a question. "What is your relationship with your father like today?"

"Non-existent. He might as well be dead."

"Is there any hope for your relationship with him?"

"I don't think so."

"Why?"

Nick searched for the right words. "If you must know, I don't think I can forgive him."

Brett paused briefly and then asked, "Nick, tell me, what impressed you most about what you saw at breakfast yesterday?"

Nick thought for a moment, wondering where this was going. "I suppose it was the compassion the son demonstrated for his father, especially since he said his father didn't deserve it."

"Then why do you think the son was so compassionate?"

"What do you mean?"

"Do you think the son actually *felt* compassion for his father?"

"Yes, but not at first."

"So, the son *chose* to be compassionate?"

"I suppose," Nick replied, considering the implications of Brett's question.

"Could that work for you?"

"What do you mean?"

"If you alter your attitude toward forgiving your father, maybe your emotions will follow, and you can restore your relationship with him. Sounds like the son you met yesterday did just that, and it worked for him."

"It's more complicated than that. Plus, I haven't seen or spoken to my father in years. And there's so much baggage. From my point of view, there really is no hope."

Ally could hear the pain in Nick's words, and he sensed her attitude toward him slowly shift from anger to empathy. Her face began to reflect her feelings, but she left the direction of the conversation to Brett.

"Maybe you need a different point of view," he suggested.

"I don't follow you?"

"Well, I don't have all of the answers, Nick, but you should look at your relationship with your father from another perspective."

Intrigued, Nick asked him to continue.

"Have you ever looked at your life as if it were a movie?"

"Not really. Where are you going with this?"

"Nick, as you know, movies allow us to see events from a different point of view—the director's point of view. In a movie we can see events close up, from a distance, from a unique angle, through a different pair of eyes or from inside someone else's shoes. A movie can speed up the action, slow it down, or freeze it to be sure we see exactly what the director wants us to see."

"And your point is?"

"My point is, to some degree, God sees our lives much like a movie."

Nick stiffened. "Is this turning religious because...?"

"Just hear me out a second," Brett interrupted. "Our lives are a story with a beginning, a middle and an end. And nothing escapes God's notice. In other words, God sees all of the events and circumstances that ultimately shape and define our lives. You could think of these events or circumstances as chapters or scenes in our lives."

"That's all fine and good, Brett, but I'm not God, so I can't see all of the events and circumstances that shaped my father's life."

"That's right, Nick, you can't, but isn't it enough to know that there *were* events or scenes in your father's life that shaped who he is today?"

"At this stage, I'm not sure those events or scenes are relevant, Brett."

"I think they're very relevant!"

"Why?"

"Go on!" Ally chimed in.

"Because if you knew the events or circumstances that shaped your father into who he is today, you might be able to understand him. And if you could understand him, you might be able to forgive him. Most importantly, if you could forgive him, you might be able to restore your relationship with him—like the father and son you saw at breakfast yesterday."

Nick listened to Brett. He could not deny his arguments were compelling and his logic was sound. Most of all, his voice was compassionate, and although Nick didn't understand Brett's faith, it was genuine.

Brett wasn't Nick's closest friend by any means, but he was the most loyal and sensitive. Even now, Brett somehow knew that in the secret places of Nick's heart he was struggling with his relationship with his father. And if Nick could be honest with himself, he would like to see his father again. However, as far as restoring his relationship with him, that would take more faith than even Brett had.

"You know, Nick," Brett added, "In some way; I think you saw a glimpse of God yesterday."

"A glimpse? What do you mean?"

"Well, I believe God is at work in our lives every day, and if we watch for him, we can catch a glimpse of him or sense his presence."

"I hate to disappoint you, Brett, but I don't exactly hang out with God, so I don't think I have had the pleasure of his company!"

"Perhaps, but I'm sure, at times, you've sensed his presence," Brett countered.

"And when might that be?"

"Have you felt God's presence through the beauty of a sunset?"

"I guess."

"Through the smell of spring?"

"I suppose..."

"Through the exhilaration of love?"

Nick glanced at Ally, and then looked away. "Yeah, but..."

"Have you ever sensed him when you pondered how the stars hang in the sky?"

"Well, I have wondered..."

"Have you noticed the intricacy of a snowflake?"

"Sure, but..."

"The immensity of the sea?"

"Of course."

"Ever feel the hope a sunny day brings?"

"Okay, Brett, you've made your point."

"Nick, you got a glimpse of God yesterday through a son's compassion and willingness to forgive his father. If we watch and listen closely, when we least expect it, I believe we can catch a glimpse of God, his work in the world and, most importantly, his work in our everyday lives. That includes your life."

Nick heard the confidence and sincerity in Brett's voice and while he didn't fully understand it, it moved him. Silence followed for a moment before Brett reached for the bill.

"I got this," he said. "This conversation was worth the price of admission."

"It certainly was," Ally agreed, as the trio quietly left the restaurant and walked back to the office.

CHAPTER 6

It was Friday, just before 5:00 p.m., and Nick was busy typing his weekly project report for Sam Morris. Another week had come and gone. It had been very productive and, as usual, Nick was anticipating a weekend at his lake house. It was his respite from this madness known as the advertising business.

Earlier in the week he and his creative team met with Sam and presented their two initial ideas for the print ad campaign. As the team had hoped, Sam selected the concept they favored, and he gave them approval to create detailed layouts for presentation to Tom Sullivan and the Transitions Board of Directors. John pre-sold Tom on the creative direction to gauge his initial reaction and preempt any surprises during the presentation to the board.

Yesterday, Brett and Ally also developed first round concepts and generated headlines for Phase Two of the campaign. Nick was proud of the creative approach they presented to Sam, and he wondered if it would pay dividends down the road. Sam stopped by Nick's office early that morning to compliment him on his staff choices for the creative team. Sam liked the way they worked together and, more importantly, he liked their work. He also asked Nick to have Brett crank out a few more headlines for Phase Two of the campaign.

Sam Morris was a creative guy who started his career in advertising as a copywriter, much as Nick did. Today, Nick thought of Sam more as a numbers man. At sixty-three, Sam never missed an opportunity to preach to new entry-level employees that "creativity and productivity are the lifeblood of Morris, McGowan & Tate." And Nick had grown accustomed to his sermon conclusion: "creativity plus productivity spell profitability."

Sam wasn't shy about reminding Nick that the Transitions account had the potential to be very profitable for the agency. "No pressure," he said with a slight elbow to Nick's ribs.

Nick tolerated Sam's manipulative techniques because Sam helped launch his career at Leo Burnett and brought him along quickly. They separated when Sam and his two partners left to launch Morris, McGowan & Tate. Nick eventually left the Leo Burnett agency for short stints at two other big agencies in town. They were reunited when Sam got his agency off the ground and asked Nick to join him. It was a welcome invitation because Nick had just about enough of big agency politics.

Sam brought him in as the senior creative director and recently threw in the VP title, a big raise, and a few extra perks. Nick owed him a lot. And Sam, a master manipulator, wouldn't let him forget it.

Nick realized that his career had always been characterized by three things: positioning, promoting, and performing. He had skillfully positioned himself to be in the presence of the top dog. He had promoted himself, his work and his accounts to get noticed, and he had performed at a high level to ensure career advancement. He never wasted much time with his peers. In fact, in his mind, he felt his peers were, well, "the little people."

Nick proudly called himself a "loner" as if it were badge of courage. In truth, his social status may have been attributed more to group consensus than self proclamation. Nick's short list of friends was exactly that—short. And, with the exception of Ally and Brett, his friends could not be described as anything that resembled loyal.

Nick spent most of his time thinking about how to get ahead. Yet, this week had been different. Instead of thinking about how Sam and the Transitions account could catapult his career, he'd been thinking about Ally.

Before asking her to be on the account team, he had strategically avoided her. And perhaps he never bumped into her because she was skillfully avoiding him too. Now that he was in her presence daily, he found himself dwelling on her—like right now.

Nick walked to his office window and stared at the hustle and bustle in the streets thirty-one stories below. He wondered how his life would be different today if he hadn't ruined his relationship with Ally. He had loved her once. And he believed that she had loved him, but the events that separated them made the depth of their feelings for each other foggy and fleeting.

"Office romances never work out," Sam often reminded him. "You should focus on your career." Nick was never sure if he told him that because Sam's first two marriages had failed or because he thought he couldn't control Nick if he was distracted by a woman.

Regardless, Nick was feeling something for Ally again, and although he didn't fully understand it, he couldn't deny it. She was a gorgeous woman. Why she was still single today, he would never know. Her long black hair accentuated her slender, curvaceous figure, while her dark brown eyes, olive skin and striking smile made her simply stunning. If Nick was honest with himself, it was more than her physical appearance he was attracted to.

There was a certain authenticity about her, a refreshing honesty, and a down-to-earth simplicity that generated hope in a complicated world. She was so frank that he always knew where he stood with her. She was also content and, unlike Nick, her contentment was based on who she was, not what she had accomplished. She didn't need more in life to be happy. Whereas her sensitivity and compassion for people could sometimes be confused with naivety, she was anything but naïve. On the contrary, Nick learned this the hard way.

In the advertising world, Nick would sometimes lose his perspective on what was real. Ally was real, and what he liked most about her was that she embodied everything he didn't. So, if the theory held, opposites attracted.

As he gazed out the window, he admitted to himself that at 39, of all of the women he had ever dated, Ally was the only one who had not only lived up to his ideal, but also had defined it. The question now was what could he do about it?

There was a tap on his door.

"Come in," Nick said, as he turned from the window.

"I have some more headlines for Phase Two of the campaign that Sam asked for," Brett said. "Do you want to look at these now, or should I throw them on your desk?"

Nick glanced at the clock. It was 5:20 p.m. "I'll take a look at them now. Do you have layouts to go with them?"

"No, I didn't bring them. I'll run and get them so you can see them before you leave."

As Brett left Nick sat and leaned back in his chair with his back to the door. He put his feet on his desk and started to review the headlines. There were five new concepts. He placed his hands behind his head and looked out the window while he mulled the headlines one at a time. He liked them all, especially Concept B.

Nick could always depend on Brett to deliver concepts that were creative and on strategy. Throughout the years, Nick had come to trust Brett for a lot more than advertising copy. Although they didn't socialize much after hours, Nick had come to appreciate Brett's point of view on many issues of life. He never knew quite how to define their friendship because they were so different, especially when, in Nick's words, "Brett got religion." Nevertheless, despite their opposing views on God and his role in this world, they shared a mutual respect.

There was another tap on his door. "Come in," he said, as

he continued to stare out the window. "I like what you came up with here, Brett."

"It's Ally," came the reply behind him.

Nick reeled around in his chair. He was pleasantly surprised to see her.

"Hey. Brett said you wanted to see these layouts."

"Hey. Yeah, I was just looking over his new headline concepts for Phase Two of the campaign," he replied stiffly, attempting to conceal how excited he was to see her this late on a Friday.

"I really like them, especially Concept B," she offered, glancing at the papers he held in his hand.

"Me, too." Suddenly, he felt like a high school underclassman star struck by a senior cheerleader. He wondered if it was obvious to her that his heart stirred when she walked in the room. *Why is this happening? And why is it happening now? I have no chance for a relationship with her again. And, I don't deserve a relationship with her again.*

"You and Brett are really doing a nice job on the campaign," he said, floundering for words. "In fact, Sam stopped by this morning and complimented me on choosing you both for the creative team."

"Really? That's great."

"Yeah, he likes what you two bring to the whole effort."

"I enjoy being a part of it. And it's a pleasure working with Brett. I really appreciate his insight."

Nick found himself waiting for her to compliment him, too. He paused to give her time to express it. It never came, so he felt compelled to cover the awkward moment.

"Yeah, I really appreciate Brett, too. And you're right, he has great insights. That's what I wanted to talk with you about," she said, changing the subject. "I've been thinking a lot about what Brett said at lunch on Monday. You know, about our lives being like a movie with a beginning, middle and end. And from God's perspective the events and circumstances that shape our lives are like scenes..."

Nick finished her sentence, "...and if we witness these scenes, we may understand why people are the way they are?"

44

"Yeah, what do you think of that?"

Why is she asking me this? Is she trying to understand me better?

"I think there is something to it, Ally, but somehow I don't think that is the real question you stopped by to ask me," he said coyly. Nick hoped she would somehow bring this around to their relationship so he could express to her some things that nagged him since they broke up a few years ago.

"You're right, that is not the real question I came to ask you," she admitted. He waited for her next sentence wondering if it would go in the direction he hoped.

"What I wanted to ask you is," she said, pausing. She furled her brow and seemed to struggle for the right words. "Based on what Brett said, do you think you should see your father again? You know, try to reconnect with him?"

Nick became suddenly still, he was sure she could see the disappointment in his face. He didn't want to talk about his father. This topic was a waste of breath.

"Why in the world would I want to see my father again?"

"Because he is your father."

"He's an alcoholic."

"He's your father!"

"He's a drunk."

"He's your father!"

"He's a drunk, and he's hopeless."

"He's your father, and he needs your help."

"My help? Where was he when I needed *his* help? Where was he when I graduated from high school? Where was he when I graduated from college?" Nick's voice continued to escalate.

"Where was he all of the times a boy needs his father?"

"Probably in the same place," she replied honestly.

"That's right. He was in the *same* place—a bar!" Nick felt his anger burn, so he turned away from her and walked toward the window to stare at the city lights far below. This city had always brought him a certain comfort because it made him feel anonymous. When he walked the streets, he was just another face in the crowd. The peace and privacy of anonymity was such a safe place.

She was getting too close—trespassing on his personal space. Even when they dated, he carefully drew boundaries he would not allow her to cross. He stared out the window for a moment until he felt himself begin to cool. She stood behind him in silence. He could see her reflection in the window.

"Look," he said, in a softer tone with his back to her, "I know you are just trying to help, but you don't know what it is like to have an alcoholic father, much less try to keep him in your life."

"You're right, I don't know what it is like to have an alcoholic father, but I do know he is the only family you've got, and if you don't at least try to restore your relationship with him, you could regret it later in life—when it is too late for second chances."

Nick turned toward her. "I'm not sure I want a second chance at a relationship with him," he said, trying to convince himself as much as her.

"You say that now, but you could regret it later. I know I would give anything to have another chance to talk to my father again."

"What are you talking about? I've met your father and you had a good relationship with him."

"You met someone you thought was my father."

"What? What are you saying?"

"I'm saying you're not the only one with family secrets."

"No?" he said coyly, to see if she would offer more.

"No!" she said firmly.

Nick was astute enough this time to know he had just waltzed into another sacred moment and, once again, he wasn't in control. He also realized he was in a dilemma. Should he ignore her comment and let the moment slip into oblivion or should he ask, as so many of his married friends had to ask, "Do you want to talk about it?"

Nick could hear his heart pound as this internal debate ratcheted up a notch with every tick of his wall clock.

If I say nothing, I will just leave Ally hanging out there. If I ask if she wants to talk about it, she can politely decline and dismiss the subject. However, if she elects to talk about it, then, hey, I'm a sensitive guy. Besides, I really wouldn't mind spending some time alone with her.

He took a few steps toward her. Her arms folded, she turned her back to him.

"Do you want to talk about it?" he asked, stiffly.

"How much time do you have?" she responded, sensing Nick may be simply patronizing her.

"All night. Want to grab a cup of coffee?"

A coffee shop was within walking distance of the agency. When they arrived, Nick noticed that most tables were occupied, but he didn't have to wait long to order. He asked Ally what she would like, and she looked for a seat.

"A grande caramel macchiato and a tall black coffee," Nick said to the barista. While he waited for their order, Ally found a cozy table in the back, away from the door.

Nick set their drinks on the table, took off his coat and draped it over the back of his chair. As he sat, he wrapped both hands around his cup to warm them while Ally sipped her macchiato. He didn't know if he should invite her to continue where she had left off or just sit quietly and let her collect her thoughts. He chose the latter. After a few sips of her drink, she looked in his eyes. He didn't know if she was as uncomfortable as he was so he just let it play out to see where the conversation would go.

"I guess every family has its secrets," she started.

He simply nodded so as to not interrupt her.

"My father," she started again, "or at least the father you met when we dated, was my stepfather," she said quietly. "My father died of prostate cancer at age forty-seven."

"I'm sorry. I didn't know."

"I know." She stared at her drink for a moment.

"They don't even screen for it before the age of fifty, so we never saw it coming. I was thirteen when he died, but I remember most things about him because we were close." Tears welled in her beautiful brown eyes and Nick started to squirm in his seat. He was not adept at listening to sentimental stories. He didn't know if it was because he harbored so much anger or if he was simply insensitive. Either way, he was uncomfortable and took a sip of coffee every time he shifted in his chair.

He had never been very good at friendships, especially with women, at least not when they required any form of sympathetic response from him. He didn't behave this way intentionally; he felt emotionally-challenged with women.

"I remember his laugh, I remember his touch, I remember his silly sense of humor, and I even remember his scent," she said with a smile.

He listened intently so he wouldn't break her train of thought, but he didn't fully understand why she was telling him this or what he should do with this new revelation.

"My mother remarried three years after my father died. Roger seemed nice at first but he was very domineering. He brought two kids of his own into the marriage, Katie and Kari. They're twins, and they were ten at the time."

"Twins, three years younger than you? Sounds like you were the odd child out in the attention department."

"You got it. At times, I felt as though both my father and my mother had died. I was very lonely during that time in my life, and I missed my father immensely. As a teenager, I really needed him."

"Tell me about it!"

"Roger had little time or inclination for me. He had his own daughters and I was, well, optional. I felt abandoned. I was so frustrated that I would throw tantrums just to get *some* attention. He would tell Katie and Kari, 'See how teenagers act? Ally behaves like she is younger than you. Promise me you will behave like big girls when you are her age.'

"I always looked to Mom for support. 'Roger, Ally has a point,' she would begin. He would cut her off, give her a dirty look, and say condescendingly, 'Didn't we agree that there is only one authority in this house, and that authority is not a teenager? A little discipline is what is needed here.' To Mom's credit, she never let him lay a hand on me."

"I see what you mean about every family having its secrets and how difficult it is to forgive. I'm sure it's hard to forgive your stepfather."

"Actually, I'm not struggling to forgive my stepfather."

"You're not?"

"No. I'm struggling to forgive my mother."

"You lost me."

"What I just told you wasn't the family secret I referred to."

"No?" Ally was about to take Nick to a place he didn't want to go. Yet, he figured if she was comfortable enough to take him there, he needed to be comfortable enough to go.

"The family secret," she said, looking in his eyes, "is my mother was having an affair with Roger while my father was dying." Nick looked away in disbelief. He had just arrived in the "no-comfort zone." He didn't have a clue as to what to say, and he certainly didn't know how to change the subject.

"How long have you known this?" he said, fumbling for something, anything, to say.

"Since I was fifteen, about a year before they got married."

"How did you handle this?"

"For awhile, I didn't. At fifteen, how do you cope with something like that? All I felt was anger and hate. My mind was filled with questions. Why would my mother be unfaithful to my father? Why didn't she love him anymore? How could she do this when he was dying? How would he feel if he knew?"

Tears started to stream down her cheeks. Nick mechanically reached across the table to take her hand. To his surprise, she held it tight. He was really out of his element now and at a loss to comfort her. He noticed her cup was almost empty.

"Can I get you something else?"

"Black coffee."

When he returned to their table, she was carefully wiping her eyes trying not to smear her mascara.

"You must think I'm crazy to drag you into all of this after all these years," she said.

"No, I don't think you're crazy, just..."

"Just, what?"

"I don't know. I guess I just wonder *why* you would want to share this with me."

"Well, I didn't intend to tell you *everything*. I didn't mean to ramble on and on. It's just that I had a great relationship with my father when I was young and, well, I just hoped you could experience that for yourself before it's too late. But that will never happen if you don't take the first step to contact him."

"I appreciate your concern and your sentiment, but I just don't think that's possible."

"All week I have been thinking about what Brett said at lunch on Monday. And I believe it is possible, Nick."

"Just what did Brett say that would give you that hope?"

"You know, when he explained how God sees our life in its totality, and the events and circumstances are like scenes. And if we view those scenes from God's perspective, we might be better able to understand why people are the way they are and then we might be able to forgive them."

"Like your mother and stepfather?"

"No, like my mother and *your* father," she countered. "Our situations are very different, but the impact of those circumstances has left us both feeling very much the same—angry, abandoned, alone, and unloved. I'm tired of feeling this way. I want some kind of resolution. I want to stop feeling this angry. I want to forgive her and get on with my life. I want to restore my relationship with her again. And, yes, I need to figure out how to feel about my stepfather, but that will come later."

"So, what are you suggesting?"

"I don't know, talk to Brett, reestablish contact with our families again and see where it goes."

"I told you, I don't want to reestablish a relationship with my father."

"I know, but if you don't, things will never change. Never. And I think a day may come when you regret that."

"Things don't have to change. Things are fine the way they are."

"They are not fine and you know it. You're living in denial," she said with the brutal honesty that he had admired about her. "You lived with a certain amount of anger even when we dated. And you're still not over it!"

"Why would I risk seeing my father again?"

"Because you could make things better."

"Or, I could make things worse."

"I just thought with Brett's insights, we could help each other confront some of this baggage in our lives—and somehow set ourselves free."

Nick looked away because he knew she was right. He had been carrying this burden much too long. *But I shouldn't have to make the first move with my father. He should come to me and ask for forgiveness.*

Ally stared into her coffee, smiled to herself, and then looked into Nick's eyes. "Do you know what I remember most about my father when I was young?"

"No, what?"

"At bedtime he would never *read* me stories. Instead, he would *tell* me stories."

"Really? Why?"

"He made up his own stories so he could see my reaction," she explained.

Nick wondered where this was going.

"I overheard him tell my mom he didn't want to read me stories because he would have to look at the book and he would miss the real story unfolding in my eyes. He told her he loved to watch my eyes widen, my brow rise and my mouth drop when he told me a story. He said that looking into my eyes while he told a story made him feel connected to me. And every story he told had some kind of moral to it so I would learn something about values."

"Sounds like a great guy."

"He was. He used to tell my mom that children may never remember everything you teach them, but they will always remember how you made them feel."

"He must have been very creative to come up with his own stories every night."

"I suppose he was creative," she said reflectively, "but what I remember most about him was his kindness. I could see it in his eyes when he spoke. I think you can tell a lot about a person when you look into his or her eyes," she said, looking directly into Nick's. The truth of her comment suddenly made him squirm but he played along to hide his feelings.

"Oh, really? What can you tell when you look into my eyes?" he said, trying to diffuse the impact of the statement.

Ally leaned forward and looked him square in the eye. "Hmmm," she said, acting like a TV psychic. "I see fear and false bravado."

"Really? Fear and false bravado? Tell me more, O' Wise One." She leaned toward him again. He opened his eyes wide.

"Ah, yes," she said, "I see fear in revealing who you really are to others, even those close to you. This causes you to overcompensate for your true feelings and, thus, the false bravado."

"You're on a roll. Anything else?"

"I see fear in confronting the truth, fear in being vulnerable and honest. But there is some good news," she concluded, as she leaned back.

"Oh, really, what could possibly be the good news?" he replied, feigning disbelief.

"You have great potential to alter your path, restore broken relationships, and live a rich and meaningful life."

"That last part sounds a little canned, like something you would read in a fortune cookie."

She laughed. "Yeah, I did. But you get the point."

Actually, Nick did get the point. Ally, with her penchant for honesty, had nailed him on a few of his many weaknesses: denial, fear, and false bravado—all of which hid his innermost feelings from others. All he could do now was not let her know that she was right.

"Hey, are you hungry?" he said, changing the subject.

"I'm starved."

"Well, then, let me take you out for a bite."

"Oh," she said hesitantly, as she pondered the implications of his offer. He could see the sudden reservation in her eyes and her body slowly recoiled at the suggestion.

"It's not a date, Ally. Just two friends catching up on old times," he reassured her, realizing that she still would not let him cross the bridge from friendship to relationship.

"Okay," she agreed, hesitantly.

"Just one rule over dinner," he suggested.

"What's that?"

"The conversation has to be on happy things, not heavy things. Deal?"

"Deal!"

Yen's Chinese restaurant wasn't far from the coffee shop so they walked together in the brisk night air. It was very mild for March and Nick could smell the fresh spring air. The hostess seated them after a twenty-minute wait. After they ordered drinks, Ally ordered an oriental chicken salad and sesame chicken. Nick ordered the same salad and the sweet and sour pork.

"So where do we begin?" Ally asked.

"Well, let's start with what you're doing this weekend or what you're doing with your life."

"Okay, I am going on a photography outing tomorrow afternoon here in the city. I just bought a pretty pricey digital SLR camera I'm dying to try out."

"That's great. As an art director that seems to make perfect sense. How long have you been interested in photography?"

"I've been toying with it for the past year. But I started getting serious about it when I met Ron."

"Really," Nick said, as he felt his stomach tighten at the sudden mention of another man.

"I really love photography. It ties into my career, but I am studying it for personal reasons." Nick wondered what she meant by that. But most of all, he wondered, "Who is Ron?"

The waiter returned with their drinks and salads. Ally took a bite and told Nick about her newfound love for photography, but he was undeniably more interested in her newfound love.

"Why is photography so compelling to you?"

"It helps me slow down and see the world."

"Really," he said, "go on."

"Well, think about it. You have to observe a subject, consider its environment, explore various perspectives, experiment with camera angles, and manipulate the effects of light. Photography, like my art, helps me develop an eye for detail. I'm noticing things I have never noticed before."

"And the benefit is?"

"Well, Ron says, by seeing things I never noticed before, I can better appreciate things I took for granted."

"Is Ron a photography instructor?"

"No, not exactly. He's a professional photographer. Why?"

"I don't know," he fumbled, "it just sounded like you were dating him."

"I am dating him—casually," she responded.

"Oh, nice," he said, once again choosing words that would not compromise his true feelings. He felt a sudden emptiness. *We split up three years ago. I shouldn't be surprised that she is dating. I should be feeling no pain—yet, I am feeling—something.*

"So, what are you going to shoot on the photo outing?"

"Ron is visiting from New York, so I'm going to take him

on a tour of the city on foot. We'll shoot some of the interesting architecture."

"The sesame chicken?" the waiter inquired before placing it in front of Ally.

"Sir, the sweet and sour pork."

"Yes," he replied, as he lifted his hands off the table and leaned back so the waiter could place the entrée before him.

"Will there be anything else?"

"No, thank you," Nick replied.

"Enough about me," Ally insisted. "What are you up to this weekend?"

"Me? Well, I'll do what I do most weekends, I guess. I'll drive up to the lake house and inspect it so I can make a list of what I have to do to get it ready for summer. And I'll take time to kick back."

Ally took another bite of her entree. "Do you spend a lot of time at the lake house. Other than the beautiful setting, what else do you love about it?" There was warmth in her question and although he knew it was one of those warm and fuzzy questions, he wanted to answer it.

"You'll have to come and see," he replied. He took a sip of his drink and waited to see if she would bite on his invitation. Another long awkward pause followed. "I suppose I love the solitude the most," he said finally.

"You're such a loner."

If she only knew how much I wish she would come to the lake house for a visit. The truth is I am not a loner. I'm lonely. There is a difference.

"You didn't let me finish," he interjected. "Just as you love the way photography makes you slow down and *see* things, I love the way the lake house makes me slow down and *feel* things—especially in the summer."

"You have *feelings*?" she said in disbelief. A smile curled around her lips. "What *ever* do you mean?"

"Well, the lake house is a place where I can totally relax, be myself, and enjoy the very best the seasons have to offer—especially summer. I love the balmy lake breezes, the warmth of the sun, a cloudless blue sky, and the energy I feel among boats cruising the lake," he said, his passion rising. "But that's not all."

"Oh, there's more?"

"Yes, but I don't know how to describe it. It's an exhilarating feeling I get when I go to the lake house. Think about the most enjoyable summer you ever had. Do you remember it?"

"Yes."

"How did it make you feel?"

She thought for a moment. "It made me feel *alive*."

"Right, and everything around you fueled that feeling. The warm weather, the smell of summer in the air, and knowing that your best days were ahead of you."

"You feel all of that when you go to the lake house?"

"Yes, and one other thing."

"What's that?"

"Complete freedom. Freedom from responsibility. Freedom from expectations. Freedom from stress. Freedom to enjoy life at its best. Most of all, I love the freedom to take my watch off and go with the flow. I eat when I'm hungry, not when it's time. I rest when I need a nap, not when my watch suggests I should be tired. It's not just the lake house. I love Lake Geneva as a tourist town."

"Why? I thought you didn't like people, or at least being around them."

"Because I love the energy of a summer town that has more bed-and-breakfasts than hotels, more specialty shops than retail chains, and more quaint coffee shops than big name coffee chains. I enjoy the feel of crowded ice cream parlors on the corner of Main Street and bustling open-air art fairs along a sandy beach. And I savor a summer walk around the lake on the front lawns of elegant lake homes and sprawling mansions."

"Wow, Nick, I have never heard you talk so passionately about anything other than your work. Maybe I was wrong about you."

"What's that supposed to mean?"

"Maybe you *do* have a life."

"You're such a cynic. There are lots of things you don't know about me." *Like how much I'm beginning to care about you again.*

"Really, so now you're a man of mystery?"

"No, I'm not a man of mystery. It's just that you don't know everything about me."

"I found that out the hard way once, remember?" In one sentence, she killed the light-hearted tone of the conversation. Nick quickly turned the conversation around.

"The real question is, are you a woman of mystery?"

"Oh, absolutely."

"Really? What don't I know about you?"

"Well," she hesitated.

Nick egged her on. "Name one thing that will surprise me about you."

"Well, I might take a new job at a big agency in New York this summer," she said, tentatively.

Nick sat there with a blank look on his face. He didn't expect this to backfire on him so quickly. The moment the words left her lips he felt his chest constrict.

"You're kidding, right? I need you on the Transitions account."

"I'll be able to finish Phase One, possibly Phase Two, of the Transitions campaign. Besides, it isn't certain that I've got the job yet."

"Who is the job with?"

"McCann Erickson."

"Really? Wow. Congrats. Where are you in the interview process?" Nick's tone shifted from playful to somber.

"I've made it through the first two rounds, and I am one of three finalists. Don't worry, it's a new position they don't need to fill until mid-August, so I'll complete most of my work on the Transitions account before I leave—if I'm offered the job."

"If you get the job that will work out great for Ron, won't it?" he said, with a subtle hint of sarcasm.

Ally picked up on his reference but chose to ignore it. "Yeah. He freelances for McCann Erickson. In fact, he got me the interview."

The evening ended there. Nick lost his appetite and his interest in the conversation. Ally finished her entree while he waited quietly.

"Have you saved room for dessert?" the waiter asked as he refreshed their water.

"No, thank you," they answered in unison.

Nick turned to the waiter. "Would you bring me the check?"

After he paid the bill, Nick walked Ally back to the garage. He was sure they talked on the way back to their cars, but he couldn't remember what she said. He was numb and still reeling from the news that she might move to New York. His thoughts vacillated between the two juicy components of this news; she was not only possibly moving to The Big Apple, she also had a new boyfriend waiting in the wings.

Madison Avenue in New York was the advertising capital of the world, so to get a shot at one of the biggest agencies in the country would be the goal of anyone serious about a career in advertising.

When they got back to the garage Nick walked Ally to her car. She politely thanked him for listening to her over coffee and for dinner. He opened her door and she slipped behind the wheel, rolled down the window and closed the door behind her.

She started her car. "Ally, thanks for caring enough about my father to challenge me to reconnect with him. Although I'm still not completely sure why it is so important to you, I do appreciate your concern. I really do."

She nodded and spoke softly. "Everyone deserves to have a relationship with their father. Besides, it's important to me because underneath all of your anger, it's important to you. And..." her voice trailed off.

He prodded her. "And?"

"And." She paused before looking up at him. "And...I loved you once, remember?"

Nick smiled and nodded at her as she slowly drove away.

When he drove back to his apartment he thought about Ally's last sentence and about heading up to the lake house tomorrow. He couldn't wait to get there. She had given him a lot to think about.

CHAPTER 7

It was a beautiful Saturday morning in March; the kind that hints that spring will be gorgeous. Nick arrived at the lake house just after ten. He dropped his duffle bag inside the front door, raised the blinds, and opened a few windows to invite the morning in.

The bright blue sky was punctuated by a few clouds that slowly glided across the lake. The sun radiated through the windows and began to warm the lake house. The weather was unpredictable this time of year. In late March you can wear a t-shirt one day and be snowed in the next.

It was just shy of seventy degrees, and the fresh smell of spring permeated the air. The view of the lake was spectacular. Nick paused in front of the window, intrigued how a warm week alters the ambiance of the lake. Since he bought the lake house, he had observed the temperament of the lake in all four seasons. In summer alone, he witnessed its volatility. Much like the human temperament, the lake expressed itself in a range of emotions. He'd seen it roar like a lion, sending waves crashing against the shoreline at the onset of a storm, and he'd witnessed its tranquility as sailboats languidly glide across its smooth surface. Summer was coming, and when he wasn't on the water, he enjoyed watching the drama of the lake unfold from his deck, patio, or pier.

This weekend would be a relaxing one since it was too early for Nick to prepare the lake house for summer. Instead, he made a list of all he had to do before June to get ready for those sacred three months everyone in Wisconsin craved after a long hibernation during the deep freeze.

Nick grabbed a pen and paper from the kitchen drawer and stepped onto the deck. He righted a patio chair that had blown over during a winter storm and began to jot down his wish list. It was actually a "to do" list, but its name came from the fact that he wished, for once, he could accomplish everything he put on it.

As he sat on the deck, the bare tree branches split shafts of sunlight that speckled his patio table. Birds were already in full chorus, and the waves rhythmically slapped the fieldstone shoreline spitting wisps of water high into the air.

As he looked across the lake, his mind drifted to his conversation with Ally the previous night. Although he initially resented her suggestion that he visit his father, he was impressed that she cared enough, and dared enough, to tread on this shaky ground. He would never admit it to her, but when she confessed that one of the reasons she wanted to help him reconnect with his father was because she once loved him, it cut him clear to the core. The mere mention of it stirred his feelings for her and ignited hope that she could feel something for him again—if he played this right and if he could somehow eliminate the X-factor that went by the name of Ron.

Ally had a way of distilling pretense into truth, and she had done it again last night. When it came to his father, Nick lived in denial. And he clearly feared revealing himself to others because he couldn't, or wouldn't, trust people. And, yes, the best way to compensate for this was with false bravado. Ally had him pegged. Sadly, she was the only one in his life who was close enough to call him on it.

Nick pushed back from the table, folded his wish list, stuffed it in his shirt pocket, and let his body sink into the patio chair. He glanced across the lake at Stone Mansion and let his mind wander. It kept going back to Ally.

She had stopped by his office last night to suggest that he consider reconnecting with his father. She wanted to help by giving him hope, and he had given her the third degree. She challenged him to face his demons and confided in him that she had her own. Perhaps she hoped they could face them together. Once again, however, Nick never gave her a chance to tell him everything on her heart. Nick chastised himself at the thought of it. *Seems old habits die hard.*

A gentle breeze blew off the lake and through his hair. As he replayed his conversation with her last night, he realized how much courage it took to tell him about her mother's affair when her father was dying. It occurred to him, once again, that when it came to character, Ally was everything he wasn't.

He laid his head back in the chair and closed his eyes. He could feel the sun warm his face. Ally was right about many things, even the lake house. It was an escape from everything that troubled him, distracted him, and overwhelmed him. But his catharsis wasn't just the lake house; it was Lake Geneva. This quaint yet vibrant city was the epitome of a small summer tourist town.

As he looked out over the water, he seriously pondered Brett's and Ally's assertions that if he visited his father and discovered the scenes in his life that sent his dad down the alcoholic road, he might better understand him and one day forgive him.

If he could just have last night back, he would alter the outcome. He felt the weight of regret and wondered if his father had ever felt similar remorse. Nick struggled with the notion that seeing his father again would change anything, yet he was intrigued by Brett's faith and Ally's hope that miracles could happen not only to ordinary people but also unworthy people.

Lake Geneva was a place where even a workaholic such as Nick could slow his life down, untangle his thoughts, and listen to his troubled heart. Whether he would admit it or not, he had a troubled heart. And he was afraid he might be falling for Ally again.

Nick closed his eyes for what seemed like a few minutes and slept for an hour. He awoke slowly and glanced at his watch. It was just before noon, and he could feel hunger tug at his gut. Just seven minutes from downtown, he decided to drive into town for lunch. He spotted the distinctive yellow and white awnings and parked across the street from one of his favorite lunch spots.

As he walked in, he heard the hardwood floor gently creak under his feet. The ceiling fans slowly turned in their counter-clockwise direction. The restaurant was about half full, and he was seated immediately in the bright, sun-filled dining room. The restaurant was lined with windows on three sides so every seat in the house had a remarkable lake view. The hostess seated him at a table for two in the corner and handed him the lunch menu.

"Your server's name is Sandy, and she will be right with you," she said with a hint of apathy. *Maybe she needs a day off or she is having a day like me: a little confused or disillusioned,* he thought.

Nick knew the menu by heart so he set it aside and glanced at the lake. The waves were starting to churn. He could see the wind pick up and the waves develop white caps. The clientele was an even blend of young and old couples with the same thing in common: they were tourists. And the worst kind; young parents toting kids, cameras, strollers and backpacks; old folks sporting white socks, walking shoes, an occasional cane and ridiculous-looking sun caps that screamed, "I'm a tourist and I'm old!"

Most of them were flatlanders, and the license plates on the vehicles across the street confirmed it. This batch though was primarily bused in from who knows where. They didn't pose any real threat. They were friendly enough, but annoying, like a swarm of gnats buzzing around your face, never biting but a constant irritation.

Nevertheless, it was a beautiful weekend to be with someone

to love, and he couldn't help but notice that he was, once again, a party of one seated at a table for two.

"May I get you something to drink?" a young girl asked, breaking his train of thought.

"What do you have on tap?" he replied. She ran through her short list, he thought for a moment, and then opted for a bottled beer.

"I'll be right back with that," she said as she turned and disappeared into the kitchen.

Nick continued to stare aimlessly at the lake and reflect on his conversation with Ally yesterday. He didn't know what troubled him more, the fact that she might leave Chicago for New York or that this Ron character might prevent him from ever winning her back.

It was obvious that Ally's life had gone on without him after they broke up. Nick couldn't say the same. His love life died a slow death, and any dating he did was meaningless to him and, thus, unfair to the women he dated. *I admit it: I used people to get what I wanted in life or what I thought I wanted. The truth is, I never found what I was looking for again. Was that because Ally was what I really wanted, and needed, all along? And if it was that simple, why didn't I see it in the first place?*

Nick had long reconciled himself to the fact that life offered only a few second chances, especially with matters of the heart. *Sure,* he reasoned, *we may love again if we lose our first love, but if we are honest, brutally honest, is that love ever quite the same? How can true love be better the second time around if it was genuine the first time?*

"What can I get you?" Sandy, his waitress asked, not realizing her simple question was an abrupt intrusion. She placed his beer in front of him.

"I'll have the tuna melt," he retorted, hoping she would return to the kitchen and not engage him in trite conversation.

"Okay," is all she said, as if reading his mind.

Nick noticed the restaurant was filling up now, and people were waiting to be seated. His thoughts drifted back to Ally. *Could I really be falling in love with her again—or do I just think I'm falling in love with her again because she may love another man and be moving to New York? Is it love, or is it jealousy?* He needed to sort this out.

Sandy brought drinks to the table across from him and placed his tuna melt alongside of his beer.

"Is there anything else I can get you?"

"No, this will do it," he replied, anxious to curb any extraneous conversation so he could lose himself in his thoughts again.

Nick took a bite of his sandwich and took a pull on his beer before finding his way back to his thoughts. *Ron. What am I going to do about Ron? Who is this guy and what does Ally see in him?* He laughed derisively. *I bet he doesn't know a thing about advertising.*

His thoughts shifted to Ally's father. From their conversation earlier, it was clear how much she had loved her dad. He wondered what it must be like to love one's father. It occurred to him that he did not know what it is like to have a father worthy of his love. Since his mother was killed when he was ten and his father was an alcoholic, for all practical purposes, Nick had grown up like an orphan. His mother couldn't be there, and his alcoholic father, well, wasn't there.

He took another pull on his beer and bite of his sandwich. His thoughts were now meandering. Ally told him that her father loved to tell her stories rather than read her stories so he could look directly into her eyes as he told them.

Nick remembered looking into his father's eyes, too. They were bloodshot and glassy. He wasn't reading Nick a story; he was reading him the riot act.

Late one night, shortly after his mother's death, his father woke him as he stumbled up the stairs after a night on the town. He crashed through the door to Nick's room and wrapped his large, calloused hands around Nick's throat, shaking him. Nick fought to breathe as his father pulled the boy's face close to his. Nick could see the hate in his eyes and smell the stench of alcohol on this breath and cigarette smoke in his clothes.

"You killed her," he slurred in a blind rage, throwing Nick to the floor. As he attempted to kick his son, he found the bed post instead. He wailed like a dog before falling backward to the floor in a drunken stupor.

Nick laid motionless in the darkness, too frightened to move. He listened to his father's labored breathing, heavy at first before slowly trailing off into sleep. As Nick lay in the darkness, he clutched his blanket and wondered what he had done wrong and what he should do now. He was too young to report his father, too afraid to stop him, and too naïve to hate him. Every night he went to bed fearing it would happen again. Although it never did, once was enough to etch it in his memory.

Nick finished his lunch and wandered outside. He strolled across the street to the water's edge and wondered: *How do you ever forgive a father like that? Do Brett and Ally really understand what they are asking by suggesting that I reconnect with him?*

He realized once more that he had more questions than answers, but it was a beautiful day to take a walk—a very long walk.

CHAPTER 8

Nick pulled into a coffee shop on his way into the office Monday morning. As he waited in line, he marveled at how successful this industry had become. *Who would believe that you could elevate something as common as coffee to gourmet status and make millions doing it?* Vanilla lattes, cappuccinos, espresso and mochas, nothing more than coffee with a gourmet image. *I wish I had thought of it.*

Advertising guys make the world a better place, or more accurately, advertising makes the world appear to be a better place, he thought. *We did the same thing with water. We elevated it from mere tap water to gourmet water by giving it an upscale name, a healthy image, and packaging it in a fancy plastic bottle. And look how many brands of bottled water proliferate today. Who would have believed you could repackage something as generic as water and sell it at a premium price when it is readily available out of your tap? Blame it on us advertising people.*

When he got off the elevator at work, cup of gourmet coffee

in hand, he walked to his office. He turned on his computer and reviewed his notes from last week on the Transitions account, a new pharmaceutical account, and some new business development proposals John had drafted for his review.

When he glanced at the clock it was almost nine and time to meet with the Transitions account team to finalize the creative approach and discuss implementation.

As usual, he was first in the conference room. A few minutes later John entered followed by Brett.

"Everybody have a good weekend?" he asked, before starting the meeting.

"Same old, same old," John replied.

"We took the kids to Navy Pier and the Field Museum," Brett added.

"I bet they loved that. How are the twins?" Nick inquired, referring to Brett and Karen's ten-year-old twin sons. Brett was a committed family man. He and Karen had been married for fourteen years. Karen enjoyed being an at-home mom, and they worked hard to balance their careers and their family life. Brett and Karen both walked away from more than one promotion, unwilling to compromise family time for financial gain.

Karen, a director of marketing for a small cosmetics company, put her career on hold for nine years to stay at home with the twins. She returned to work last year to ensure that they would be ready to finance college for the twins eight years from now.

Nick was never quite sure how to feel about Brett and Karen's approach to the work-life balance. On one hand, he knew if he was in the same situation, he wouldn't sacrifice one income to babysit kids—even if they were his kids. There are simply too many other things he wanted in life—yes, material things.

On the other hand, he deeply respected Brett and Karen for having the guts to sacrifice a director's income simply to "be there" for their kids. When it came to matters of the heart, Brett typically put people before profit. It was a life philosophy Nick didn't fully appreciate nor emulate. However, he couldn't deny there was something enviable about it.

Nick glanced at his watch. It was almost 9:15.

"Have you guys seen Ally this morning?" he asked. "She's usually not late for team meetings."

"Haven't seen her," John offered. "Maybe she is catching up on the latest office gossip," he teased, knowing Ally seemed to be above idle chatter.

"I haven't seen her, but she knows we're meeting. I'm sure she'll be here any minute," Brett added.

"Well, let's get started without her," Nick suggested. "Let's review Phase Two headlines. We'll look at layouts when Ally arrives. Brett, what have you got?"

Brett passed out his list of headline concepts and intro body copy. Before he could take them through his ideas, they were interrupted by an urgent knock on the door. Sam Morris let himself in. He looked at Nick with a grim face.

"What's wrong Sam?"

"There's been an accident."

"Ally?" Nick knew instinctively.

"Yes! She was involved in a car accident early this morning. We don't know very much. Shelly Marsh from accounting was driving behind her. She witnessed it, called 911, talked to the ambulance driver and the cops and then called the office.

Nick swallowed hard. "How much do you know?"

"All I know is an SUV blew through a red light and hit her broadside.

"Driver's side?" Brett asked, anticipating the worst.

"Yes, rescue workers just freed her from the car."

"How long was she trapped?" Nick asked, his voice rising with concern and his breathing suddenly becoming labored.

"Maybe an hour, but they got her out, and she was just taken to emergency at Cook County General Hospital. The details of her injuries are sketchy. I'm sending Judy there now to see how she is doing and…"

"I'll go," Nick said, interrupting Sam. Yet, he shuttered at the sound of his own voice. He once promised himself he would never step into that hospital again, and now he inadvertently was jumping at the opportunity.

"I need you here today. Judy will call us as soon as she knows something. Besides, Tom Sullivan called earlier and will be in this morning. He wants to review the creative strategy and execution of both campaigns with you. Plus, he wants your feedback on some PR initiatives."

"That will have to wait," Nick insisted, his tone firm and direct as his fear conceded to his conviction. "I need to know if she is all right. I'll go."

Nick knew better than to defy a directive from Sam, especially in front of his colleagues. He also realized the urgency in his voice revealed his feelings for Ally, so he attempted to cloak them in professional etiquette.

"Look, Sam, Ally is a key member of my creative team for the Transitions account. It only makes sense that I go. Besides, once I assess the situation, I'll call you with the details."

"I said I prefer that you stay here. I'll send Judy," Sam countered.

"No, Sam, I'll go. Reschedule the meeting with Tom for this afternoon. I won't be gone long."

Nick's comments were met with a long pause. He knew Sam was contemplating how he should quench his deliberate insubordination in front of the creative team. Although Sam was Nick's mentor, he valued his ego more than he valued Nick. He knew he would pay a price for this in the future.

"Okay, fine, you go," Sam conceded. "But get back here as soon as you can and call me when you know Ally's condition."

When Nick arrived at the hospital, he stalled outside the revolving door. He couldn't bring himself to go in. He backed away from the ER entrance and intuitively reached for a pack of cigarettes in his breast pocket. His pocket was empty. He had stopped smoking several years ago. Funny how bad habits surface to cope with stress. Nick had kept his promise to himself and hadn't set foot in this hospital since his mother had died. To this day, he didn't know all the details surrounding her accident. His father never talked about it, except in his drunken stupor when he blamed Nick for it.

All Nick knew for sure was his mother fought for her life for three days in this hospital after a head-on collision with a drunk driver. Part of him still wanted to know exactly what happened on that rainy night, but that would mean talking to his father.

As others passed through the revolving doors before him, Nick paced the sidewalk fidgeting with loose change in his pocket. He remembered the ER on that night long ago: the chaos, the panic, the pace, flashing lights, sirens, scents and his feelings of helplessness—feelings long buried until they gripped him now.

He sheepishly glanced at the large red block letters above the door:

E M E R G E N C Y R O OM. It's a room a ten-year-old should never end up in, especially in the middle of the night. But there he was—at the request of his dying mother. It's as if she knew she would slip away shortly after seeing him. Gus Milloy, a long-time family friend who lived nearby, watched over Nick that night when his mother went to pick up his father. Gus roused him from a deep sleep and brought him here in the dead of night. It was the night he first wondered if there was a God and concluded, if there was, he was not good. And now here he stood again, twenty-nine years later. The players had changed, but the script was the same.

He summoned the courage to walk through the revolving door and approached a white-haired woman at the information desk.

"Excuse me, a friend of mine was just involved in a car accident. I assume she is still in emergency. Can you confirm this?"

"What's the name?" she asked politely.

"Allison Grant."

She tapped the keys of her keyboard and tilted her head back so she could read the screen through the bifocals perched at the end of her nose. "Yes, it looks as though she is still in emergency."

"How do I get there?"

"Just take this main corridor past Radiology and turn right. There will be signs from there to guide you. I hope she's okay."

"Thank you."

The emergency room turned out to be what Nick expected, chaos. He slipped behind another family, walked through some doors he knew he wasn't supposed to, and started looking for Ally. He peeked in three exam rooms before he found her in Exam Four.

"Ally," he shouted, relieved to see her. She was groggy but appeared to have only minor cuts and abrasions on her face and arms.

"Excuse me, are you family, sir?" a nurse assisting the attending physician asked.

"No, I'm a friend and co-worker."

As the nurse approached Nick, he backpedaled out of the exam room. When they were both out of the exam room the nurse pulled the curtain closed and faced him. "I'm sorry, you can't be in here unless you're family."

Nick had lost someone he loved before in this hospital, and he wasn't going to let it happen again.

"Could you ask her if I can see her? I'm sure she would want to see me." Nick wasn't sure that would fly with Ally, but he had nothing to lose.

"What's your name?"

"Nick Conway."

"I'll ask her, but we have to conduct a procedure first. You'll have to go back to the waiting room and I'll come and get you."

"Okay, thanks."

The nurse returned to Ally and pulled the curtain behind her. Nick could see through the gap where the curtains came together. He backed away and found the best vantage point to see Ally.

She was conscious, her eyes were open, but she groaned as she shifted her weight on the gurney. A neck brace was firmly in place.

71

Her forehead had superficial cuts, and bits of broken glass were in her hair. The nurse took a scissors from her tray and rapidly cut through Ally's clothes, gingerly peeling them off. *I can't believe this is happening.* Nick had seen Ally wear this outfit before. She looked gorgeous in it. Now they were cutting it off her body as if they were shearing sheep. As the nurse worked her way around Ally, she stepped in the gap of the curtains and blocked Nick's narrow view.

Nick waited until he no longer heard the scissors and the distinct sound of fabric ripping. The nurse was wrapping Ally in warm blankets. She placed her clothes in a plastic bag. Another physician entered the exam room. There were so many conversations going he couldn't keep track of them.

He heard something about blood work, blood pressure, heart rate, X-rays, an MRI and a CAT scan and on and on. This is what he remembered about this hospital when he was ten: confusion, voices, big words, and no clear understanding of his mother's condition. In the flurry of activity, he simply stared at Ally's beautiful face.

When the nurse stepped out from behind the curtain, she was surprised to see Nick still standing there.

"Mr. Conway, you're still here. I was just coming for you. We're going to take Ally to Radiology. There is a waiting room there."

"Very well," he replied, and he followed the gurney.

When he arrived in Radiology the attending physician turned to Nick. "We're going to take a few tests. This may take a while. Ally has given us permission to talk to you and for you to see her. You can have a seat in the waiting room. When we know more, we will come and get you. We can talk then."

"Can you at least tell me the type of injuries you're looking for?"

"Well, a number of things in this type of accident: concussion, broken bones, fractured ribs. I'd like to take a picture of her lungs, major organs and her spinal column."

"Her spine?" Nick asked, nervously.

"Yes, she complained of back pain when she was first brought in, so we want to check it out."

As they rolled Ally away on the gurney, Nick walked to the waiting room. *It's funny how one minute everything is right with your world and the next it's unraveling.* Nick took a seat in the corner, grabbed his cell phone, called the office, and left a message for Sam indicating what little he knew.

When he got off the phone, he noticed the waiting room was empty. As he stared at the bland hospital walls, it occurred to him that at times like these most people would lean on God. Not Nick Conway. To this point in his life he had never given himself permission to yield control of his life to anyone, including God. He was not certain there was a God. *Worse, if there is a God,* he thought, *I don't think I could believe in him because he would be too much like my father—never there when I need him.*

Brett is convinced there is a God, and he is a God of love and justice. I don't get it. In my book, a God of love wouldn't allow my father to be an alcoholic and my mother to be killed by a drunk driver. And a God of justice wouldn't allow Ally to be injured seriously in a car accident by a guy who blows through a red light.

It's so much easier to dismiss God than to acknowledge him. And that's why I keep him and his Good Book in the same place: a remote corner on the top shelf of my bookcase—just beyond my reach.

In Nick's view, the only benefit of a crisis was that it revealed your true feelings for someone. When he saw Ally's cuts, the abrasions on her beautiful face, and the nurse crudely cutting her clothes off her body, he felt a strange sense of clarity. Clarity as to what really mattered in life. Clarity as to how he felt about her. Indeed, he knew he was falling in love with her all over again. Yet, he wondered why it took a crisis to bring clarity. *Why can't we tell someone how much we love them when all is well instead of when all is lost?*

Although he did not understand this God of the Bible whom Brett spoke so personally about, he was willing to make a deal with him. *After all,* Nick reasoned, *God is really no different from a client. Yes, a big client perhaps, but a client just the same. The rules of negotiation should apply, especially if there is something to gain for all parties.*

Nick glanced around the room to ensure his privacy and whispered under his breath, "God, if you exist and if you elect to hear me, I want to make a deal with you. I haven't done business with you before, so I'm not very good at this. But if you will spare Ally's life—and heal her—I promise to make a few changes in my life."

Nick paused and looked around again. He didn't want to have to explain why he was talking to himself. He was still alone in the room, so he continued. "God, if you heal Ally, I'll play it straight with you. No more denial. No more false bravado. And no more running. I'll even attempt to see my father again. I can't promise I will ever forgive him, but I'll try to make it right—but, hey, I'd appreciate a little help." He paused again to ponder how to close the deal, and more importantly, how he would live up to it.

"I'll give you my word if you give me yours. Deal? And God, it would sure help if you would go first."

Nick felt a strange peace subtly settle over him. It was as though God had accepted his end of the bargain. Nick started to fidget in his chair. He had never talked to God before, much less made a deal with him. Talking to him felt surreal, yet real; ludicrous, but legitimate; unfamiliar, but comforting; and contrived, yet genuine. Suddenly, Nick sensed what just happened was authentic, and it scared him.

About an hour later, a nurse came to get him in the waiting room and brought him to the attending physician. He had good news and explained her injuries.

Nick called the office. Sam was on the conference call he wanted Nick to handle with Tom Sullivan, Brett and John. He left a message with Judy, Sam's secretary, simply telling her Ally would be all right, and he would explain more later.

Nick stayed with Ally for a few more hours, until she was admitted to a room on the third floor. He didn't make it back to the office until late afternoon. When he arrived, he was met by Sam and Brett.

"What's the situation with Ally?" Sam demanded, clearly upset that he did not leave any details when he called in.

"She should be fine. X-rays and an MRI revealed six cracked ribs, a punctured lung and a mild concussion. The attending physician said it will be a slow, painful recovery, but she should be okay and will be back to work in a month or so."

Nick could see the concern on Brett's face. "What happened exactly?"

"A witness confirmed what Sam heard earlier. Apparently, some guy driving an SUV blew through a red light and hit her broadside on the driver's side. The impact pushed the door of her Acura into her ribs, injuring most of them. One of the ribs punctured her left lung. Shelly Marsh said her car was practically bent into a U-shape. Ally was pinned under the dashboard. That's why it took so long to get her out."

"This could have been much worse!" Sam muttered under his breath.

Sam excused himself and proceeded to explain Ally's status to Lisa, Michelle, and other employees in the art department while Brett followed Nick back to his office and briefed him on their earlier conference call with Tom Sullivan.

"Tom likes our creative direction and signed off on the headlines and copy," Brett said.

"Great. Did he like Ally's layouts?"

"He loved them. He wants to meet next week to discuss the media plan. I'll set something up."

"Thanks, Brett."

"How long will Ally be in the hospital?"

"Probably most of the week. She could be home by Friday."

"Well, I'm glad she's going to be okay," he said, as he turned to leave Nick's office.

"Brett, before you go, can I ask you a question?"

"Sure."

"Ally's accident—it wasn't her fault."

"Yeah?" Brett replied, not knowing what Nick was thinking.

"Well, you've talked with me before about the love of God and the wrath of God."

"Go on."

"When bad things happen to good people it doesn't seem like the love of God."

Brett interrupted him before he could finish. "So, you're wondering if Ally's accident is an example of the wrath of God?"

"Yeah."

"No," Brett replied confidently. "I think her accident is an example of the *grace* of God."

Nick looked bewildered. He ran his fingers through his hair and scratched the back of his head. He wondered if Brett was implying that Ally's accident was a part of some master plan.

CHAPTER

It was a very long day, but by quitting time Ally was resting comfortably at the hospital. Her mother had flown in from St. Louis leaving Ally's stepfather, Roger, behind. For a fleeting moment Ally felt hurt Roger didn't come too.

Brett invited Nick to dinner at his home. His wife, Karen, was a great cook, and it beat Hamburger Helper. Nick knew he would enjoy dinner, and he needed the company, so he gratefully accepted Brett's invitation.

After Brett greeted Nick at the door and hung up his coat, he returned to the kitchen counter where he took vegetables out of a steamer, placed them in a serving dish, added a dash of seasoning salt, pepper, and a slice of butter. Karen was behind him at the stove simmering slices of green peppers and onions. Her hair was up, she was wearing a slim cut pair of jeans that accentuated her fit figure, and she padded around the kitchen barefoot. Her casual attire suggested that Brett hadn't told her he had invited him for dinner until the last minute. Nick thought about how lucky Brett was to have her. It didn't seem to matter that he had caught her by surprise. Karen rolled with the punches and was one of those women who looked elegant in just about anything.

Brett warned him at the office that dinner would be nothing fancy. "We're not going to try to impress you," he stressed, "dinner is nothing more than glorified meatballs. Karen's recipe for Mad Hatter Meatballs is a favorite of our sons."

When Nick entered the kitchen, Karen greeted him with a smile and a warm embrace.

"Hey, Nick. How are ya? It's been a while," she said as she kissed him on the cheek.

"Yeah, long time. I'm good," he replied as he returned her kiss. "I don't hear the twins. That means they're not here, or they're into something."

"They're with Grandpa and Grandma Stevens. Brett called me at the last minute and said you were coming for dinner. It was too late to change the menu but not too late to change the atmosphere." She smiled. "Brett's folks are good about taking the kids on short notice. So, we can enjoy a quiet dinner tonight. We're glad you're here."

Nick could hear the kindness in her voice and see it in her eyes. It was one of her trademarks. Karen was a striking woman. She was a natural blonde with sculpted facial features. Her clear blue eyes, deep dimples and alluring smile not only made her the girl next door but also the gorgeous girl next door.

Her personality would charm anyone, but she had a gleam in her eye that conveyed a mischievous, yet playful sense of humor. Brett bore the brunt of that sense of humor, but he played right into her hands. They had an enviable marriage, but it hadn't always been that way. Nick remembered they had struggled early in their relationship with communication and financial issues, and they often laid unrealistic expectations on each other. Yet, unlike most young couples, somewhere along the way they got professional help and simply figured their relationship out. When most couples would have given up, they learned, with practice, how to navigate through their sea of differences.

Whereas Nick never took the time to examine what worked in their marriage, he did notice they never bailed on each other, and their commitment to "this God thing" seemed to work for them. They had no idea how much he envied them.

"Nick, can I get you something to drink?" Karen asked without taking her eyes off the frying pan.

"You know, just water with a lemon for me."

"Why don't you have a seat at the table then?" Brett added as he grabbed a bottled water and lemon from the fridge. "We should be ready to serve in a few minutes."

Brett poured the chilled water into a goblet, sliced a lemon and perched a slice on the edge of the glass. Nick took a seat at the kitchen table just beyond the breakfast bar and stared out the window that overlooked a wooded lot and a large pond. In a few months color would burst around their patio from their landscaping and perennials.

"I love your home, Karen."

"Thanks, we love it too. Have you been here before?"

"No, but it's my fault. Brett has invited me, but I could never seem to break away. How long ago did you build this house?"

"Just over two years ago," Brett answered.

"I think we're ready," Karen said as she brought the mashed potatoes and steamed vegetables to the table. Brett followed her with a fruit salad of strawberries, bananas, grapes and blueberries then returned to the stove.

He carefully poured Karen's special recipe of Mad Hatter Meatballs into a serving dish and brought them to the table. He sat alongside her.

"Will you say grace, Brett?"

"Let's give thanks," Brett said as they bowed their heads.

Nick felt himself squirm in his chair. He never knew what to do when someone prayed publicly. Yet tonight it felt different. He found himself clinging to every word, especially when Brett asked

God to heal Ally. Brett was speaking to God in such a personal way, almost as though he knew him or as if God was in the room. Prayer was all very new to Nick, and Brett's prayer seemed natural, sincere, compassionate and confident.

I remember Brett telling me once that prayer reveals the heart of man and unleashes the power of God. I don't know if that is true, but I feel something. Maybe it's just the sincerity of Brett's heart and my desperate hope that God, the God of the Bible as Brett always says, will allow Ally to recover quickly.

When Brett finished his prayer, he relished the aroma that wafted through the kitchen.

"It smells delicious, honey."

"Thanks, why don't you pass the meatballs to Nick and get started?"

Steam rose from the dish. Nick served himself a generous portion before passing them to Brett.

"This recipe really looks good. What's in the sauce?"

"It's a blend of tomato soup, chicken with rice soup, chopped onions and green peppers," Karen said. "And while it is not exactly a gourmet meal or a steak dinner, I know two ten-year-olds who love it."

"I warned you, Nick. We're going to treat you like family tonight, not a VIP," Brett reminded him.

"That's fine, I would rather be treated like family. I'm just happy to be here and to enjoy your company. It's been a long day. I'm concerned about Ally."

"I think we're all concerned about her," Karen agreed.

Nick dished up some steamed vegetables and fruit salad and then passed them to Karen.

"I just can't believe this happened to her today," Nick stated.

Brett nodded. "Yeah, one minute life is good--the next, everything you ever cared about is at risk."

"But why Ally? Of all people, why did this happen to her?" Brett and Karen could hear the frustration in Nick's voice and see the anxiety sweep over his face.

Karen was blunt. "You still love her, don't you?"

Embarrassed, he didn't know how to respond. He remembered what Ally had said about his false bravado, so he simply surrendered. "Is it that obvious?"

"Let's just say I've noticed it for awhile," Brett added.

"You two had something special once," Karen said gently. "It's not unusual for those feelings to be rekindled, especially in a crisis."

"My head seems really messed up. I honestly don't understand how I feel."

"Well," Brett said, "I'm just glad that, by God's grace, she's going to be okay."

"I've been thinking about what you said this afternoon about God's grace. Do you really believe God spared Ally's life?"

"Yes, I do."

"Why?"

"I can't answer why. Only God knows why. I suspect that he has more planned for her life and for the people she will impact during the course of it."

"I'm not sure I believe in God, or ever did, but I find the concept of grace interesting, yet contradictory."

"Contradictory?" Karen said, raising her eyebrows. "What is contradictory about it?"

"Obviously, I'm very thankful Ally's life was spared, but I don't understand how God chooses."

"What do you mean?" Brett asked.

"Well, what about all of the other people in this world who have died in car accidents? I mean, how does he choose whose life to spare?" The impact of the question sucked the air out of the room.

"Take my mom for example. Why wasn't she saved from the drunk driver by what you call the grace of God?"

Brett put his fork down as Nick's question lingered. "I can't answer that. No one can, simply because we don't know the mind of God. All we know for sure is, according to the Bible, God loves us, he is in control, and he is sovereign."

"Sovereign? What do you mean?"

"The Bible tells us that nothing happens by accident and nothing happens without God's knowledge and control. But *why* it happens, I cannot answer," Brett explained. "I can tell you that the Bible says that God's thoughts are not our thoughts and his ways are not our ways. Yet, it is very clear concerning the character of God—his deep love for us, and that he is at work in our daily lives. But we won't always know *how* he is working or *what* he is doing."

"Then why should I trust him?" Nick countered. "I'm sorry, Brett, but that just doesn't cut it."

"Fair enough, let's backtrack then," he suggested. "Let's start with a definition. God's grace is receiving unmerited favor. In other words, grace is like receiving a blessing you don't deserve. Think about your own life. Have you ever received a blessing you knew in your heart you didn't deserve?"

Nick paused to consider Brett's question. Karen got up to refresh their drinks and slice the dessert. Brett took a sip of his water and waited for Nick to answer. This is what Nick respected about Brett and Karen. They never attempted to stuff their beliefs down his throat. Instead, they left it up to him to come to his own conclusions. And regardless of their differences, Nick never felt judged by them.

Nick took the last bite of a meatball and pushed his plate away. "That was delicious, Karen," he said, and he turned his attention to Brett's question. "I guess I remember an example of what you would call unmerited favor or a blessing I didn't deserve.

"I used to go into this old hobby store most of the summer when I was a young teen. I longed for this gas-powered plane on display. I didn't have any money and I knew my dad would never buy it for me, so I would hang around the hobby store and learn as much as I could about the planes. The store owner, a kind old man named Les, got to know me and eventually let me handle a few display models."

Karen placed a piece of French apple pie in front of Nick as he continued his story. "After hanging around that store all summer, I worked up the courage to steal one of the model planes. I didn't think about how it would make Les feel. I just wanted a gas-powered airplane, and the only way that I saw to get it was to steal it.

"So, one Sunday afternoon when a new clerk was working, I stuffed a small gas-powered plane into my gym bag and sneaked out the back."

"What happened?" Karen asked.

"Well, I got caught by an employee I didn't see taking his break in the back of the store."

"Then what happened?" Brett asked.

"The new clerk said he was going to call the police. But he called Les at home first and told him he caught a young teen stealing. Les asked him to detain me until he arrived and then he would call the police."

"Were you scared?" Karen inquired.

"Yes, but I wasn't as scared of the police as I was of the look of disappointment on Les's face. When Les arrived, as you can imagine, he was shocked to see that this kid who had won his trust was now stealing from him."

Brett took a drink of his water. "How did you *feel*?"

"Can you say, Benedict Arnold? I was humiliated."

"What did Les say?"

"Well, he gave me a 'how could you' look of disappointment. I'm sure he expected to see anyone but me. Then a funny thing happened. He said, 'Let's go for a ride.' Naturally, I thought he was going to take me to the police station himself, and I started thinking that my dad would kill me when he found out."

Nick took bite of his pie and then wiped his mouth with a napkin. Karen and Brett waited for him to continue.

"I got in his car and he drove downtown toward the police station, but before we arrived, he pulled into an old drive-in diner. The next thing I knew he was buying me a hamburger and a root beer. Les was silent while I ate, and I felt the guilt of betrayal creep over me. Soon I feared the guilt more than the police or my dad.

"Les kindly asked me why I stole from him. I told him the

truth. 'I always wanted a gas-powered plane, and I had no money. My father will never buy it for me—so I stole it.'

"Then he said something strange. 'If you had the money would you have bought the plane from me?'

"'Sure,' I said. 'It's not like I'm a thief or anything.'

"Les laughed and then looked me in the eye. I felt like he could see through me. 'You're not a thief?'" he asked, surprised.

"'No,' I said, with great conviction.

"'Are you sure?' he pressed. 'Well, that's nice to know,' he said with a laugh. 'For a minute there I thought you were a common thief. But you're not a thief. You're just an honest man with no money—and one of my planes. That's different. I can fix that.'

"'Huh?' I said, perplexed. 'How can you fix that?'

"'Well, an honest man with no money is a simple fix. He simply needs a job, and I happen to be looking for a young man who knows something about gas-powered planes to work in my store every other weekend. You would be paid, of course. Are you available?'

"Before I finished my hamburger, Les hired me. He created a simple payment plan, and I eventually paid him for the stolen plane. He never told the police or my father."

Karen was visibly moved. Brett nodded with approval before he spoke.

"Nick, that's grace. Les granted you unmerited favor. He gave you a blessing you didn't deserve."

"Yeah, and I really needed that job!"

"He gave you much more than a job. He gave you a second chance. He restored your dignity. And, he gave you a reason to believe in yourself and in others again," Brett added.

"Most importantly," Karen chimed in, "he gave you your relationship back because he was willing to trust you again."

"As a kid, I thought he simply cut me a break. Gave me a pass."

"Just a random act of kindness?" Brett asked.

"Yeah, something like that."

"No, I think it was more than that. In fact, I think Ally's

accident today and your childhood experience with Les gave you a second glimpse of God. A glimpse of his grace—unmerited favor—in the everyday events of life."

Nick thought for a moment. He was unfamiliar with this whole concept of grace or unmerited favor. Who in this world, he wondered, grants unmerited favor, and who would ever give you what you didn't deserve?

CHAPTER 10

Nick spent most of the next day thinking about Ally, not his work. Since he was adept at playing roles, he thought no one in the office noticed just how distracted he was except for Brett and possibly Sam. He was wrong. In client briefing meetings he found himself obsessed with the clock. During conference calls he drummed his fingers on the table, stared out the window, and asked questions that had been answered earlier in the conversation. And during new client introductions he asked them their names immediately after they had been introduced to him. Nick may have been in the building, but he was clearly not *there*.

He left the office before five o'clock and was on his way to see Ally. He stalled momentarily before entering the hospital but found it easier this time because he used the unfamiliar main entrance.

When he arrived at her room she was sleeping. A woman's coat was draped over the visitor's chair, and the window sill was lined with flowers. No one was in the room with her, so he slipped into the chair beside her. As he brushed against the bed she awoke.

"Mom, is that you? I must have drifted off," she said squinting before opening her eyes.

"No, it's me, Nick."

"Hey, stranger," she said with a slight boost of energy that encouraged him.

"Hey. How ya doing?"

"All right, I guess," she replied softly. Her punctured lung created labored breathing and short, shallow breaths.

"Are you going to be okay?"

"Yeah, but I'm sore all over. It even hurts to eat. And it really hurts when I laugh. It's a little hard to breathe, but I guess I'll live."

"Well, you've got a lot of people at the office worried about you."

"Some people will do anything for attention I guess," she said with a sideways smile. Nick laughed quietly, admiring her spirit. The moment reminded him of how she had always accepted adversity. Forever the optimist.

"You remember what happened?"

"Not much." She spoke in short sentences and took a breath between each sentence. "I remember the intersection. I remember the light turning green. That's all."

"You never made it through the intersection. Some careless fool in an SUV blew through a red light and nailed you. Witnesses said you never saw him coming. Can you believe that guy? He was probably running late for work and tried to beat the light."

"Yeah. They said he had been drinking, too." Nick looked away, glancing out the window at this new revelation. *Why does alcohol seem to follow me?* he wondered. *Everything that has ever mattered to me has, in some way, been affected by alcohol or an alcoholic. Why? I wonder how Brett would answer this?*

"Where is your mom?" he said, changing the subject to mask his anger.

"Downstairs getting dinner in the cafeteria."

"It's nice she's here for you."

"Yeah, I'm glad they're here."

"Oh, did Roger decide to come?"

"No," she said, as she labored slightly to catch her next breath. "Ron flew in from New York. Met her at O'Hare. Brought her here."

"Nice," Nick replied with a slight smile that couldn't possibly cloak how rattled he felt inside. In the midst of his emotions, he failed to account for Ron. *This clown is back in the picture. Actually, he isn't "back" in the picture. He never left the picture.* Nick realized that his emotions were deceiving him again. Just because he might be falling in love with Ally again didn't mean she was falling in love with him.

A woman's voice came from behind him. "Oh, who is this?" It was Ally's mother, Helen, accompanied by a tall handsome man Nick's age.

"Mom, remember Nick Conway?"

"Oh, yes, of course. Hello, Nick."

"Hey, Mrs. Grant."

"It's not Mrs. Grant anymore, but please, call me Helen."

"Okay. And this is?" Nick asked, as he turned to the dapper gentlemen smartly dressed in pressed casual clothes punctuated with a classy tie.

"This is Ron, Ally's *new* boyfriend."

"Mom, please!" Ally replied, clearly disappointed her mother made her feel like Ron was her flavor of the week. Nick didn't miss the underlying message: Ally had moved on with her life, and Nick represented nothing more than the past.

Nick extended his hand and noticed Ron's firm handshake. He read into it as most men do; he was a strong man, probably stronger than Nick. Ron's hand was slightly rough and calloused. He probably was no stranger to manual work. Maybe he was a handy guy or enjoyed wood-working or weightlifting in his spare time. What troubled Nick most was he was so easy on the eyes. Handsome. Pressed and starched shirt. Tie centered and carefully held in place with a gold tie chain. Perfect knot. Thick, five o'clock shadow. Jet black hair, like Ally's, with every strand in place. *He must be one of those hairspray guys,* Nick thought. *Most women would find him very attractive. He looks more like a news anchor than a freelance photographer.* Yet, judging by appearances alone, it looked like they belonged together.

"How you feeling, sweetheart?" Ron asked, as he leaned over to kiss her on the cheek. "Sweetheart." It was term of endearment Nick never understood. It seemed like such a meaningless term. *"Sweetheart." I even hate the sound of it. It's so superficial,* he thought. *A sweetheart can be your high school girlfriend, your five-year old daughter, or, your waitress at a chintzy restaurant. The word doesn't remotely convey the depth of a relationship which, in this case, may be its saving grace.*

Despite his rationalization, the term troubled him for a simple reason. While the term was meaningless to him, he could not deny the fact that only Ron knew the real meaning he attached to it, and, more importantly, the weight it carried with Ally.

"Look, I'm going to give your mom a ride home and then grab a bite to eat. I'll come back later to see you," Ron offered, to offset the "Two is company, three is a crowd" phenomenon taking place in the room.

"Okay. See you tomorrow, Mom."

"Try to get some rest, dear. I'll see you first thing," Helen promised, as she leaned over and kissed Ally's forehead.

"Nice guy," Nick said, after Ron and Helen left the room.

"Yeah, he's a sweetheart," Ally responded, reinforcing Nick's viewpoint on the "Sweetheart" theory and adding further confusion regarding the depth of their relationship.

"Nick, I'm going to be out for a week or so. Will you follow-up with Michelle on the layouts?" She paused to take a breath. "You know, for the Transitions account? Michelle knows what to do."

"I'll take care of it. You just take care of yourself."

"I will. I always have."

"Yes, you have," Nick replied, picking up on her reference to their past. Ally could read the reservation in his eyes.

"What's wrong?" she asked as she carefully repositioned herself in the bed.

"What makes you think something is wrong?"

"That look in your eyes."

"What look?"

"The empty stare."

"Nothing's wrong."

She smiled in resignation. "Still won't talk to me, eh?"

"I was just thinking..."

She paused for him to continue.

"I was just thinking that I, I should have..."

"Go on?"

He looked away then returned his gaze to her. "I should have taken better care of you when I..."

"Yes, you should have," she said, as a smile curled around her lips. "A little late—but it's about time you realized it."

Nick exhaled heavily feeling both the embarrassment for their past and the loss of a future together. "Must you be so frank all the time?" The question hung in the air. Ally didn't have the energy or the inclination to answer it.

"That was a long time ago, Nick. Thanks for coming tonight."

"Get some rest now. See you tomorrow."

When he walked to the elevator Ally stared at the ceiling. She wondered if Nick would actually visit her tomorrow or if his comment was nothing more than a convenient cliché so often used to close a conversation.

When he got in the elevator and pushed the button for the ground floor, he replayed the conversation in his head. He wondered what he meant by his last sentence, too.

CHAPTER 11

At work the next day Nick found himself preoccupied with Ally again. *Should I go see her after work or just check in over the phone? It would be much easier to call.* She wouldn't see him so she couldn't read his face, or his mind. He wouldn't run the risk of bumping into Ron, and he wouldn't have any polite but clumsy conversations with her mother.

All day he wrestled with the notion of calling or visiting Ally. He stopped by Brett's office after his four o'clock briefing meeting with a new client. Brett was editing body copy for the Transitions account.

"Hey, Brett. How's it going? I wanted to let you know that we got approval today to develop the online campaign for Tyler Medical."

"Great, when do you want to sit with the client?" Brett asked without taking his eyes off his computer monitor.

"In a couple of weeks. They gave me a strategy brief today and want to regroup later this month. This is going to be a big account for us. John is really building our medical portfolio."

Brett wheeled around in his chair to face Nick. "Yeah, he's on a roll. Hey, by the way, have you talked to Ally today?"

"No. Actually, that's one of the reasons I stopped by. I was thinking about seeing her tonight, but I saw her last night and it was a little awkward."

"Awkward?"

"Yeah, you know, her mom was there, and her new boyfriend was there, then I showed up."

"Ally has a boyfriend? Interesting."

"Yeah. Ron somebody. He's a freelance photographer from New York. Seems like a nice guy. I don't want to get in the way, but I would like to see her. You know, update her on the Transitions account and make sure she's doing okay."

"Yeah, right," Brett said with a smirk.

"What's the smirk all about?"

"Nothing."

"Come on, Brett!"

"I heard that Michelle updated her on the Transitions account this morning. She said Ally was doing okay except she was having a little trouble breathing. So now you know. So, there is no reason to see her today."

"Well, yeah, but..."

"Look, Nick, I'm just yanking your chain. You and I both know you want to go see her. So, go see her! I know it's complicated and awkward but if you really care about her don't be afraid to show it."

"That's easy for you to say. You don't have anything at risk."

"And what do you have at risk?"

"Well, obviously she has a boyfriend. If I show too much concern and she's in love with the guy, I'll look stupid."

Brett laughed. "In every meaningful relationship, when love is on the line, one of the two parties has got to put his or her feelings out there first. At some point in every relationship someone always says, 'I love you' first—and the minute he or she does, there's a risk if the other party doesn't respond the same way, right?"

"Right, but this is not about telling her I love her."

"No, but it is about showing her you are deeply concerned about her even if it puts your feelings at risk."

"Okay, but I am not ready for that."

"Has she ever put her feelings for you out there first?"

"Yeah, once. Okay, maybe twice."

"So, she was willing to risk her feelings for you?"

"I guess."

"So, she was willing to be vulnerable for you?"

"Okay, where are you taking this?"

"I'm just saying that if you know you love her, don't be afraid to risk something for her. You don't have to say anything or commit yourself to anything. But if you *know* you're falling in love with her again, and if you're concerned about her, don't be afraid to show her even if you feel it puts you and your feelings at risk. She did it for you. Twice."

Nick's struggle about visiting Ally again ended when he left Brett's office. He drove straight to the hospital. Once he committed himself, driving to the hospital felt as comfortable as driving home.

When the doors of the elevator opened there was only one person inside. Nick didn't look at him. Instead he simply stared at the floor and said, "Three, please," as the man pushed the button.

"Hey, Nick."

It was Ron.

"Oh, hey, Ron. How are you?" he said, stunned by his sudden predicament. He smiled as he realized there are few situations in life more ironic than being alone in an elevator with the boyfriend of your ex-girlfriend, especially when both were on the way to see her.

"What's the latest with Ally?" Nick casually asked, feeling a certain amount of security by asking a question that suggested he had some emotional distance from her.

"I talked with her this morning. She's feeling a little better."

"Still in a lot of pain?"

"Yeah. The cracked ribs are extremely painful, but the doctors are more concerned about the punctured lung possibly filling with fluid. They don't want the complications of restricted breathing or pneumonia."

When the elevator doors opened, they walked to Ally's room together and exchanged small talk. Ally raised her eyebrows when they entered the room together. Nick felt the pressure of the sudden side-by-side comparison: last year's model versus this year's model; the past versus the future; what might have been versus what's yet to come. Typically, Nick would be cavalier in such a comparison, but today he felt very much the underdog.

"Look who has come to see you, Ally. Your boss," Ron announced.

The statement caught Nick by surprise and made him wonder just how much Ron knew about him and his former relationship with Ally. This question created a host of others.

Just what does Ron really know about me? Did Ally really tell him I'm her boss, or did he make this erroneous assumption? And if he assumed it, why didn't she correct him? I know it's safer, cleaner and less complicated to be considered her boss, but I think I would rather be known as her former boyfriend. At least there's some status to that! And it levels the playing field. As an old boyfriend I would be considered a former player in her life, unless, of course, she minimized that too, and relegated me to an asterisk. *A guy I once dated. A mistake. No big deal.

"Hey, stranger," Ally said in a whisper. It made Nick feel good that she somehow addressed him first. Ron reached over and grasped her hand.

"Hey, Sweetheart. How you feeling today?"

She spoke in shallow breaths. "I'm having a little more trouble breathing."

"Is there anything I can do? Anything?" Nick spoke in kind, soothing tones to match Ron's approach. Ron adjusted her pillow, helped her sit up, and filled her glass with fresh water. Nick watched, a mere spectator in the drama unfolding before him. He was not in control, and he hated it. He had no legitimate role here, at least not the one he wanted, so he looked for a reason to excuse himself.

"Have you guys eaten?" Ally asked before he could find his way out of the room.

"No," Ron replied. Nick remained silent.

"Well, if you're hungry, you should get something before the cafeteria closes downstairs," she suggested.

"I'm really not hungry, and I can't stay long. You go ahead, Ron," Nick offered.

Ron didn't appear to be the kind of guy that would settle for fast food, much less hospital food, so it surprised Nick that he accepted Ally's suggestion so readily. Before he left, he adjusted Ally's covers. "Okay, I won't be long."

Nick watched as Ron left the room, then gazed at Ally.

"Bad day today?"

"Yeah, I felt better yesterday."

"It's going to take awhile before you're feeling normal again. You took quite a hit. I'm really sorry this happened to you."

"It was an accident. It's no one's fault, really," she said, dismissing the severity of her situation.

Nick took exception. "Yes, it was someone's fault! That man blew through the red light."

"It happens, Nick. Besides..." She took a breath, and then elected not to finish her sentence.

"Besides what?" Nick inquired.

Ally hesitated.

Nick raised his eyebrows as if to say, "Go on."

"Besides, I've been hurt worse."

"When?"

Ally just looked at him and he knew. "You might say, I was side-swiped once before, remember?" she said.

"I'm sorry for that, too, Ally. I..."

She cut him off. "Forget it. It was a long time ago."

"Yes, but if I could go back—" He stopped short. He walked over and closed the hospital room door. He pulled the chair closer to the bed so he could sit next to her.

"If I could go back, I would do things much differently."

Ally shifted her weight to face him.

"I've made a lot of mistakes in my life, Ally, but none as great as I made with you..."

Suddenly uncomfortable, Ally interrupted him and redirected the conversation. "Remember the time," she said, pausing to take a breath, "we went to that outdoor summer concert at Alpine Valley?"

He was surprised she abruptly changed the subject, but he followed her lead. "Yeah, it was a clear night as we laid under the stars. Seemed like we talked for hours."

"We did. Remember what we talked about?"

"Not really, but I do remember how I felt."

"How did you feel?"

"Honestly?"

"Yeah."

"Exhilarated. Alive. In love. Why do you ask?"

"I felt the same way. Two young people. Our whole lives ahead of us. Lying on the ground. Staring at the stars, talking, laughing, dreaming..."

He finished her sentence. "...and loving life on a beautiful balmy summer night. I remember that feeling we all have in our twenties, that feeling of invincibility. Life doesn't get any better than that."

"It doesn't."

"What *did* we talk about, Ally?"

"A little bit of everything I guess, but mostly the future."

"Really, the future?"

"*Our* future, Nick. Do you remember asking me, 'Where do you think we will be in five or ten years?' It could have easily been a rhetorical question except for the key word."

"The *key* word?"

"*We*," she said. "Where do you think *we* will be in five or ten years?"

"The question assumed we would still be together, didn't it?" he said, as he began to recall the moment.

"Yeah. Funny how life is different from dreams." She paused again to take a breath. "Somehow I didn't picture myself in a hospital bed having trouble breathing at thirty-something."

As she repainted the past, Nick suddenly felt the full impact of this memory. He looked into her eyes. She returned his gaze. Time seemed to stop. They could no longer hear the din of the hospital in the background. They no longer felt confined to the present. If only for a moment they seemed to leave the room, the hospital, even the time zone. They were in a different place, a comfortable place, a safe place, and an uncomplicated place: the past. Younger. In love. And ready to embrace the future with energy, optimism and, most importantly, each other.

A sudden tap at the door shattered the silence and suspended their travel through time. Simultaneously, they came crashing back to this place called reality, confined to a time called the here and now, and a space called a hospital room. From bland, sterile walls to painful broken ribs, the present engulfed them once more.

The door squeaked as it slowly opened and Ron stepped in. "I'm back," he said, oblivious to the moment he altered forever.

"How was your dinner?" Ally asked quietly.

"I didn't eat much. What can I say? It's hospital food." He chuckled.

"Now you know why I wasn't hungry," Nick added. "Well, it's getting late and I'm sure you guys want to visit for awhile. I'd better be going."

"Thanks for coming, Nick." Ally offered.

"Yeah, sure. Nice to see you again, Ron. Catch you later."

"Okay. Thanks for stopping," Ron said gently. "You have all been so kind at the agency. It's great that you and Ally's co-workers have taken the time to come and see her."

"No problem," Nick replied, as he left the room.

When he drove out of the parking lot, he took what seemed like a very long ride home.

CHAPTER

During the next few days Ally's breathing became more labored as her left lung began to fill with fluid. Ron and Nick showed up every day, and although it was noticeable that Ron began to grow uncomfortable with Nick's daily visits, he never said a word. Nick varied the times he visited Ally, assuming, by the law of averages, that he would never arrive at the same time as Ron. However, Murphy's Law somehow put them in the same room with her at the same time most nights. When they arrived this day, a physician was talking with Ally. He turned to face them as they entered the room.

"Gentlemen, I'm going to take Ally downstairs for a short time. Would you like to wait in the waiting room on the first floor or grab a cup of coffee in the cafeteria?"

"What's going on?" Ron asked. Nick stepped back to take it in knowing he had no say in the scene that was unfolding.

"I was just explaining to Ally that we need to insert a chest tube," the physician explained.

"We need to aspirate the fluid in her lungs. It won't take long. You're welcome to wait."

"Ally, I'll wait in the cafeteria and come back in a half hour," Ron replied, clearly concerned.

Two aides wheeled Ally to the elevator while Ron and Nick walked to the cafeteria together. They each bought a cup of coffee and sat at a table in the corner near windows overlooking a fountain that had been shut down for the winter.

Nick understood why Ron was still there, and he knew Ron must be wondering why he was still there. Nick couldn't blame him; he wondered the same thing. The physician gave Nick a reason to excuse himself and come back tomorrow. Yet, he hung around making the situation a little clumsy and intense. Ron gazed out the window while Nick pondered what he could possibly say.

"Ally tells me you are a freelance photographer," he offered to blunt the awkwardness. "How long have you been on your own?"

"About eight years."

"Enjoy it?"

"Yeah, I like being my own boss, and I like the variety of assignments I get. It doesn't hurt to name your own price, too."

"It's everyone's dream, isn't it? To run your own business and make a good living at it."

"I guess so. It's nice chasing your dreams and doing what you love."

Ron spoke with a quiet sincerity that was easy to detect, and Nick felt that in a different time and place he would have liked this guy.

"How long has Ally worked for you?" Ron asked, catching Nick off guard.

He wondered how to answer. He was not technically Ally's boss. In fact, she only reported directly to him on the Transitions Addiction Recovery Center account. But, since he selected her as the art director for this account, she did, in effect, work for him.

"Ah, just a few months. I got a promotion to VP a short time ago, and she works for me on key accounts. But we worked together for several years at various agencies right after college."

"So, you've known each other for years?"

"Oh, yeah."

"So, you're old friends?"

"Right. Old friends." Nick replied in a confident tone to reinforce friendship rather than suggest *relationship*. Ron exhaled hard, took another sip of his coffee and seemed to relax and become a little more comfortable.

"Ron, how did you and Ally meet?"

"Actually, I met her quite by accident," he replied, staring into his coffee cup. "I bumped into her at an art museum in New York when she was there visiting her friend Kate."

"Kate Codell?"

"Yeah. You know her?"

"I do."

"Well, I had a small exhibit of my work on display. You know, every so often they have exhibits of local artists and photographers. Ally said she was interested in photography, so I asked if she would like to see my exhibit. She agreed, so I showed her, and we talked for a while."

"Nice," Nick said, dreading every word.

"It didn't take long before I could see her love for art. She has genuine passion for art and her work."

"Yeah, she is a very creative person, and she enjoys self expression through the medium of art," Nick confirmed. "She could easily spend a lot of time in a museum."

"I found that out. I told her that in a former life I was a tour guide in that museum, so I offered to give her the two-bit tour."

Nick raised his eyebrows. "But it turned into the premium tour?"

"Something like that. We had a good time. I enjoyed her company. Her free spirit and easy smile were very attractive to me. So, after our tour, I asked her if we could have a cup of coffee together." Ron stopped abruptly. "Am I boring you?"

"No, go on," Nick assured him. He hung on every word. Nick had always believed that, in every relationship, knowledge was power. The more you knew, the more weapons you had in your arsenal to manipulate future circumstances. He needed to know everything possible about Ron and his relationship with Ally, so he encouraged him to ramble on.

"Over coffee, Ally shared a little more about her life, her love for art, and her career in advertising as an art director. I loved her spunk, the way she presented herself and her optimistic outlook on life. After coffee, I asked her how long she would be in New York and if I could see her again before she returned to Chicago. She arranged a double date with Kate and her boyfriend."

"Sounds like that worked out great."

"It did. We've stayed in touch. She has come to see me in New York a few times and stayed with Kate. When I've been in Chicago on business, I've stopped to see her."

"It was good of you to come now, Ron," Nick said, not sure if he honestly believed what he was saying. "Ally said you were in the middle of a big photo shoot in New York for a demanding client when you got the call. Must be tough to drop everything when you run your own business, the client is breathing down your neck, and the deadline looms."

"It is. But wouldn't you do the same thing if you loved someone?"

The answer was obvious, but Nick wrestled with the way he posed the question. It was rhetorical and seemed to skirt what Nick longed to know. *Does Ron really love Ally? If he did, why didn't he say, "You do what you got to do when you love someone." At least that would have removed all doubt about how he felt about her. Yet, Ron framed the question differently. He seemingly removed himself and his feelings from the equation. He said, "But wouldn't you do the same thing if you loved someone?"*

Nick knew he was splitting hairs. He knew he was looking for a loophole, and he knew he was, once again, living in denial. Denial was such a familiar and comfortable place for him. After all, he had lived there a long time.

Nick observed Ron's gentle yet confident demeanor as he spoke of Ally. He knew Ron deserved her—yet he stubbornly refused to believe that Ron loved her; and worse, that she might love him. He convinced himself that by acknowledging another man's love for Ally, she would somehow no longer be available for him—and he certainly wasn't willing to do that.

CHAPTER

After Ron and Nick had talked for awhile in the cafeteria, they walked back to Ally's room. Nick stopped briefly at the nurses' station and asked the head nurse, Gwen, if Ally had returned to her room from the chest tube insertion procedure.

Gwen was a bright and attractive nurse around Ally's age, and she ran a very tight ship. Nick clearly noticed that her second shift appeared more efficient than the first shift. He was sure that Gwen had a lot to do with it.

"She's back," Gwen said with a smile. "But I'll have to warn you. She's going to be tired now, guys."

"We understand," Nick said.

"Okay, I just wanted to remind you that she has labored to breathe all day, so she's exhausted. The insertion of the chest tube will drain her lung of excess fluid and make it easier to breathe but it will also make her weary."

"Fine, we won't be staying long," Ron assured her. Nick gave Ron a fleeting glance. He wasn't sure how he felt about Ron speaking for him, but he agreed.

"Yeah, we won't be long."

When they reached Ally's room an aide was placing pillows behind her head and pulling the covers up to her shoulders.

"You warm enough, honey?" she asked. Ally nodded and turned to Ron and Nick.

"Hey," she said in a weak attempt to greet both of them.

"Hey," they replied in unison.

"Look, Ally, you need your rest so I'll hit the road," Nick said. "I'll catch you tomorrow."

"Thanks for stopping by again." She took another shallow breath. "But don't feel you have to stop by every day."

"Yeah, don't go out of your way, Nick," Ron concurred. "You've done enough."

Nick let the final three words ring in his ears and instinctively attached more than one meaning to them. Nick then uncharacteristically stepped toward the bed, held Ally's hand and said, "Good night. I'll see you soon."

Ron's eyes followed him out of the room.

When he was in the hallway, he stalled just beyond the door out of their line of sight but within earshot. He wanted to hear what they would say. He wondered if Ron would question Nick's frequent visits. Instead, he spoke to Ally in loving tones. "You should get some rest, Sweetheart..."

With that, Nick walked down the corridor to the elevator. Ron lingered for ten more minutes before Gwen entered the room.

"Hey, Ally, I just need to change your IV and take your vitals, and then we'll turn the lights down and close your door so you can get some rest tonight."

"That's a good idea. You need to get some sleep," Ron echoed. "I'll see you tomorrow morning."

As Ron left the room, Gwen pulled a fresh IV bag from her cart, hung it, and started the drip.

"Tired?" she asked sensitively.

"Yeah, it's been a long day," Ally said quietly, her breaths short and measured.

"And you've had a lot of company. That tires you out more than you realize. But your last two visitors are a nice kind to have," she said with a wink.

"Why do you say that?"

Gwen smiled warmly. "Well, most women in the hospital would feel a little better having two handsome men come visit them every night."

"Yeah. But it's also complicated."

"How is that?" she asked, as she attached a blood pressure cuff to her left arm. Ally wondered if she should divulge what she was thinking. She trusted Gwen, but she was used to keeping her feelings to herself. She remembered sharing one of her problems once with a stranger who sat next to her on a flight to California. She got sound advice and enjoyed the relief that only venting can bring.

"It's complicated because," she whispered, pausing for a moment, "they're former boyfriends."

Gwen hesitated. "Well, then, maybe now is not the best time to take your blood pressure," she said with a smile. "Two old boyfriends back in your life? Hmmm, I can think of worse problems to have."

Ally felt the warmth in Gwen's teasing and started to relax. "Actually, they are not both old boyfriends," she said slowly, taking time to catch her breath. "One is a current boyfriend. The other is an ex-boyfriend."

"Oh, well, what's so complicated about that?"

Ally drew a deep breath. "I think the former boyfriend is trying to make a comeback."

Gwen raised her eyebrows and removed the blood pressure cuff. "Oh, that *is* a little complicated. Your blood pressure is good."

Ally cleared her throat. "And I'm not sure how I feel about the current boyfriend."

"Now that's a *lot* complicated," Gwen said, as she folded her arms.

Their eyes met. "Gwen, I can't believe I could love two guys who are so different."

Gwen laughed. "That's why we are so mysterious, girl. We don't want guys to figure us out. Maybe I can help you sort this out. How are they different and what do you like most about them?"

"You're on duty. I'm sure you don't have time for this."

"Hey, I came in early and worked first shift today, remember? So, I'm going home after I talk to you. That is, if you want to talk."

"Where do I start?" Ally spoke in short sentences to control her breathing. "Nick is witty and outgoing. Ron is sincere and reserved."

Gwen interrupted. "Wait a minute. Which one is Nick, and which one is Ron?"

"Nick has brown hair and is about my height. Ron is tall and has jet black hair like mine."

"And which one is the ex-boyfriend, and which is the current boyfriend?"

"Nick is my ex. Ron is current."

"Okay, got it. What else do you like about them?"

"Nick is exciting and adventurous, and Ron is quiet but strong. They both love the outdoors."

"What else?"

"They are both creative. Nick is a writer and can paint beautiful pictures with words. Ron is a photographer and can paint a beautiful world with pictures."

"This is getting romantic. Don't stop now."

"Nick is organized, yet impulsive, and a risk taker. Ron is conservative, and, at times, controlling."

"So far things are leaning toward Nick in my love meter, Ally."

"Nick comes from a broken family, actually a shattered family. His father is an alcoholic and his mother was killed by a drunk driver.

Ron comes from a solid family. His family is the farthest thing I've seen from dysfunctional."

Gwen walked across the room and draped her stethoscope around her neck. "I see what you mean by complicated."

Ally went on. "Oh, let's see, what else? Nick can be selfish and sarcastic. Ron is unselfish and sincere."

Gwen brought her hand to her chin. "Now it's starting to balance. Anything else?"

"Despite his moodiness, Nick is fun, a good listener, and helps me figure out things." Ally took a breath.

"And Ron?"

"Ron is safe, and the answer man. He prefers to tell me the answer rather than listen and let me vent. So, what's your verdict now?"

Gwen thought for a moment. "Can I give it to you in a broad brushstroke?"

Ally shrugged her shoulders. "Why not?"

"Well, one sounds like a boyfriend and the other sounds like a husband. What I mean is, one is wild and crazy, fun and unpredictable and the other is conservative, safe and reliable. The kind you can settle down with for the long haul."

Ally rolled her eyes to the ceiling and paused to digest Gwen's evaluation. "I guess that sums it up and should make it easy, huh?" Ally said, impressed with Gwen's logic.

"It's never easy, Ally. Maybe it will add clarity to focus on just one attribute. Tell me, what is the *one* thing you like most about each of them?"

Ally exhaled and took a fresh breath. "Ron is very sincere, so he always has my best interests at heart."

"Any drawbacks?"

"He is over-protective, so he can be a little controlling and suffocating at times."

"And the thing you like most about Nick?"

"Back in the day, we had fun. Nick made me feel alive. He

always made me feel *free*. Free to be myself. Free to dream. I always knew he believed in me, and he pushed me to chase my dreams.

"And the drawbacks?

"Let's just say, he wasn't always there for me."

"Okay, so where do you want to go from here?" Gwen asked as she dimmed the lights in the room and lowered the bed so Ally could sleep.

"I don't know. I thought I did but..." her voice softened to a whisper.

Gwen walked to the door that Ron had closed when he had left. "If it were me, as much as I like wild, crazy, fun and a little unpredictable, I'd go with the sure thing at this stage of my life. But..." Gwen wondered if she should continue.

"But what?" Ally asked.

"But...you sound like you've got your boyfriends mixed up."

"What do you mean?"

"Well, when I listen to your heart, I think I'm hearing you say Ron should be your ex and Nick should be your current."

"How are you getting that?"

"The same way we girls get anything. Intuition. Telepathy. Magic? Let me ask you this. Are you falling for Nick again?"

Ally blinked and looked away. "I'm not sure. I don't think so. Before today everything was clear. Now, well, it's just that I think Nick is changing. And I like what I see."

"Maybe it will be clearer in the morning, Ally," she said warmly, as she opened the door to leave. "Just sleep on it."

When Gwen closed the door, Ally laid in the darkness and stared at the ceiling. There were several things she was not sure of, but one thing she was sure of; at least for today, when it came to Ron and Nick, she couldn't trust her heart.

CHAPTER 14

March soon turned to April, April to May, and May to June. Ally returned to work later than expected due to a serious lung infection from the insertion of the chest tube, but by early May she was working fulltime and by mid-June she had no residual effects from the accident and the subsequent complications. The same couldn't be said about the residual teasing she received about the entire ordeal by Nick and company. She rolled with the punches and found comfort in the fact that people often used humor to diffuse tension and mask relief. So, she took it as a compliment when Nick teased her about milking her accident to avoid work.

Nick folded his hands behind his head and gazed out his office window on this warm Friday afternoon. He recalled the deal he had made with God in the hospital. If Ally recovered, he would attempt to see his father again and try to make things right. *Surely God doesn't expect me to keep this idle promise,* he reasoned. *After all, would God really hold me to a promise whispered under duress in a hospital waiting room?* Yet he couldn't shake the notion of how different today would be if God reneged on his part of the deal and Ally had died.

I made a deal with God. He kept his end of the bargain. I guess I need to keep mine. It's payback time. I need at least to attempt to see my father again. Maybe I should see him this weekend and get it over with. But how should I approach him—and what on earth should I say?

As Nick shuffled a stack of papers from the Transitions campaign, one sheet slipped out of the stack and fluttered to the floor. Before he could bend over to retrieve it, Sam marched in.

"Oh, good, at least you're still here," he said sternly. "I was hoping to catch you before you left."

"What's up?" Nick asked, knowing this typically meant Sam was about to ruin his weekend.

"I just got off the phone with Tom Sullivan. He wants us to generate one more headline concept for Phase One of the Transitions campaign."

"What's wrong with the two concepts they previously approved?"

"Nothing, they just want a third concept to test with focus groups."

"Focus groups? They're going to put our ads through focus group testing again?"

"They want to test a few more concepts. They don't want to risk offending potential patients and their families with the direct approaches you developed, so they want to test one with a softer approach. It's due diligence, Nick."

"Okay, okay. When do you need it?"

"Monday morning."

"Monday morning? I'm going to be out of town this weekend."

"Then I guess you'll be burning the midnight oil tonight."

Nick rolled his eyes.

"What's the matter, you didn't think that promotion wouldn't cost you something?"

"No, that's not it. I..."

Sam cut him off. "Look Nick, do you want to be a partner in this agency someday?"

"Well, yes, of course."

"Good. For a minute I thought you might not have the commitment necessary to run this firm. I'll look forward to seeing your new headline first thing Monday. I'll ask Ally to stop by in a few minutes to help you start generating ideas."

"We will need Brett."

"I stopped to see him first, but he sneaked out before you. So, it's up to you and Ally. Have a nice weekend," he said, with the arrogance Nick loathed, yet often emulated.

It was times like these that Nick hated the advertising business and the control he allowed Sam to wield over him. Early in his career he let Sam control him *and* his weekends. He tolerated it because it was the road to the fast track. Now, the older he got, the more he resented it.

He bent to pick up the piece of paper that had fallen to the floor just before Sam had come in. It was face down. He turned it over. *This just might work,* he said to himself. *And maybe this will appease Sam and free up my weekend.* It was one of the initial headlines Brett developed for Phase One of the campaign but never showed Sam or Tom Sullivan. Nick looked at it long and hard. He slowly read it aloud: *The Difference between Addiction & Recovery is Admission.* It was definitely a softer approach than the former concepts. *Hmm, yes, I think this will work.*

His eyes focused on the key word—*admission.* As he mulled over the headline again, a funny thing happened. It spoke to his heart. *The Difference between Addiction & Recovery is—Admission.*

When Brett wrote that headline, Nick liked the double meaning. Now his mission was coming into view. When he reconnected with his father, he knew one thing he must talk to him about—*admission.*

I haven't seen him in years. How in the world will I talk to him about admitting he has a problem, much less admitting himself into an addiction recovery center?

There was a soft tap on his door. Ally walked in.

"Hey, friend."

"Hey."

"Sam just stopped by. Sounds like we're going to be spending the weekend together."

"Yeah, but I don't think we're going to be working," Nick said with a mischievous look.

"Okayyyy, what are you thinking?" She dubiously arched her eyebrow at him.

"Well, I was just planning my weekend before I was so rudely interrupted by Sam and his little assignment."

"Go on."

"Remember this?"

She glanced at the paper he handed her. "Yeah, I remember. We never presented this to Sam and Tom, right?"

"Right," Nick said with a laugh.

"So, we're going to present this idea on Monday instead of developing any more ideas for Sam? Would you really risk that?"

"Oh, we'll develop some more, but not here."

"Where?"

"It's going to be a beautiful weekend, Ally, and I was heading up to Lake Geneva. I'd like to invite you to join me as my guest at the lake house. We can work on a few more ideas there or on the deck or patio. Besides, we'll be more creative outdoors. What do you say?"

Nick knew it was a bold invitation, but he had to see how Ally would respond. They had grown close during the time he had visited her in the hospital and during her recovery at home. She hadn't mentioned Ron much in the past few months, so now was as good a time as any to find out where he stood with her. Besides, that was subsidiary next to his real motivation. He needed her support if he was going to follow through with his part of the deal with God this weekend. Ally was the only person he could trust.

Ally furled her eyebrows. She was conflicted.

"What's the matter? It'll be fun. Besides, you said you would like to see the lake house someday, remember?"

She paused and walked toward the window. With her back to him she spoke. "I don't think it is appropriate, Nick."

Excited about preserving his weekend, he recklessly rambled on knowing he was crossing the boundaries of propriety.

"Don't be ridiculous, Ally. You'll love the lake house and Lake Geneva. Specialty stores. Art shops. Quaint restaurants. And we can catch some sun on my boat or tour the area as we walk the Shore Path around the lake."

Ally was resolute. "I don't think it is a good idea, Nick."

"What's wrong? Don't worry about Sam. We'll have plenty of time for his assignment."

Ally turned and faced him. Nick had seen this look before when he would cook up a scheme she wanted no part of.

"Look, Nick..." She paused again. Then she hit him with the two by four he should have seen coming. "Nick, I'm not interested in sleeping with you." Her words were biting cold and reminded him once again of just how much he had hurt her in the past.

"Ally, I—I didn't mean to imply, in any way, that we would sleep together. After all, you and Ron are..."

"Are what?"

"Are—" he fumbled for a safe word, "involved."

"Nick, my relationship with Ron is undefined, but ..."

"Look," he interrupted, "it's none of my business. You don't have to explain your relationship to me. I didn't intend to put you in such an awkward position." Nick bit his lip and continued. "Ally, trust me. I have no hidden agenda. I'm inviting you as my guest. The lake house has three bedrooms, mine and two guest rooms. My bedroom is on one end of the house. The guest rooms on the opposite end. I just thought you would like to see the lake house on a beautiful weekend and—I need you to help me..."

"You need me to help you what?" she asked, waiting for an ulterior motive.

"Well..." He bit his lip again and exhaled hard. He didn't know how to ask her.

"Nick, you need me to help you—what?" she persisted.

"I need you to help me...talk to my father."

"You're going to *see* your father?" she asked, stunned. "And *talk* to him?"

"Yeah, that is, with your help."

She paused, gauging his sincerity. "What in the world changed your mind?"

"Let's just say I made a deal with God, and I need to pay up."

"What do you mean you made a deal with God? You? What kind of deal would Nick Conway make with God?"

Nick stalled to collect his thoughts. *How do you tell an ex-girlfriend you might still love her—when you destroyed the relationship the first time? Not to mention she has a new boyfriend. How do I weasel my way out of this?* Nick reverted to a familiar technique—misdirection. "Let's just say the past few months I have been thinking a lot about what you and Brett said regarding reconnecting with my father, and I would like to see if this God thing works."

"What God thing?"

"You remember! Brett said that God sees our lives like a movie sometimes, right? And if we could see the background scenes of a person's life, we may better understand why they are the way they are."

"And you want to reenter your father's life and view a few background scenes to see if you can better understand him—and forgive him?" she asked with a tenderness that drew him toward her.

"Yeah, sort of. Plus, for the past few months while you were recovering, I've been thinking about what you said. I don't want to carry the baggage of a broken relationship anymore. I just thought it would be easier if—well—if you would go with me."

Ally folded her arms and looked away. Nick could see tears

well in her eyes. He wondered if she started to think about her father and how much she cherished her relationship with him.

"Nick, I'd love to visit the lake house and help you reconnect with your father again," she said as a warm smile broke across her face. "But, I want a private lakeside room," she said coyly.

He laughed. "Hey, I'll even throw in a private bathroom."

Nick picked Ally up after dinner about 8:15 and they headed north to Wisconsin. He wasn't quite sure how to manage their conversation during the ninety-minute drive. There was a lot to talk about. He wondered how he would approach his father and what he would say to him. *Will he recognize me after all of these years? Will he throw me out of his place? Does he even live in the same house?*

There was a great deal Nick wanted to know. He wasn't sure of anything except that he was relieved to have Ally with him. As she stared out the window, he realized anew just how much he had longed for the companionship of a woman again. Not just any woman—a woman he could love. He could feel himself craving a deep relationship with her. He wondered if her status with Ron had changed in the past few months and if he would ever have a shot with her again.

CHAPTER 15

Ally was quiet through most of the drive through Chicago. They both needed the serenity of silence after a long week at the office. They felt at peace with each other, and the stillness was refreshing.

Ally started to get excited about the lake house when they entered Wisconsin. She didn't realize it, but she asked him many of the same questions she has asked him in the past. When did he buy the lake house? What improvements had he made? She was like a kid on vacation nearing the final destination. Nick enjoyed her enthusiasm, and he answered every question as if he was hearing it for the first time.

They arrived at the lake house just before ten. He grabbed her bag from the trunk while she got out of the car and stretched under the star-filled sky. The fresh balmy night air carried a hint of Ally's perfume and reminded him of happy times they had shared in summers past.

Ally surveyed the property from the driveway, nodded in

approval, and expressed her first impression. "It's charming," she said with a grin. "It's cozy the way it's nestled among the trees."

"And this is just the curbside. Wait till daylight tomorrow and you see the lakeside," he added. "There's nothing like seeing the sunrise over the water."

He carried her bags inside, turned on a couple of lights, creating a warm glow in the room and opened a few windows. The outside air swiftly filled the room with its alluring summer fragrance. He gave Ally the nickel tour, saving the real tour for daylight. He showed her to the lakeside guestroom and bathroom. She freshened up while he prepared some cheese and crackers and uncorked a bottle of red wine. She joined him a few minutes later in the great room and, in true form, folded one leg under her as she plopped on the couch. He swirled her glass of wine as he handed it to her.

What would have been awkward just a few months ago now felt natural. They had grown comfortable being alone together again. She took a sip and glanced around the room. "I love the openness of this house," she said, as she reached for the plate of cheese and crackers he had placed on the coffee table. "I like the way the kitchen spills into the great room. I love the fieldstone fireplace. And you have a wall of windows! You're right. I can't wait to see the sunrise. I can even hear the waves crashing below us."

"The sound of the waves will lull you to sleep tonight," he predicted, as he poured himself a glass of wine.

Nick strolled into the great room, slipped off his shoes, sank into the other end of the couch and put his feet up on the coffee table. He took a sip of his wine and released a long sigh, officially heralding the end of the workweek.

"*This* is why you love it here so much," Ally said. "It's a refuge for you."

He took another sip of his wine and nodded. "It's many, many things Ally. It's a refuge when I need an escape. It's a sanctuary when I need to be alone with my thoughts. It's a playground when I need some fun. And it's a healing balm when I need to de-stress."

"And it's a mirror," she added.

"A mirror?" he asked, surprised. She could see the blank look on his face.

"Yes, a mirror. A place where you can reflect and see yourself as you really are."

"Wow, that's a heavy metaphor. You don't want to go there," he said, laughing.

"Yes, but it is true, isn't it? You reflect much more than you would ever let on at the office. I rarely see the reflective side of you. It makes me wonder who you really are."

"The reflective side is not a side I care to share with people at the office," he admitted, as he felt the wine start to relax him.

Ally reached for another cracker as he crossed his legs on the coffee table. "I mean, co-workers don't genuinely care about your personal life."

"That's not true," she countered. "How can a person ever know you if you are never really open with them?"

"Why is it important for them to really know me? And why is it important I know anything about them other than their skill set? All that really matters is, do they have the skills to do the job, right? Everything else about them is, well, irrelevant."

"How can you say that?"

"The way I see it, the more you reveal of yourself to your co-workers, the more they can use you and hurt you."

"Tell me about it!" she said sarcastically. She wondered if he knew she was referring to him.

Then Ally leaned toward him as though she was going to scold him like a grade school teacher. Instead, she spoke in a gentle whisper. "You're missing so much life has to offer." As she leaned toward him, he smelled the faint fragrance of her perfume and looked into her eyes. He hadn't been this close to her in years. He felt his face flush, and he swallowed hard. He had no doubt he could love her again, and he wished he hadn't made so many mistakes with her.

"Oh, really? You have a better philosophy?"

"Yes. I told you once before, no more fear and false bravado."

"This sounds familiar. You did tell me that over coffee that night you were the crazy TV psychic."

"I wasn't crazy, I was right. Listen to me. Don't be so afraid to take a risk and open yourself up to people." Nick wondered if the wine was giving her this sudden boldness or if she had wanted to walk down this road for years and had just been waiting for the opportunity.

"And the benefit of openness is?" he asked, raising his eyebrows.

Ally took a sip of her wine then set her glass on the coffee table to free her hands to gesture. She spoke with enthusiasm and conviction.

"Don't you see? When you open yourself to people, you let them in. When you are vulnerable with them—when you share your heart with them—you invite them into your life and they, in turn, are more willing to share their lives with you. By being genuine with people, you have the potential to live a more meaningful life because you have allowed yourself to be known. And you become known by letting people get close, as you did with me at the hospital after my accident."

"And what if closeness makes a person uncomfortable?"

"Then the person misses out on one of the best things in life."

"Which is?"

"Relationships! Rich, meaningful relationships." Even Ally wondered if the wine was doing the talking. Although she knew her comments addressed Nick's approach to life, she wondered if she was actually addressing his approach to her life and their past relationship.

"Do you know what you are?"

"Uh-oh. Here we go."

"You're an island!"

"Another metaphor? What's so bad about that? A beautiful tropical island surrounded by water!" He was toying with her. He knew where this was going.

"No, a deserted island, cut off from the world, surrounded by loneliness."

"This is not good," he replied, attempting to interject some humor. Ally was quiet just long enough for her analogy to bite.

Nick stared out the window into the darkness. He knew she was right—again. And she knew he was playing a game with her—again. They had been here before. His unwillingness to be open with her, to share his thoughts, his dreams and his life, clearly stunted their dating relationship. Somehow, he would always encourage her to share her dreams but would rarely share his own.

But now she had him wondering, had he shut out his father, too? He had always placed the blame for their failure to communicate squarely on his father's shoulders. Certainly, Nick had no responsibility in their relationship. After all, he was just a kid and his father was the adult—albeit, the drunken adult.

One side of him wanted to blow off Ally's philosophy as nothing more than sentimental "girl talk." Men don't care about closeness. And men certainly don't live for relationships. Yet, the other side of him, the reflective side Ally believed only came to life at the lake house, knew she spoke the truth.

Deep underneath Nick's veneer, he wanted what Ally was talking about—meaningful relationships—especially with his father. He desired openness with him. He wanted closeness with him. He hoped he could communicate with him. Most important of all, like all sons, Nick wanted to love his father and to be loved by him.

Throughout the years, Nick discerned the exclusive power fathers have over their sons. Even if their relationship stinks, a son will consciously or unconsciously strive for his father's approval. Every son seems to crave it. And every father must bestow it.

Nick knew he would never have a good relationship with his father, but was there some middle ground? Was there limbo, a place where although they would never love each other they wouldn't hate each other? If so, where was this place, and how did they get there?

Nick realized with Ally's help, maybe he could find this limbo, because he knew one thing: he would rather live in limbo than this place called "hate."

"Does your father live nearby?"

"If he is still in the house I grew up in, he is just a few miles down the road in Williams Bay."

"Williams Bay—sounds like a quaint little town."

"It is. It's one of three villages on Geneva Lake. Fewer than twenty-five hundred people live there, and it is another popular vacation spot for wealthy Chicagoans."

"What does your father do for a living?"

"Well, when he's employed, he's usually a landscaper—a pretty good one, too. I remember when I was a kid, he was a very creative landscaper. He could make anything look good. After I was born, he studied to be a landscape architect but never finished."

Nick got up to pour himself another glass of wine, careful not to have too much. He never allowed himself to get caught in the clutches of alcohol. Plus, he knew from his research at Transitions that forty percent of children of alcoholics often have five genes that create a low sensitivity to alcohol. This is why people with these genes could often drink other people under the table. He never wanted to test this theory. Yet, with every sip of alcohol, Nick realized he was walking a tightrope. He knew what was at risk. *Will I be a hypocrite or a duplicate of my father?* Although he carefully monitored how much he drank, secretly it troubled him that he was willing to play with his father's poison.

He raised the bottle to offer Ally more. She held her hand up politely to refuse. He settled back into the couch. The room was quiet. A breeze wafted through the window, and Nick inhaled the fresh smell of the balmy night air. As he spread cheese on a cracker, Ally broke the silence with a question.

"So, what are you going to say to your father when you see him?"

It was the question Nick had been wrestling with all night— and most of his life. "I don't know what I'll say to him. I've never known what to say to him."

Nick continued to stare out the window into the darkness, but he could feel Ally staring at him as she pondered the weight of his statement. He found himself thinking out loud. "What do you say to a man whose parenting skills start with mental abuse and end with physical abuse? Just what would you say, Ally?"

He turned and looked at her. She looked at the floor. He didn't expect her to have any answers. How could she? After all, he had been searching for answers to these questions most of his life.

After a night of tossing and turning. Nick finally drifted off into a deep sleep in the early morning hours. When he awoke, before he even wiped the sleep from his eyes, he started to second guess himself. *Will I regret this weekend for the rest of my life? How can this possibly go well?*

He crawled out of bed, stretched and waddled to the master bathroom. He wondered how Ally had slept on her end of the lake house.

As he washed his face in a vain attempt to regain full consciousness, a fragrant aroma of fresh coffee and toast wafted into the bathroom. He pulled on a pair of jeans and a clean t-shirt, slipped on a pair of slippers and shuffled into the kitchen. Ally was already dressed and sitting on the couch munching a slice of toast and jam and sipping a cup of coffee.

"You missed the sunrise," she said cheerfully. "You're right— it's beautiful as it rises over the water. I didn't think you'd sleep in."

"I didn't either, but that's the problem. I didn't sleep, at least, not till a few hours ago," he explained, as he poured himself a cup of coffee and surveyed the fridge for eggs, bacon or anything he could make for Ally. "What time is it?"

"It's about 9:15."

"What would you like for breakfast?" he asked, realizing the options were limited.

"I ate breakfast," she replied.

"Really?"

"Yup, toast, Raisin Bran, and coffee."

"Would you like anything else?"

"You don't have anything else," she retorted, still staring out the window as she finished her toast. "I love this view. I could sit here all day."

"Sometimes I do," he replied, as he wiped his eyes.

"I see why you love this place. It feels so good just to be here. I'm so relaxed."

"Yeah, and you haven't sat out on the patio, deck or pier yet. And I think you're going to love boating and walking the Shore Path around the lake. You have a lot to see this weekend."

"I'm really looking forward to it."

After his Raisin Bran breakfast Ally sat out on the patio enjoying gentle summer breezes off the lake while Nick showered, shaved and got dressed. He later gave her the full tour, showed her his boat and where they could walk the Shore Path that surrounded the lake. They spent a few hours on the patio talking and watching the speedboats buzz across the lake. He was avoiding the inevitable, and Ally knew it so she confronted it.

"What time do you want to go see your father?"

"What time is it?

Ally glanced at her cell phone. "It's just after eleven."

"Well, let's grab some lunch and head to my dad's place at noon. We stand the best chance to catch him during the lunch hour."

"Okay, I'm ready," Ally said as she stood and stretched.

Nick was anything but ready, but he grabbed his car keys off the kitchen table and they headed for his car.

After a quick lunch they headed to Williams Bay. It was a short scenic drive from Lake Geneva, and when Nick pulled up to the house he was reared in he barely recognized it. The paint was peeling, the shrubs were grossly overgrown. The lawn looked more like a field. A ladder was leaning up against the north side of the house. The front porch light was on, but the house appeared uninhabited. Nick wondered if his father still lived there. Based on the appearance of the house, it seemed highly likely.

He pulled into the driveway and left the car running. He stared at the keys in the ignition and felt the strange familiarity of being home—if he could call it that.

"We've come this far," Ally said gently, sensing his second thoughts. She reached for his hand. Feeling her warmth, he realized he had never backed her the way she had backed him.

"Let's go," Nick responded confidently, masking his inhibitions.

They walked along the uneven cracked sidewalk as they approached the house. He rang the bell and waited anxiously for an answer. Nothing.

"Looks like no one is home," he said, hoping this feeble attempt to see his father would fulfill his part of the deal he made with God. Before he could retreat, Ally put him back on the hook.

"Ring the doorbell again. If no one answers, let's walk around back."

Nick reluctantly rang the bell again and waited for an answer. Subconsciously, he rattled his car keys against his leg.

"Are you nervous?" Ally asked.

"No."

"Well, you're making me nervous shaking those keys."

Nick heard someone inside walking toward the door. He put his keys in his pocket. The curtains on the door were sheer but he could not quite make out the figure walking toward them.

The deadbolt lock clicked as it retracted and the doorknob slowly turned. The door creaked as it opened. The man in the doorway had a full head of gray hair combed straight back. He was tall and thin, and the deep lines around his eyes and a sparse gray beard put him in his seventies. He was wearing an old soiled green t-shirt with a couple of holes near the collar. It wasn't until he looked Nick in the eye that he recognized him. It was Gus Milloy, his father's lifelong friend.

"Can I help ya?" he asked kindly.

"Hi, Gus," Nick responded.

Gus looked Nick over from head to toe then leaned back and turned his head to size him up again. "Don't suppose you're Chuck's boy?" he asked.

"That's right. Hi, Gus," he said again warmly. "Is my father around?"

Gus smiled broadly. "Nicky! Come on in. He's out back," the old timer said, as he led them through the living room and into the kitchen. The living room was filled with stacks of old newspapers scattered throughout the room. A worn couch was pushed against the wall and was covered with a dirty blanket. A recliner was propped up in front of an old television. Nick couldn't help but notice the multi-colored afghan draped over the arm of the recliner. It may be the only thing he had in common with his father.

Nick's mother made each of them a multi-colored afghan. She was working on Nick's when she was killed by the drunk driver. She never finished it, leaving the tattered edge which Nick always pulled close to his heart.

"We're cutting brush out back. I came in for something to drink. Otherwise I would've never heard the bell." Gus stopped in the hallway and turned to look at him. His milky eyes bore into Nick's as he said, "Long time, Nicky."

"Yeah, a very long time." Nick acknowledged, not knowing what else to say. Before Nick could introduce Ally, Gus kept right on walking. He went out the back door to get his father. Nick and Ally waited in the kitchen.

The house was unkempt and carried a light scent of mildew and cat litter. Empty beer cans were heaped in a large brown paper grocery bag on the floor near the back door. The kitchen table told the story of yesterday's lunch and dinner and an array of liquor bottles punctuated the table.

Nick looked out the window and watched as Gus approached his father. Ally leaned against the sink filled with dirty dishes and looked around the room. It answered so many questions about Nick, she thought. She realized the irony of the moment. Just as Nick was there to view a few scenes from his father's life in an attempt to understand and forgive him, she had the same opportunity with Nick.

As Ally surveyed the surroundings, her body warmed as she felt a wave of compassion for him. He glanced at her and, without a word, was sure she now understood why he told her his father was dead.

The windows were open so they could faintly hear the conversation outside. "Someone is here to see you, Chuck. I let them in," Gus informed him.

"A bill collector?" Chuck asked angrily.

"Nope. Somebody else."

"Who is it then?"

"See for yourself."

"I said who is it, Gus?" he demanded, as they marched toward the house together.

Gus knew better than to tell him Nick was home. Gus had been a loyal friend to Chuck Conway most of his life, despite his alcoholism. He was one of the few who considered Chuck his friend after alcohol systematically destroyed his life and livelihood.

As a boy, Nick admired Gus. He was an old timer who always seemed to see the silver lining. Even when alcohol influenced Nick's father to use or abuse Gus, he would find a way to let friendship prevail.

Nick didn't remember a lot about Gus, but he did remember how he made him feel. The old man's kindness cut through this childhood pain and made him believe that the future would be brighter with his pet phrase, "Better days are coming, Nicky." And when his mother was killed, Gus was there for Nick and his father.

Gus pulled open the screen door and walked through first. Nick glanced at Ally, and she winked to reassure him. Chuck stepped through the door and stopped abruptly the moment he saw Nick. Then silence. Nick could hear his heart pounding. Ally swallowed hard feeling a slight twinge of guilt for putting Nick up to this. Chuck looked at Gus, then back at Nick.

It was obvious that the years were hard on him; the alcohol was harder. He was nearly bald now. His dirty white t-shirt stretched tightly around his bulging belly. His hands were grimy, and his forehead was smudged from wiping sweat from his brow. His eyes were what Nick expected—glassy, red, and perpetually angry. Chuck stood just a few feet from his son so Nick could smell the alcohol on his breath. The bottles on the kitchen table suggested a liquid breakfast.

Chuck glanced at Ally, then Nick. "So, what do you want?" he said, disgustedly. Immediately, Nick felt his defenses rise and his good intentions fall.

"It's good to see you too, Dad."

"Who is the babe?"

Ally stiffened at the address, stood up straight and grasped her hands together in front of her.

Nick turned to Ally. "This is Ally," Nick said pausing slightly, not knowing what title to put on their relationship. "She's a good friend of mine."

"Hi, Mr. Conway," Ally said warmly. "It's nice to meet you, I've heard good things about you," she offered in a tone intended to help Nick's cause, but it came out sounding weak, flat and contrived.

"You've heard *good* things about me?" he asked sarcastically. Then he laughed. "You certainly didn't hear good things about me from *him!*" He looked at Nick with distain. "Look, you don't have to lie for him, Cutie. He knows how to do that himself."

"Now just a minute, Dad," Nick said, raising his voice to defend Ally. "I didn't come here to..."

"Just why *did* you come here?" he fired back.

It took everything Nick had to answer honestly. He preferred to blow him off. "I came here..." He paused to consider how he should respond. He looked at Ally, regained his poise and elected to stay the course. "I came here to see if you were—okay."

Chuck guffawed. It was the laugh he had used to mock Nick in the past, and once again he found himself standing before his father feeling humiliated.

"What do you think of that, Gus? After all these years,

Nicky-boy came here to see if I was okay. Tell him I'm okay, Gus. And tell him to check back in *another* twenty years!"

"That's enough, Chuck," Gus intervened. "Your boy has come to see you. You ought to treat him with respect. After all, he's the only kin you got."

"Whose fault is that?" he demanded, as he walked to the refrigerator and cracked open a beer. Nick felt a sudden flash of anger at the gall of drinking in front of him. This was a familiar scene. Nick had grown up seeing it, hearing it, hating it. He could not believe his father was numb to the fact that this simple act, which epitomized his life, would infuriate him.

Despite the strength Nick derived from Ally, he felt his conviction for coming start to fall and his temper rise. This is what he had come to expect from his father. They would speak a few sentences to each other and then the shouting match would begin.

"You think it is my fault that I'm your only relative?" Nick countered. "I'm your only relative because *you* killed my mother."

"I killed your mother?"

"Yes! What's the matter, too drunk to remember? Let me refresh your memory."

"Nick!" Ally interrupted, trying in vain to salvage his purpose in coming. It was too late. Nick should have known better than to come. His anger ignited after being on a slow burn most of his life. Even she couldn't stop him now. He continued recklessly.

"You went drinking at your favorite bar. You had too much—as usual. You called Mom to pick you up so you wouldn't have to drive home. She was killed by a drunk driver on the way to pick *you* up. Ring any bells?" Nick could hear the hate in his voice, and it scared him. Ally took it all in and wondered how she could possibly stop the inevitable train wreck.

Chuck took another slug of his beer, sat at the kitchen table and stared at the floor like a defendant ready to admit he was guilty as charged. Nick expected the shouting match to escalate. Instead, an eerie silence filled the room. He hit a nerve.

"I didn't kill your mother," he said quietly.

"Then who did?" Nick demanded, refusing to let him deny it.

"You did!" he shouted.

"You drunken fool," Nick screamed. "How dare you blame that on me! How could I kill my mother?"

"You killed her in childbirth! Rose was never your mother. She was your stepmother!" the old man confessed, still staring at the floor.

Nick's mouth dropped, Ally covered hers, and Chuck leaned back and guzzled his beer till he could see the bottom of the can. He wiped his mouth with the back of his hand and tossed the empty can on the heap in the brown paper bag. He spoke again. This time in a whisper.

"You killed your mother. I killed your stepmother," he repeated, and then he walked out the back door. For the first time in Nick's life he could detect regret in his father's voice.

The room was still, and Nick found himself replaying this new revelation over and over in his head to make sense of it. "I killed my mother?" he kept repeating to himself.

"Sometimes ya got to wonder if the truth is worth knowing," Gus offered compassionately.

Nick wasn't sure what stunned him more: that his mother died giving birth to him or that the mother he had loved so dearly wasn't his mother at all.

"I can see from the look on your face this is news to ya. Somehow, I thought your dad would have found a way to tell you long before now," Gus said.

"Nick, I'm sorry," Ally offered feebly, as she lowered her hand that had covered her mouth.

"Gus, my father never talked to me about anything, so it is not surprising that he never told me this."

"Sorry to hear that. But then, I figure it makes sense. Your dad never was the same after he lost Mary. Your mom, I mean. He took it pretty hard. He didn't drink much in those days, at least not while she was alive."

"Gus," Nick interrupted, "thanks for supporting my father all of these years, but whatever happened then is in the past. I think it is best to leave it there. Ally, we're done here. We better head back."

"No wait. Gus, tell me more about what happened after Mary died."

Gus sat down at the kitchen table, and Ally pulled up a chair next to him. Nick crossed his arms, leaned against the sink and looked out the window for his father. He was not in the yard.

"After Mary died, Chuck was real determined to raise Nicky on his own. He left his landscaping job in town. He thought he could make more money if he started his own landscaping business. He was good at it, and he did really well for a while.

"Thing is, he started to get pretty lonely being a fairly young man with no wife and a kid to support. Not much of a social life for someone in that situation. At first, he was okay with it. Fact is, I remember him telling me that he cared more about his son than having a social life.

"But, over time, he lost touch with people his age. Most of his close friends were married except for me, so we stuck together. He never liked the idea that he sort of became a forgotten man. You know, if you're not married but your peers are, well, you're sort of left out. Never bothered me because I was never married, but once you been married, then you're not, well, it's hard. I think it slowly started to eat at him."

"What did he do?" Ally probed.

"Well, seems the best way to meet women was over a drink. So, he started to frequent the bars. He didn't seem to have too much trouble attracting single women but..."

"But once they found out he had a kid..." Ally interrupted, as Gus nodded.

"Yup. Eventually, I think the alcohol and the loneliness started to mess with his head," Gus continued. "He started to blame Nick for his troubles, and he started looking for a way out of fatherhood. Thank God he met Rose, your stepmom. Don't remember where she met him, but it wasn't a bar. In fact, she was the one that got him out of the bars. But it didn't last long.

"She really loved you, Nicky, and after she married Chuck, she tried to give you a good life. Eventually, I think she figured she couldn't save him, but she might save you."

"I loved her, too," Nick added, staring out the window. "Well, we should go, Ally."

"Tell me about Rose," she asked, prolonging the conversation.

"Well, she was a joy, carefree and outgoing. She saw the best in people, and she believed she could make a positive impact on just about anyone.

"She knew what she was getting into with your dad—but she saw something she loved. And she believed a good woman could turn any man around. She almost did it, too."

"How so?" Ally asked inquisitively.

"Well, she never gave up on Chuck or his recovery. She almost got him into a recovery program once. Would have been the best thing that ever happened to him. He knew she loved him and would not quit on him. He once asked me, 'How can she love me when I can't love myself?' Don't remember what I told him. Something like: 'God puts angels on this earth to watch out for us. You got lucky. You got to marry yours.' He loved that answer and would play it back to me over the years.

"By now he was having drinking binges. He was on a binge the night Rose was killed. It was his fault, and he knew it. To make matters worse, it turns out the drunk driver who killed Rose had been drinking with Chuck earlier that night."

"How could he live with that?" Ally asked, thinking out loud.

"He couldn't," Gus continued.

"How awful," she whispered.

"It was awful. Here you have a guy who gets a great start in life then loses his first wife in childbirth and his second wife from a drunk driver who spent the night drinking with him. From this point on, I think your dad didn't drink because he wanted to. I think he drank because he had to—to put himself out of his misery. But I suppose it could have been worse."

"What do you mean?" Nick asked, surprised by this comment. "How could it possibly have been worse?"

"Well, as you know, Rose died at the hospital three days after the accident so your dad had plenty of time to punish himself for what he had done. But Rose, being the kind of woman she was, sort of let him off the hook."

"How?" Ally asked.

"By what she said to him just before she died."

Nick turned to Gus. "What did she say?"

"She simply said, 'I forgive you, Chuck.'"

Nick and Ally didn't say a word to each other during the entire ride back to the lake house. She stared out the window, and Nick kept his eyes firmly fixed on the road. Neither one of them could believe—or fully comprehend--what had just happened.

CHAPTER

Neither Nick nor Ally could anticipate the bomb that was dropped when they visited his father. All the way back to the lake house they replayed in their minds the stories Gus had told them. Each story filled in a few more blanks in Chuck's life so Nick could connect the dots. What Brett had been saying all along was beginning to make sense. Nick could see how the circumstances or scenes of his father's life had permanently altered his life course. Now came the painful task of sorting it out and understanding what it would mean—for both of them.

Nick reflected on the advice Gus gave him when he walked them to the car before they left for the lake house. "It took a lot of courage to do what you've done," he said. "You've stepped back into his life. Don't give up on him now, Nicky. Your stepmother never did. You just broke the ice. It will never be easier than now to come back again. And you never know what you might learn if you stand by him. Think about stopping by more often."

When they pulled up to the lake house it was late afternoon. "Do you want to get something to eat?" Nick offered.

"No, I'm not hungry. Are you?"

"Not really," he admitted. "It's a beautiful day for a walk. Would you like to take the Shore Path and see some of the lakefront homes and mansions? I think you'll enjoy it."

"I'd really like that. I need to stretch."

The Geneva Lake Shore Path was a catharsis for Nick. It always melted away his stress and focused his attention on the things that really mattered. The Shore Path was a beautiful walk around the perimeter of the lake. It provided public access across the front lawns of every lake home.

Nick usually walked just a few miles, but he had promised himself that someday he would take the entire twenty-six-mile trek along the lake shore. He could not imagine a more scenic walk because this narrow winding footpath offered the natural beauty of sprawling lake frontage, enormous oak trees, willow trees, vibrant wildflowers and steep, rocky bluffs among the architecture of majestic mansions and luxurious lake homes.

They grabbed bottled water from the fridge and caught the narrow foot path on Nick's property between the patio and pier. As they walked, Nick noticed the sun sparkled off of Ally's dark hair. She looked beautiful as she crossed her arms and walked beside him. He carried water and a snack in a backpack he had thrown over his shoulder.

They hadn't walked far when Ally stopped and took in the beauty around her. Pink coneflowers and brilliant yellow black-eyed Susans lined the narrow stone foot path. Blue flag iris and bellflowers grew along the wrought iron fence line that bordered some of the lake houses. Tall natural grasses and a palette of colorful wild flowers created an alluring ambiance and filled the air with a fresh summer fragrance. The waves gently lapped against the jagged shoreline while the summer breeze put the wind in the willows.

Ally stopped to touch a black-eyed Susan. She carefully ran her fingers along the tall, hairy leafstalk to the flower head with a brown button-like center disk surrounded by bright yellow daisy-like petals. "This is such a gorgeous place. I get it now. I really understand why you escape here most weekends. It's a magical place."

"And it's a place where I can recalibrate. And after today, I've got some serious recalibrating to do."

Ally looked away to the horizon over the water. "I'm really sorry. This was my fault."

"It's not your fault. I made the decision to go see my father."

"Yes, but you wouldn't have gone if I hadn't pushed you so hard. I should have kept my mouth shut. I just thought..."

"Forget about it."

"I just thought if you saw your father again you would be able to get rid of some of the baggage you've been carrying for so long."

Nick could hear the sincerity in her voice, and it made him want to stop and take her in his arms. "Really, forget about it. I'm going to."

"Even if I could, how can you? I mean, your birth mother and all."

She made a good point. Nick was kidding himself if he thought he could ignore the truth and forget the facts. He would never forget that his mother died bringing him into the world. Whether he knew it or not, whether he would admit it or not, he would have to deal with this new baggage no matter how hard he tried to convince himself it didn't really matter.

"Learning about my birth mother today was a shock. I'll admit it. And I'll admit I have to think this through. But does it really change anything? Think about it. I never knew her. She has had no impact or influence on my life, and it doesn't alter anything my father has ever said or did to me. So, it is just a fact, a new revelation that should have no real relevance, right?"

"I think it is very relevant. And I think it changes everything. That's why I am so sorry."

"Thanks for your concern, but really, my life hasn't changed since yesterday. I'm still the same guy, in the same circumstances, regardless of what my father revealed today."

"I think what you learned today has the power to hurt you—or change you—*and* your relationship with your father."

"How?"

Ally walked toward the lake near the fieldstone shoreline. She gently touched the coarse petal of a purple coneflower. "Well, again, it goes back to what Brett said about God seeing the circumstances of our lives like scenes in a movie. Today, we saw two major scenes in your father's life that helped to explain why he is the way he is."

As the deep blue water of Geneva Lake gently lapped against the shoreline, Nick felt his numbness for his father faintly fade and a slight sting of regret for abandoning him.

They walked along a sprawling white wooden fence line and over an arched fieldstone bridge to a cluster of weeping willow trees that gently swayed in the wind. Long spike clusters of purple loosestrife flowers grew along the water while fragrant white hydrangeas bloomed along the precisely trimmed hedges of the lake houses. It took Ally's breath away.

"This is unbelievable," she said, as they stopped. She opened a bottled water and took a sip beneath the enormous willow trees.

"I call this spot The Willows," he said with a smirk.

"Very creative," she teased. "Look how the willow tree trunks are pitched. The tree trunks are cantilevered over the surface of the water. They're almost parallel to the water. Let's walk out over the water," she said, with a playfulness that Nick loved.

They walked the trunk like a tightrope then sat, talked, and laughed while dangling their bare feet in the water.

"Do you come to this spot often?" Ally asked, as she gently paddled her feet.

"Sometimes. When I need to clear my head."

"Like now?"

Nick gave her a sideward glance. "Yeah."

"You know, the news you received today wasn't all bad."

"How so?"

"Well, remember Gus said that after your birth mom died your dad was determined to rear you. He even started his own business to create a better life for you. That must count for something. Unfortunately..."

Nick waited for Ally to finish her sentence but she stopped short. He coaxed her to complete it. "Unfortunately...?"

"Unfortunately... his *pain* got in the way."

Nick now knew he was deluding himself if he believed he could ignore the events of the day. He felt the impact of Ally's statement, and for the first time in his life he noticed himself feeling deep compassion for his father.

They walked a few miles along the Shore Path. Nick pointed out a few tourist attractions: Green Gables, once called the jewel of the Wrigley Estate, the Lakewood, and the House in the Woods, all three among the most enchanting homes on the lake.

As they walked in the warm summer sun, he knew that Ally had given him a small but enduring gift today, the gift of encouragement. She lifted his spirits and gave him a reason to believe that, in time, he would make sense of the revelations of the day.

When they returned to the lake house, they relaxed and had a drink on the patio. Later, they slipped into their swimsuits and went out on the lake in his boat. Ally looked like a swimsuit model. Slender, curvy, tan, gorgeous.

They darted around the lake like two crazy teens. Nick later found a quiet spot in shallow water in Buttons Bay and set anchor. The boat gently bobbed along as they laid across the bow, soaked up the sun and enjoyed the view of the lake homes and mansions. It was a breathtaking way to spend a day.

Ally kept him off balance with her probing. "Do you think you can ever forgive your father, knowing what you know now?"

"I don't know. Don't you have to ask for forgiveness first?" he countered, trying, as he always did, to duck penetrating questions.

"I don't think so." A pause followed. Nick was going to change the subject, but Ally persisted. "Well, do you think you can ever forgive him knowing what triggered his alcoholic behavior?"

"I'm not sure. It would really help if he asked for my forgiveness. Isn't that how it *should* work?"

"Your stepmother forgave him, and he didn't ask."

"Yeah, but..."

"I forgave you, and you didn't ask."

There it was. The Ally Grant two-by-four. It just blindsided him square in the head. He never saw it coming. Suddenly, she took him back to their past and his indiscretions.

"Must you always be so frank—Ally?"

"Must you always be so evasive—Nick?"

"Maybe we should head back," he suggested, trying to dodge a bullet.

"You're evading the subject. I asked you a question."

"Okay, yes, I guess I could forgive my father, someday."

A long and uncomfortable pause ensued. Nick wasn't sure what Ally was thinking. But he knew exactly what he was thinking.

"When did you forgive me?" he asked, tentatively. He could not believe he had just broached this subject...a subject that secretly and silently tormented him the last few years.

"Two years ago, I guess."

"Really? And we broke up what, three years ago?"

"Something like that."

"Wow."

"Why are you so surprised?"

"I don't know. I guess I'm just surprised you could forgive me at all."

"When I forgave you is irrelevant. There's a more important question."

"Really, what's that?"

"*Why* did I forgive you?"

"Okay, *why* did you forgive me?"

"Because I couldn't carry the baggage of the past anymore. I felt imprisoned as much by my anger as by your unfaithfulness. I had to let it go. My anger began to change me, control me and devour me. I wanted to master my emotions, but they mastered me—and they made me miserable. I needed to be free.

"I never understood why you slept with our boss when we were dating. Over and over I asked myself if she was really that attractive, or would it crush your ego to see me get the promotion you wanted but I deserved?" Ally felt her throat tighten and her stomach rise and fall. How many times had she practiced this speech never thinking she would ever deliver it, she wondered. How many times had she convinced herself that she had forgiven him and was over it only to doubt it now, at this critical moment, as she confronted him? This wasn't supposed to happen. She knew in her heart she had forgiven him for his unfaithfulness, but she had to vent. She needed this final release.

Nick fumbled for words as the conversation took a sudden about-face. Ally continued to vent, needing finally to release the safety valve that had been bottled up for the past three years.

"You slept with her to steal my promotion, but you stole so much more. You stole my career, my dignity, and my trust. And you severed our relationship. Was getting a promotion really worth that much to you? Was I worth so little?"

Tears welled in her eyes. She looked away from him. Despite the years, despite the forgiveness, venting was the healing balm. She felt the relief of the release, and Nick heard the pain in her voice. This was the confrontation he had skillfully avoided for years. And he did not want to face it here—in a boat—with nowhere to run. There was no place to hide and no way to disguise his disgrace.

How do I answer her? What do I say to this beautiful woman I once betrayed but still love? Yes, I had the affair. Yes, I did it for the promotion. And, yes, it was the biggest mistake of my life. I live with regret every day. I'm ashamed of it. Humiliated by it. But how do I tell her that? And how could I ever make it right?

"Ally, I don't know what to say," he stammered. "Betraying you was the darkest moment of my life. It was wrong. It was selfish. It was despicable. I know I'm a snake," he confessed, feeling some relief for finally admitting it.

"And you have no idea how much I regret it. How much I hate myself for it. Please believe me. I know I never asked you for your forgiveness, but you forgave me. So, I want to ask you now. Will you, could you, forgive me? I don't want you to forgive me just because you don't want to carry the baggage anymore. I want you to forgive because I'm sorry. I'm truly sorry."

Ally felt something tingle in the back of her neck, and he leaned into her. They looked down but as she felt his arms gently slide around her waist, she glided her arms slowly around his neck. He nudged her close. He saw tears glide down her cheeks. Their eyes met, and he moved into her, softly, tentatively, bumping his lips against hers to see how she would respond. She kissed him slowly and with reservation. He tapped his nose against hers in a gentle caress. She parted her lips, opened her mouth and captured his lips, once, twice, then in full embrace. He kissed her once more with a passion he had never felt before, and then he slowly pulled back and wiped the tears from her cheeks with his thumbs.

As he held her in his arms and they felt the gentle sway of the boat, Ally spoke in a whisper. "Nick, I accept your apology. And as I've said, I forgave you two years ago when I didn't know if you would ever ask for it."

Ally stepped away and sat on the bench seat, opened her purse and reached for a tissue. As she wiped her eyes, Nick glanced at the horizon and wondered if she just felt what he felt or if it was just a kiss to her. A kiss means different things at different times. He knew what this kiss meant to him, but what, he wondered, did it mean to her? *Was it relief for the pain of the past, or was it passion for the promise of the future?*

"You know, in some ways our situation is similar to your relationship with your father."

"How's that?"

"Well, I forgave you when you didn't ask for it, and now you need to forgive him if he doesn't ask for it."

As the seagulls soared gracefully overhead, Ally's words vibrated in his ears and spoke to his heart. He had never seriously contemplated this before.

On Saturday night, Nick grilled dinner and they ate on the patio overlooking the lake. Since their talk on the boat, and the kiss, the evening had taken on a somber tone. Yet, after Nick built a fire and poured a couple of glasses of wine, they quietly and peacefully talked the night away.

On Sunday morning Ally took a long walk alone on the Shore Path while Nick took the boat out on the lake for most of the day. He had much to think about.

Nick took Ally out to dinner at the Grand Geneva Resort on Sunday evening. They ate at his favorite restaurant overlooking the pond and golf course.

After a glass or two of wine, they reminisced about some of the good times they had together in the past. Ally even recounted the first time he asked her out and how he fumbled to ask her. She had no idea how he was taken by her appearance and the belief that someone so attractive could never be interested in someone like him.

As the wine began to take hold, they laughed together as she described their first kiss and how he muffed it by bumping noses. She must have thought he'd never kissed a girl before.

He reminded her of one of their early dates where he planned a picnic on the lawn of Grant Park. It started out as a beautiful day when he built the fire to grill burgers, but the weather changed abruptly when they sat to eat. The wind picked up and the rain began gently to fall. He refused to give up on the picnic, and they continued to eat in the rain.

She didn't want to spoil the moment, even though it was ruining her hair. Instead, she cheerfully went along with him and they ate their burgers on their blanket in an eventual downpour. It became a game to see who would acknowledge the rain and give up first. He held his ground, drenched. She sat beside him acting as if it were still a sunny day.

"Would you please pass the Grey Poupon?" she said, in a pathetic British accent as the rain fell in sheets.

"Why, yes, madam. Can I get you anything else?"

"No, I have quite enough," she said, as her hair flopped in her face. "Sir, could you tell me, is there any rain in the forecast?"

"Not that I know of, madam, but we sure could use some. Everything is so dry around here."

"Everything but this soggy potato salad," she said laughing.

They sat there for at least twenty minutes laughing and acting as though there was nothing unusual about a picnic in the rain. When he was soaked to the bone, he stood first. So, Ally won. It was fun. It was exciting. And it was surprisingly romantic. Although it was early in their dating relationship, it was the first time Nick realized that Ally was a woman he could love.

Late Sunday night they headed back to Chicago, sunburned, exhausted, and ambivalent about the weekend and what it all meant. Yet, inwardly, Nick thought they both sensed something else; the love they once had for each other was real, very real.

CHAPTER 17

Nick hadn't even had a chance to grab his first cup of coffee when Sam was in his office Monday morning.

"Nice weekend?" Sam asked cynically. "I see you're sunburned. I hope that doesn't mean you don't have a new headline for me today for the Transitions account."

"No, Sam, I have both a sunburn and a headline," Nick said, with similar sarcasm and just enough conviction to compensate for the fact that he totally forgot about this assignment during the weekend.

"Okay, let's see what you've got."

Nick flipped through the papers on his desk and produced the headline he rediscovered on Friday before he left with Ally. He gave Sam his rationale as to why it would work, and surprisingly Sam bought it. He walked toward the door then turned to face Nick.

"Heard you spent the weekend with Ally Grant. I wouldn't get too involved with her or anyone for that matter. Office romances never work. You don't want to lose your focus at this stage of your career. You follow me?"

Sam met with Tom Sullivan and sold the headline idea to him. With that issue off Nick's back, he reviewed the status of his other accounts, checked in with John Gesh regarding new developments with the Transitions account, made a few phone calls, and answered urgent e-mail messages. Despite his attempts to stay busy, the revelations of this weekend and the guilt of his past with Ally sidetracked him. He didn't know exactly what to do with what he had learned.

He wondered what Brett would do. One thing was certain; Brett could offer him insights that would give him hope and perspective. He pulled up Brett's calendar on his computer to check his schedule for lunch. If he was free, Nick had a few things he wanted to run past him.

When they connected, Nick offered to buy lunch at Maurice's. They left just before noon to beat the crowd and slid into a private booth in the back. To put their lunch on automatic pilot and prevent interruptions they ordered the pizza buffet.

As they ate, Nick detailed his conversations with Gus and his father. Brett seemed content to let Nick dominate the conversation, occasionally nodding to convey his understanding. His gracious demeanor made Nick feel so comfortable that he did something he never thought he would do. He shared his past about Ally, even his unfaithfulness.

"Wow. Interesting weekend," Brett said when Nick finally gave him a minute to respond. As Nick expected, a clumsy pause followed as Brett sifted through this new information and wondered what he could possibly say. He elected to focus his comments on Nick's relationship with his father.

"Sounds like you had a chance to view a few significant scenes of your father's life that led to his alcoholic lifestyle. That explains a lot, doesn't it?

"Think about it, Nick. Your dad had to deal with the loneliness of losing his first wife in childbirth and the guilt and anxiety of losing his second wife due to a drunk driver—that he helped intoxicate.

Sounds like he couldn't cope. I'm not making excuses for him, but I can see why he opted to numb himself to the pain, can't you?"

"I guess so, but I still can't rationalize his behavior."

"I agree. You have a lot to sort through. I'm not sure where to begin. Let's narrow it down. What is the one thing troubling you most right now?"

"I guess it's Ally's question: 'Can you forgive your father knowing what you know now?' I know I *should* forgive him, I just don't know *how* to forgive him."

"I know where you're coming from. Believe me, I did not always see life the way I do now. My circumstances were different from yours, but I too once struggled with forgiveness."

"Really? So, how did you learn to forgive?"

"For me, it was simply realizing that I *could* forgive, if for no other reason than I had been forgiven," Brett started. "Plain and simple, I believe that since God has forgiven me, I, too, can forgive others."

"So, your primary reason for forgiving others is a spiritual one?"

"I think the basis of forgiveness *is* spiritual."

"How so?"

"Well, forgiveness flows out of the character of God. And there is no forgiveness more complete than when we place our faith in him. Think about it. To forgive is essentially to forfeit your right for revenge. To not forgive is, in some way, to continue to seek revenge. Even if we don't seek this revenge in our actions, we can seek it in our thoughts."

"I've heard this somewhere before, years ago, in church or Sunday school or something."

"So, the real question is, will you forfeit your right for revenge?"

"I never thought of it that way. So, you're saying, in my heart, by not loving or caring about my father, I am, in some way, seeking revenge for what he has done?"

"Only you can answer that. Search your heart. Ask yourself, 'Do I feel compelled to get even with my father in some way?'"

"I'm not sure it's that blatant."

"Well, how did it feel when you left him? How does it feel

when you talk about him negatively? How do you feel about the Transitions account and alcoholics in general? You know, 'those kind of people.'"

"Okay, okay, I see what you mean. Deep down I guess I want him to pay for what he has done. Wouldn't you?"

"Probably. But it doesn't matter what I think. It only matters what you think. You told me you wanted to forgive him, but you didn't know how. I'm telling you that once you forfeit your right for revenge, you will be able to forgive him. But I don't think you will be able to do that until you get to know him better, and that means you will have to walk back into his life again. And that won't be easy."

"Tell me about it. He certainly didn't seem happy to see me this weekend."

"Based on what you told me, your father sought some verbal revenge when he mocked you for being gone for twenty years. Sounds like he is having trouble forgiving you, too."

"Forgiving me? How twisted is that?" Nick asked, raising his voice. "Can you believe he has the audacity to think I offended him after all he has done to me?"

"Well, apparently he was wounded when you abandoned him."

"Brett, I abandoned him to save my life. I simply left home one day—the first day I was old enough to bail out on him. I was nineteen, I had a job, and I found a way to leave home by renting a place with a few other guys. I suppose I should have said 'good-bye' or left a note, but I didn't think he cared if I was dead or alive. It was about survival for *me*, not abandonment for *him*."

"I understand. But your father has his point of view. Maybe, in his mind, having you around was actually survival for *him*. All I'm saying is he may be having trouble forgiving you too—for leaving him. It is just something to think about."

Nick sensed Brett was right. He and Ally seemed right about everything lately. He wondered if he was too close to the situation mentally and emotionally to evaluate it accurately. He continued to talk with Brett, and the more he did the more insights he gained. Brett and Ally were becoming steady sources of encouragement for him, and he feared he would come to depend on them. He had to remind himself that he did not need other people. While he appreciated their help, he should be able to figure his problems out on his own.

As they walked back to the office, Brett said something that got him thinking.

"You know, as I reflect on everything you've told me, I think you've just seen your third glimpse of God."

"What do you mean?"

"Well, remember I told you that if you watch carefully, you can see glimpses of God at work in the everyday lives of everyday people?"

"Yeah."

"What do you think the third glimpse is?"

"Forgiveness, I guess."

"Yes, I think so. Just look at how many times God has spoken to your heart about forgiveness in the last three days. First, your stepmother was killed by a drunk driver. Your father was partially at fault, she knew it, yet she forgave him on her death bed.

"You were once unfaithful to Ally. Instead of exercising her right for revenge she forgave you. Now she enjoys the sweet freedom of forgiveness. And now, you're wondering how you can forgive your father."

They stopped at a busy street corner in front of their building and waited for the light to change. Nick mulled what Brett was saying. He glanced at Brett while he talked and sensed the depth of his convictions. Nick wished he could be more like him. He wished he had faith, Brett's faith. *Any* faith.

"Yes, I think you just saw your third glimpse of God this weekend when you witnessed the essence of forgiveness, Nick."

"I suppose," he agreed, realizing everything Brett told him about God in recent weeks was beginning to come together. Then, as they stepped inside the lobby of their office building, Brett posed a question that intrigued him.

"Do you think God is trying to get your attention?"

It was a question Nick would ponder the rest of the week.

CHAPTER

Tom Sullivan had been brought to Transitions as the vice president of marketing about a year ago and was fully committed to putting its facility and its approach to addiction recovery on the map. He was aggressive, intelligent, sincere, and tireless in his mission. Yet, unlike some vice presidents Nick has worked with throughout the years, Tom appeared genuinely motivated to help his clients—rather than get rich off of them.

Whereas Nick admitted that he was suspicious of most people and their motives, particularly the profit motive, Tom Sullivan was slowly winning his trust.

After working with Tom for the past few months and seeing him in action, Nick noticed his opinion of him gradually shift. Suspicion gave way to sincerity. Tom was genuine, and Nick could see his personal conviction that alcoholics, with proper treatment, could recover even from severe addiction. He noticed that Tom was one of the few people he had met in his life who inspired hope virtually every time he talked to him. It made him seriously consider if Transitions could give his father his life back.

⚮

Nick, Ally and Brett spent the day at Transitions with Tom and his staff. They immersed themselves in the addiction recovery business and invested "a day in the life of a recovering alcoholic." Their goal was to learn as much as possible about Transitions's addiction recovery services so they could develop a public relations initiative to support the advertising campaign.

"I have shared with you most of the components that make up our addiction recovery services in the past few months. Today, I'd like to give you an opportunity to ask questions," Tom said, as he walked toward the front of the conference room where he was projecting an overview of their services and treatment outcomes on a slide.

"As you know, our program is multi-faceted and includes a blend of traditional drug and alcohol abuse therapies, a twelve-step approach and scientific techniques. The program includes detoxification, dependency education, individualized treatment, group therapy, family therapy, nursing services, physician services, psychiatric care, recreational activities and rehabilitation," Tom explained. "Which areas would you would like me to address to help you develop the PR campaign?"

"Tom, you did a nice job explaining the detox program for acute patients and the twelve-step program earlier, but can you tell us more about your family and group therapy components? Why are these so important to recovery?" Brett asked.

"Good question, Brett. Family therapy services are offered because, let's face it, addiction is a disease the whole family must face. Everyone is affected. In these sessions we remind the family that the addiction their loved one faces is not the family's fault. The family did not cause it, they cannot cure it, but they do play a major role in recovery."

Nick's ears perked up and he hung on every word.

"We also help the patient address co-dependency issues while helping the family repair the damage they incurred as a result of their loved one's addiction. We have several free workshops on various topics designed to give the family help and hope."

There they were again, the two words resonating with Nick the past few days: help and hope. Nick broke his own train of thought with a question. "Tom, what type of issues do you address with the patients in the group therapy sessions?"

"Well, it depends on the patient population. We tailor our sessions to the needs of the group at the time. To give you an idea, some of the things we have talked about are relapse prevention, psychiatric issues, medications available, and issues that specifically affect men or women."

Ally asked about the nursing and physician services offered, and Nick could tell by the way she glanced at him during Tom's explanation that she wasn't asking for the sake of their PR campaign. She was asking for the sake of his father. And Nick had to admit, he also asked most of his questions with his father's recovery in mind.

This was the first time Nick ever remembered linking his father and recovery in the same thought. Ally continued to feed Tom questions that would not only benefit the development of the PR campaign but also address the questions on Nick's heart. Tom's answers were steadily erasing any doubts about recovery for long-term alcoholics if they had some help—and some hope.

Tom stressed that any alcoholic could transition to a better life if they were fully committed to change *and* if they had at least one person willing to go the distance with them. That was what troubled Nick most. Was he willing to stand behind his father at this stage of their lives? *I'll be forty in August. He will soon be seventy. Can I go the distance with him if he, by some stretch of the imagination, agrees to seek help?*

Since it was inconceivable that his father would ever consider the notion of getting help Nick realized these questions were moot. After all, his father seemed perfectly content being miserable.

As the morning wore on, Tom touched on Transitions's rehab

services, chemical dependency education, recreational services, and psychotherapy by its board-certified psychiatrist. Nick and his creative team witnessed advanced scientific treatments, such as brain mapping and neurocognitive rehabilitation.

A comprehensive tour of the facility coupled with up close and personal patient interviews confirmed that the Transitions approach often led to long-term recovery.

Throughout the afternoon, Nick, Brett and Ally conducted interviews with the medical staff, and Nick understood like never before what the medical community meant by a holistic approach to addiction recovery. Alcoholics need to heal physically, mentally, and spiritually.

By the end of the day, Tom and his team had answered all of the questions of Nick's creative team.

"Our goal is simple: to give our patients their lives back," Tom reiterated, "clean and sober lives, happy and useful lives, productive lives, lives that will allow them to enjoy everything life has to offer—substance-free.

"Every patient," he continued, "has a right to a loving and caring environment designed to help him or her identify and address underlying core issues, treat those issues and become whole again. In other words, we will give every addict or alcoholic a second chance to *transition* to a better life. Together with the patient's family we strive for long-term recovery by blending treatment with tenderness. We will provide the treatment; a loved one must supply the tenderness."

Tom's final words cut Nick to the core. He didn't want to hear them. He didn't want to believe them. And he was uncertain if he could ever commit himself to fulfill them. Nevertheless, the truth in them sliced through him and his disdain for alcoholics. Tom's words, like a surgeon's scalpel, skillfully severed every layer of pride, resentment, and anger. Nick felt as though his chest were sliced open and his heart fully exposed. If he wanted his father to recover, he had to convince him to accept treatment and then fully support him through it. And, thanks to Brett and Ally, Nick realized that before he could ever love his father again, he must first forgive him—even if he never asked for it.

CHAPTER

Nick spent most of June fully immersed in the Transitions business. The PR campaign was anchored in testimonials from recovering alcoholics. As Nick and Brett conducted extensive patient interviews and wrote their success stories explaining how the Transitions treatment plan was helping patients reclaim their lives, Nick was clearly troubled. One warm June evening when they were working late in Nick's office he confided in Brett.

"Brett, take a look at this case study I just wrote and tell me what you think."

Brett glanced at the headline and scanned the body copy. Nick waited as he read through the two-page document.

"Nice," Brett said. "I think you captured the patient's battle with alcohol, the events that culminated in his cry for help, the challenging journey through Transitions's treatment plan, the family's role in his recovery, and a positive final outcome. It's well written."

Nick nodded and glanced out the window. Brett wondered what he was thinking.

"Did I miss something?"

"No."

"Then what's wrong?"

"I don't know. At least, I don't know how to explain it."

"Try."

"Are my case studies written with enough conviction?"

"Conviction? Well, they're certainly compassionate and compelling. And they demonstrate that treatment at Transitions works. Why?"

"I don't know. I guess I wonder if they're believable."

"Why would someone doubt them?"

"I don't know. Maybe because—I doubt them."

"*You* doubt them?" Brett asked, as his eyes widened. "After all of our research? After all of our interviews with physicians and recovering patients? After all of the positive outcomes you've witnessed of the Transitions treatment plan?"

Brett was confused by Nick's admission. "So, you're telling me that suddenly you don't believe the Transitions Addiction Recovery Center treatment plan works? Not exactly the best way to write convincing PR for the client, Nick."

"That's not what I'm saying. But I am saying I'm not sure if I believe the Transitions treatment plan will work on a *long-term* alcoholic."

Brett leaned back in his chair.

"Like your father?"

Nick looked away.

Brett exhaled hard then leaned toward Nick. "Okay, I get it. You're doubting what you are writing about Transitions because you have something at stake, your father. Hey, it's okay to have doubts. But that doesn't change the fact that Transitions has had very positive outcomes with other long-term alcoholics. Look what we've learned about Transitions in the past few months. I think they can help your father! How would you admit him?"

"I don't know. I'm not even sure if I could hang with him through treatment. I'm not sure of anything. I want to believe in the system, but I'm afraid to. And my dad is such a loose cannon."

"I hear you," Brett said, "but if you can convince him to seek treatment and you stand by him, Ally and I will stand by you." Brett paused. "This won't be easy."

"I know. And I'm not sure what I doubt most: Transitions, my father, or me."

Nick's voice came out in a whisper. "But I think it is the right thing to do. And there's never been a better time to do it."

A smile cracked across Brett's lips.

"What's so funny, Brett?"

"It's funny how God works, that's all."

"What does he have to do with it?"

"It's interesting that about the time you start thinking about reconnecting with your father God puts you in charge of an Addiction Recovery Center account."

"It's coincidental."

"Right, coincidental."

Nick didn't know quite how to respond. *It's coincidental,* he replayed in his mind. *Okay, it's too coincidental.* He didn't have an explanation, but he found a strange peace envelop him. He trusted Brett, and he realized that his friend had just given him one more reason to slow down, pause, and at least consider the providence of God in his life.

In the days to come Nick confronted his doubts by taking action. He acted on the deal he made with God and the challenge Gus issued; he stepped back into his father's life—with both feet.

When Nick traveled to the lake house each weekend, he stopped in to see his father for a few hours every Saturday morning. It was thorny at first. Chuck Conway was not particularly interested in seeing his son, and, of course, he routinely questioned his motives.

"Trying to ease your conscience?" he chided.

How can you possibly think that I should feel guilty? After all, you are the alcoholic, not me.

When Nick showed any kind of compassion, Chuck made it crystal clear he was not a charity case. Nick ignored his banter. Instead, he showed up most Saturdays and quietly put on a pair of old work gloves and worked alongside his father as they cut back overgrown shrubbery from years of neglect.

Gus was usually there when Nick arrived and served as a convenient buffer between them. With Gus present, Chuck could mumble under his breath, strategically ignore Nick, and when it suited him, toss a few barbs.

Nick realized that he benefited from Gus's presence too. Whenever his father stepped out of earshot, Gus would interpret what transpired and why. Somehow his play-by-play commentary prolonged Nick's patience and curbed his anger.

Listening to Gus provided something else: a broad perspective that added new insight into his father's life. If Brett was right, and people's lives played out like a movie before God, then Nick was beginning to see the pivotal scenes that shaped Chuck Conway's adult life. And with each passing Saturday, the conversation eventually became more civil and sincere, and Nick's conviction to stay the course intensified.

Although he didn't fully understand why his father elected to trim back the brush and re-landscape his yard, he took solace in the fact that he could actually stop drinking long enough to do something, anything, constructive.

While Nick and Gus cut, bundled and tied the underbrush, Chuck dug up dead shrubs and prepared to plant new ones. Chuck leaned on his shovel and wiped sweat from his brow. Gus lifted a small bundle and started the long walk to the curb. Nick wiped the sweat from his forehead with his sleeve then sat on a decorative bench to catch his breath.

When Gus was out of sight, Chuck sat on an old tree stump adjacent to his son. They looked at each other and then looked away.

Although they were becoming more comfortable with each other, they couldn't hide the clumsy pauses and awkward attempts at meaningful conversation. When Gus was out of the mix, Chuck was more direct and abrasive.

"So, what do you hope to gain by all of this?" the elder Conway snapped.

"Better landscaping?" Nick retorted.

"You know what I mean. Why did you come back here after twenty years? What do you hope to gain?"

"Gain?" Nick felt a familiar rage rising and was not going to back down. He was equally direct in his response. "I was hoping to gain a relationship with my father since *we* have both wasted so much time."

Chuck felt a stab of guilt but was relieved by Nick's choice of words. By sharing the blame, Chuck softened and directed the conversation to the issue that made him the most uneasy.

"So, when did you give up?"

"Give up on what?"

"I think you know what I mean."

"No, I don't, Dad."

"When did you give up *on me*?"

"When did I give up on *you*? Don't you think I should be asking you that question?" Without Gus, he had no buffer and he felt his anger slowly rise again. "You've got a lot of nerve asking me that."

"I'm not blaming you," he said humbly. When Nick heard the conciliatory tone in his voice his anger abated. "I'm just asking, when did you give up on me?"

Nick didn't need much time to think. He spoke slowly. "I don't know. Not long after Mom died. Or should I say, my stepmom? Middle school, I guess."

"Really? That soon?" The old man paused. "How old would that make you?"

"Eighth grade? I guess that would make me twelve or thirteen."

Chuck looked away, reached for his shovel and began to dig out another dead shrub.

Nick had hit a nerve. He picked up his shovel and began to dig out a fern across from him. The ball was in his father's court. Nick waited for him to speak. When Gus waddled back into the yard, he could sense tension. He glanced at Nick. Nick glanced at his father and back at Gus. Gus nodded, understanding who had set the tone. Gus started to hum to himself while filling a wheelbarrow with underbrush he had bundled. He didn't address them, electing to let Chuck control the tone and tempo of the conversation.

Nick pried out the fern with the tip of his shovel and broke loose the clumps of soil that clung to the roots. Chuck continued to dig holes to plant boxwoods. Each stroke of the shovel was quick and deliberate. And every thrust was in sync with his sentences.

"I lost your mother at 31, your stepmother at 42, and *you* at— twelve, maybe thirteen. I'm not exactly a success." Sweat dripped from his brow. "Life is not supposed to play out this way. I can't imagine why someone as successful as you would want to drag yourself back into a relationship with a father like me."

Nick almost dropped his shovel at this admission. He glanced at his father, who continued to stare at the ground digging out one small shrub after another with efficient, yet almost violent downward thrusts of his shovel. Nick let his mind wander back to Brett's headline work on the Transitions account. He dwelled on one headline: *The Difference Between Alcohol Addiction and Recovery is Admission.* For the first time, Nick simultaneously felt the hope of this headline and hope for his father's recovery.

Gus poured Chuck a glass of ice water from the pitcher on a picnic table to break his pace. Chuck wiped the beading sweat on his forehead with a handkerchief and slowly set his shovel down. He gulped down half the glass. His breathing was labored as he worked in the hot sun.

"Yup, you're right, Chuck," Gus concurred, once again supporting his closest friend, "life is not supposed to play out that way. You got a bum deal. You had a plan for your wife and son, but it didn't work out. It's just the way life is." Nick glanced at Gus, knowing the cagy old timer had just created an opportunity for Chuck to share more with his son. Silence followed. Nick continued to dig to allow his father to manage the moment.

"Who would think you would lose your wife giving birth to your son? Anything would have been better than that—anything! That should never happen to anybody," Chuck confided.

The elder Conway wandered over to the stump, sat and finished off his water. Nick took this cue and sat on the bench adjacent to him and waited to see what would happen. Gus picked up a shovel, content just to lean on it.

"All I ever wanted was a normal life. A simple life. Nothing special. Just you, me, and your mom," Chuck confessed. "Maybe a few more kids. I didn't want a big house or a fancy car. I didn't need a big-time job."

Chuck stopped and walked to the picnic table to get more water. He gulped hard and walked back to his shovel. "I've always loved the outdoors. I dreamed of working for myself someday—you know, having my own landscaping business. Maybe becoming a landscape architect."

He paused and looked at Nick. "A father always has dreams for his firstborn, especially a son. I remember hoping that you would love the outdoors too. We would do stuff fathers and sons do. Hunt, fish, play sports. And maybe, someday, I would teach you the landscaping business."

Nick shot a glance over to Gus. The old timer nodded as if to say, "Let him ramble. Just listen."

The elder Conway wiped the sweat from his brow and from around his collar. "Just before you were born, I remember telling your mom that I hoped you would become a residential architect, and if I was a landscape architect, we could work together someday."

Chuck gazed at the horizon. He had a far-off look in his eyes. He then glanced at the ground and drove his shovel in the earth. "So much for dreams."

Nick reflected on his father's dream. It was simple enough.

Innocent enough. Achievable enough. *Why did it go so terribly wrong?* he wondered. He was deeply moved knowing his father had once dreamed that they would work together side by side. He described a world Nick never thought his father imagined, a world in which they would not only be present in each other's life but also instrumental. It was a stark contrast from reality until Gus, in his simple way, brought it all into perspective.

"Yup, life is always different from dreams, Chuck, but at least part of your dream came true."

Chuck glanced at him with a look of disgust. "Yeah? How's that?"

"You're working together with your son now."

Chuck looked at Nick. Their eyes met. With this simple truth the elder Conway felt that familiar stab of guilt while Nick's pulse quickened. Suddenly, their hearts collided. Simultaneously, they felt remorse for all the mistakes, grief for the pride that prevented reconciliation, and the sharp sting of regret for the magnitude of all the lost time.

As the summer wore on, Nick could feel an unspoken bond slowly building between them. He wondered if his father could feel it. It felt good. For the first time in Nick's life, he felt as though he had a father, a real father.

One Saturday morning they even drove into town together in the old man's truck to a local nursery to buy some boxwoods, evergreens, wet prairie wildflowers, and grasses to build a rain garden. Nick was shocked when Chuck introduced him to the landscape architect at the nursery. "Bill, this is my boy, Nick. He has a fancy job in Chicago. He's helping me fix up the yard." This led to a brief but pleasant exchange between them. Nick stood quietly acknowledging the introduction with a simple nod. It wasn't much, but Nick counted it a victory that his father acknowledged their relationship.

Nick was also surprised how hard Chuck worked when he wasn't drinking. He could dig a hole faster than Nick could pull a plant out of the pot. Most Saturdays Nick would show up unannounced and help him build his perennial Rain Garden. They planted native wetland and prairie wildflowers and grasses. Together they dug a seventy square-foot shallow depression and planted New England aster, cardinal flower, great blue lobelia, wild bergamot, sneezeweed, and stiff goldenrod. Nick would place the plants and natural grasses in the hole. Chuck would carefully shovel dirt in the hole and grade the dirt.

They redirected the downspouts to the rain garden depression by digging a shallow swale. Chuck then watered the plants every other day for two weeks to establish them. Once they were established, they would not require additional watering. In theory, rain would be enough.

When Chuck spoke, it was primarily about landscaping. Nick noticed his father lacked certain social graces, and he was not one to share his emotions freely. In this arena, it was like father, like son.

The old man taught Nick that rain gardens make good use of rainwater runoff, conserving water supplies. They also provide food and shelter for many interesting birds, butterflies, and beneficial insects. Nick assumed there was a certain comfort in talking shop and let his father lead most conversations. The more his father talked, the more Nick entered his world and observed his talents. The more time they spent together the more Nick realized how alike they were. For example, Nick noticed the similarities in their word choices, gestures, and even their postures as they leaned on their shovels. *He is my father. And for the first time in my life it feels like it.*

When it came time for Nick to depart for the lake house, Chuck never thanked him for coming. Nick, in turn, never told him if or when he would return. Instead, he would just show up, whenever he could, he would slip on a pair of gloves and assist Chuck in whatever he was doing. The old man was a good landscaper, creative and hardworking.

Ally accompanied Nick to the lake house several weekends during the summer. Secretly, he hoped she was coming to be with him and to enjoy the tranquility of the lake house and the natural beauty of the surroundings. Instead, she seemed content simply to watch them work together and see how their relationship would develop. She was not afraid to work. She would find an extra pair of gloves and pick up a shovel to help when she felt she could contribute. Nick felt something stir deep inside him when she would get dirty working alongside them. It made him feel like she was committed to him and his mission to reach out to his father and get him the medical attention he needed to beat his battle with alcohol.

Nick was never completely sure if his father enjoyed his company, but Chuck certainly enjoyed having Ally around. Anyone would be taken with the loveliness of such an attractive woman, but Nick believed it was Ally's playfulness and frankness that won him over. Chuck never minced words—and she didn't either. Nick was surprised that despite her friendliness, she didn't tolerate his language or his negative attitude when it went south. It made him wish he would have been less tolerant of his behavior growing up. She seemed to hold her own with Chuck, and he seemed to respect her for it.

"You're lucky to have her," he would tell Nick.

"I don't 'have her,'" Nick quickly retorted, knowing that Ally was not comfortable being tagged as his girlfriend, especially since that right was currently reserved for Ron.

After spending most of the morning with his father, Nick and Ally would return to the lake house and take long walks on the Shore Path or spend hours adrift in his boat talking the afternoon away. They talked about everything: life, death, dreams, and disappointments. They talked about the way life was—and the way they had hoped it would be. They talked about the good times in their past together and about the future—careful never to include each other in their plans. And Nick couldn't help but notice that Ron seemed to have a more significant presence in her life, yet she skillfully avoided divulging details about her relationship with him. He wished she wasn't so secretive and mysterious about him.

Nick was never sure why Ally was so involved in helping him restore his relationship with his father. He assumed it simply fell under the "that's what friends are for" category. Maybe it was because Chuck was his only relative, and no one should go through life alone. Perhaps she was motivated by the deep love she had for her father. Or maybe it was just her way of telling Nick that every son deserves a relationship with his father. Most likely, it was nothing more than simply paying Nick back for being so good to her during her recovery from her car accident. He didn't know what her actual motivation was, but he knew what he hoped it was.

Despite his best efforts to prevent it, he was unquestionably falling deeply in love with her again. She was beautiful. She was vivacious. She was honest. And she cherished the things that mattered most in life. If he could have a relationship with her again, he would do everything differently. The truth was he didn't deserve a second chance with her, and if he had a second chance, he wondered how she could trust him, much less, love him again.

There couldn't be a worse time to fall in love with her. She might take that new job in New York before the end of summer and, for all he knew, she could be deeply in love with Ron. He needed to find answers to these questions, and his window of opportunity was closing.

CHAPTER

After a long week at work, Nick pulled up in front of his father's house on most Saturday mornings with the expectation of getting dirty and, if he was lucky, getting closer to his father.

He knew he could never get too close. Chuck would see to that. The old man typically put up barriers when his son attempted to cross a personal boundary. Yet Nick had his own set of boundaries, too. His own deep-seated anger was ever-present, and it was more a barrier than a boundary. Nick knew if he was going to forgive his father for the past and bond with him again, he must take his wall of anger down.

Over time, he occasionally was able to talk with his father on a personal level. To forgive the past, he reasoned, he must first understand it. So, with the help of Gus, he was able to probe his father and ask why he stopped believing in himself, why he surrendered his life to alcohol, and why he seemingly gave up on life itself.

One cool July morning he tested his father's boundaries to see just how far he could go. As they finished planting some boxwoods in the front yard and Gus watered a new grass bed, Nick stepped over a boundary to a secret place, his father's heart.

"Tell me what Mom was like."

"What?" he asked, with a hint of anger and surprise.

"Mom. Mary. What was she like?"

"Why in the world would you ask a question like that now?"

"When would be a better time, Dad? Think about it. There will never be a better time than now. I'm almost forty. I don't know a thing about my birth mother, and you're asking me why I would ask about her now!"

Gus waited a moment for Chuck to confide in his only child. When he was slow to respond, Gus took it upon himself to interject. "She was a peach, Nick. They didn't get much prettier. And she was radiant. Very outgoing. Self confident like you, and just happy to be alive. People loved being around her." Gus smiled in recollection. "I'd said she was..."

"He asked me, Gus!" Chuck retorted, cutting him off.

"Then answer him," Gus replied. He glanced at Nick. When their eyes met Gus gave him a wink.

Chuck turned a large empty flower pot over and sat on it. "She could allure you with her smile," he started, "cheer you with her humor, outsmart you with her wit, and inspire you with her laughter." The old man paused and drew a breath. "And could she dance. That woman loved to dance, and she was good at it."

"Yup, men would flock to dance with her," Gus added. "Once, they actually formed a line to dance with her. Old Chuck stood in that line, too. Come to think of it, I think he was behind me."

"You old coot," Chuck said with a laugh. "Let me tell the story." Chuck grinned at the thought of her, and Nick felt a shiver in his spine. "She loved life, and because of it most people enjoyed being around her. After we were married and she became pregnant, she was so happy. She seemed to know that we would have a boy. She spent a lot of time picking out boys' names. 'Nicholas, it's a name I'll never grow tired of' she said when she named you."

Chuck looked at Nick, then Gus and then away. "Seems unfair that the woman so excited about bringing you into the world never got a chance to see you, much less hold you. She never got a chance to call you by name. How fair is that?"

Chuck's mood suddenly shifted, and he walked in the house. Nick knew what he was going to do inside and wished he hadn't taken him there. Gus noticed a look of regret sweep over Nick's face.

"Don't blame yourself, Nicky. That was almost forty years ago. Just one of those things life throws at you to make you stronger. You would have loved your mom. She was vivacious and optimistic. She didn't complain much and made the best of bad situations. Your dad saw similar traits in your stepmom, too. I think that's why he was attracted to her a few years later when he knew he needed to move on."

"Maybe I shouldn't have asked him about her, Gus."

"Land sakes, you just asked your father a question about your mother. Nope, nothing wrong with that. Nothing will ever be wrong with that. Don't worry about it. Let's go see what your dad is up to."

When they entered the kitchen, Chuck was on the living room couch. He took a pull on a bottle of beer. Another unopened bottle sat on the end table next to him, so they knew where this was going.

Nick took a seat on the recliner across from him. "Wanna cold one?" he offered his son.

"No, thanks. Dad, look, I'm sorry. I shouldn't have taken you there."

"Where?" he replied, to mask his emotions.

"To your past."

"You didn't take me to my past. You took me to my life, my miserable life. And that's not all your fault. Some of it is, but..." He stopped short as Gus walked toward him.

"It's not his fault, Chuck," Gus injected firmly. "None of it— and you know it. We've been through this before."

Chuck took another long pull of his beer and finished it before twisting off the cap of the other one on the end table beside him. Nick stood, thanked Gus and walked toward the door.

"Bye, Dad," he said, as he left the room.

"What's this. You walking out on me again?" the old man taunted.

"Not sure there is anything I can do for you when you're like this."

"When I'm like what?" he replied, forcing Nick to describe his image of his father.

Nick thought for a minute and chose his words carefully. "When you're...not yourself. When you're under the influence..."

"I'm not under the influence—yet. Talk to me."

"Dad, you've had a tough life. I know that. I'm sorry for that. But I want to see you recover."

"Recover?" he shot back almost before he finished his sentence.

"How do you recover from the premature death of your spouse?"

"Dad, I don't know..."

"How do you recover from the premature death of your second wife...and it's your fault?"

"I don't know but..."

"How do you recover from the death of your only son?"

"What do you mean? I'm not dead," Nick replied.

"You were. When you walked out of here at nineteen and never said good-bye, never wrote a note, you might as well have been dead. For twenty years, I didn't know where you were. You changed jobs just before you left. I couldn't find you. The police weren't much help because you were considered an adult and, thus, not a runaway.

"What bothers me the most is, for those twenty years, you knew where I was but you chose not to contact me. Now you want me to recover? How can I recover from this life—this totally meaningless life?"

"Dad, listen..." He paused for a moment. "I know a place..."

"Save your breath, I don't believe in those recovery places or whatever they call them. Besides, alcohol is cheaper, and it probably works better, if not faster."

Nick turned to the door and walked out to his car. Gus had listened to their exchange and followed him out the door.

"Heading back to your lake house?"

"Yeah, not much more I can do here."

"Nope, not today maybe, but down the road. Remember, don't give up on him, Nicky."

"Gus, I'm not sure why I'm even involved sometimes. This whole thing is way over my head."

"Nope, it's not going to be easy. And many of your father's problems are his fault, but don't write him off."

Nick opened his car door and slid behind the wheel. He looked up at Gus. "You've stood by him for all of these years. How? Why?"

The old man slowly stroked his chin and spoke in a gentle tone. "When you get to know him like I know him, like your mom and your stepmom knew him, when you understand the original intentions of his heart, when you've seen the hopes he once held, the disappointments that usually followed, when you've seen how hard he worked in his life, when you've witnessed his mistakes and detected his regrets, when you've felt the pain he has felt, sensed the sudden loss and crippling loneliness he has endured, when you've observed the entire picture, then you'll see that..." Gus choked back his emotions and couldn't finish his statement.

"Then you'll see *that*?" Nick coaxed him to finish his thought.

Gus responded quietly. "Then you'll see *that*—he's worth saving."

Nick nodded and momentarily stared out the windshield as Gus's words gripped him. He turned the key in the ignition. Gus stepped back, and Nick slowly drove away.

CHAPTER

At work Nick caught Ally after a few meetings, and they had coffee in the employee lounge. There Nick played back all of the conversations she had missed, coupled with those she'd witnessed. Together they gradually pieced together his father's life like a complicated jigsaw puzzle and agreed that Nick should encourage him seriously to consider alcohol addiction recovery treatment at Transitions before the end of summer.

Everything made perfect sense. Everything was logical. Now Nick could tie all of the reasons his father should seek treatment into a nice big bow, yet something still troubled Ally.

"Exactly what are you going to say to your father when you ask him to seek treatment?" she asked.

"I don't know. I guess I'll tell him about all of the treatment options at Transitions, the positive outcomes, the great docs and how he will benefit, and how our relationship could benefit. Why?"

"So, basically, you're going to represent the advertising we created."

"Well, we've worked on this account for months, and we're convinced that Transitions is for real, right?"

"Yeah, but I don't think that is going to convince your father."

"No?"

"No. He's not interested if Transitions is for real. He's interested in if you're for real. I think there is a better way for you to convince him to seek treatment than to recite the features and benefits of Transitions Addiction Recovery Center."

"Okay, what are you thinking?"

"We talked about this before. I think you need to forgive him."

Ally accompanied Nick to visit his father and to enjoy the serenity of the lake house for most of July. When he decided to have a talk with his father on the first weekend in August, he once again invited Ally to accompany him. If things blew up in Williams Bay, they could always enjoy some time together at the lake house, he reasoned. Today, Nick knew he needed Ally's support, and she graciously agreed to stand by him.

It was a beautiful Sunday morning as they pulled up in front of his father's home. They had enjoyed a relaxing dinner on the patio at the lake house the previous night, and they had eaten brunch at the Grand Geneva Resort earlier that morning.

Nick rang the bell and waited for an answer. When no one came to the door, they walked around back in case Chuck was working in the yard. As they rounded the corner, Chuck was sitting on the patio slugging down a beer in the warm morning sun. Nick didn't count the empty beer cans on the table because he could tell by the look in his father's eyes that he was on his way to a morning buzz. Ally noticed too, but she didn't let it deter the warmth of her greeting.

"Hey, Mr. Conway," Ally said tenderly.

He turned his head slowly and Nick noticed it bob in the characteristic fashion that said, "I'm an alcoholic." They pulled up a chair and sat at the table with him. Nick wondered if this was all a big mistake.

"You've made a lot of progress on your rain garden, and your landscaping looks great," she said, trying to break the ice. Nick looked around the yard and had to agree it was turning out very nicely, especially considering what it had looked like before the project got started.

"You think so," the old man asked, encouraged by Ally's kindness.

"Yes. What are you going to plant next spring?"

Nick was glad Ally was with him. She kept the conversation going while he pondered how to ask the tough questions without confrontation.

"Maybe some prairie blazing star, mountain mint, and green bulrush. That is, if I can get any consistent help from him."

Nick knew the alcohol, not his father, was speaking, but he let it irritate him just the same. "Dad, how can you say that? I've stopped by to help you for a few hours on most Saturdays this summer."

"Like I said, if I could get some *consistent* help. Since I never know when you're going to show up or for how long, I can't really count on you, can I?"

"You can't count on *me*?" Nick said, his anger on slow burn but rising. Ally's eyes widened as she heard Nick's tone shift. She was about to get caught in a crossfire.

"Dad, how can you of all people say that? I never knew when you were going to show up through most of my childhood. I couldn't count on *you!*"

Nick heard the resentment in his voice. Chuck put his beer down on the table and looked off in the distance. Ally looked at the ground, and she sat quietly not knowing how to intervene or excuse herself. She felt a tremor of an earthquake between the two.

Nick had come here today with completely different intentions, but once again his father altered the agenda with an irresponsible remark. Nick regretted his anger and reminded himself that he was there to help him, not hate him. *Don't let him win again! Do what you came here to do. Forgive him. Get help for him. And set yourself free from the bondage of your anger.*

Nick wasn't sure how to start the conversation, nevertheless, he launched into it fearlessly. With his now toxic mix of emotions, the only way to say what he had come to say was to blurt it out. He knew he might be making the biggest mistake of his life and there was no turning back, but it was time to finally unload!

"Dad, I'm sorry. I didn't mean to get angry at you. I don't ever want to be angry at you again, and—I forgive you for not being there for me as a kid."

Chuck fired back. "Don't blame that on me, you're the one that..." Nick didn't let him finish.

"I forgive you for your anger, resentment and irresponsibility."

"How dare you!" he replied, but Nick cut him off. His momentum building.

"I forgive you for missing my Little League games. For missing my high school baseball tournaments. For missing my state championship game."

"Now just a minute," he started, but Nick talked over him again.

"I forgive you for embarrassing me in front of my friends."

"Now stop right there," the old man said lifting his hand, his voice beginning to quiver. It was too late to stop. Adrenaline propelled Nick forward.

"I forgive you for leaving me home alone as a young child. I forgive you for never making me feel secure, for never making me feel loved." A tear started to cascade down Nick's cheek, but he stuffed his emotions and forged ahead. He felt relief with every sentence.

"I forgive you for scaring me and choking me as a boy when you had too much to drink." Chuck started to weep. Nick's voice cracked.

"I forgive you for blaming me for my birth mother's death. I forgive you for loving your bottle more than your baby.

"I forgive you for abandoning me emotionally when Mom died." The old man buried his face in his large hands and started to sob. Ally gently slipped her arm around him.

"I forgive you for *drinking* like an alcoholic. I forgive you for *smelling* like an alcoholic. I forgive you for *being* an alcoholic."

"Nick, please stop," he begged, with a kindness his son had never heard before. But Nick couldn't stop.

"Dad, forgive *me* that Mom died giving birth to me. Forgive me for what it did to you. Forgive me for pain it caused."

"Nick, stop," he pleaded, as he choked back the tears. Ally remained silent but wiped streaming tears and running mascara from her cheeks. Nick felt the liberating freedom forgiveness brings. He continued to unleash the burden that, for years, had held his heart hostage.

"Dad, forgive me for hating you. Forgive me for hating alcoholics. Forgive me for not being willing to forgive you, to love you."

"Enough," he cried. But Nick hadn't finished what he had come to do.

"Forgive me for thinking you were a lost cause. Forgive me for walking out on you the first chance I got. And forgive me for treating you like you didn't exist for the past twenty years."

Chuck was leaning over now, sobbing. Nick spilled his guts all over the patio. He was empty. He listened as his father wept quietly, and Ally searched her purse for a tissue. Nick realized he was hearing the sweet sound of forgiveness and sensing the hope of reconciliation. This was what Brett and Ally had been talking about.

Nick got up from his chair and walked over to his father. He sat next to him and gently placed his arm around him as Ally did the same on the other side of him. Finally, Nick said the words he had always wanted to say.

"I love you, Dad."

They rose to their feet and faced each other. Chuck put his arms around his son, and they embraced.

"I love you too, son. I've really made a mess of things."

The moment lingered. "Dad, we can beat this thing—together. I know a place that can help you...a place that can help us..."

Ally handed Chuck a tissue and turned to Nick. Spontaneously, they embraced each other. She slipped her arms around his neck and squeezed him tighter than he anticipated. He lost himself in the pleasure of her embrace and the sweet fragrance of her perfume. He waited for her to release, but she held him. As they gently receded from each other, they both realized they had just witnessed a miracle; maybe two.

CHAPTER

Nick and Ally drove back to the lake house Sunday afternoon after a passionate discussion with Chuck on the benefits of treatment at Transitions Addiction Recovery Center. All the way home they weren't quite sure that what happened, in fact, did happen. Like his father, for more than twenty years, he carried the dead weight of negative baggage. Now, finally, Nick not only had forgiven his father, he had vowed to stand by him through his course of treatment.

"Ally, thank you. I would never have gotten through this without you."

"I didn't do that much."

"If it weren't for you, I would have never considered seeing my father again and forgiving him, much less encouraging him to seek treatment. Did you notice how he listened to you? You're the one who convinced him that Transitions could really help him."

"I don't think I convinced him, Nick."

"No?"

"No," she continued. "I think it was the hope you gave him of a renewed relationship with you. Today, you wiped the slate clean. Think about it. Now you both can start over. It's exciting!"

Nick could hear the joy in her voice. It was one more reason it was easy to love her. She was genuinely happy for the triumphs of others.

They spent the afternoon sipping iced tea under the umbrella on the patio table watching the flurry of activity on the lake. Speed boats ripped across the water while teens bounced on floating trampolines and tanned themselves on the piers below.

They discussed how well the ad campaign and PR initiatives were progressing for Transitions and two other new large accounts at the agency. While the conversation was on work, Nick took the opportunity to ask Ally about her career plans.

"Hey, what's up with your opportunity at McCann Erickson?"

"Actually," she said hesitantly. "I have been hoping to talk with you about it, but you have been so busy with your dad. They made me an offer, but I haven't officially accepted it yet." She paused a beat. "I'm going to New York on Tuesday for a few days to see if we can finalize a deal, meet a few more people, and possibly talk to a realtor. I should be back sometime on Friday."

Nick stared off into the horizon as his gut began to churn.

"Hey, congratulations," he said, trying to sound like everything was cool. For a guy pretty good at faking his emotions, he wasn't sure he was pulling it off now. "How am I going to find an art director as talented as you for the Transitions account?"

"That shouldn't be too hard. What about Tanya West? She's talented, creative and—attractive."

"Thanks, but I'm just looking for talented and creative," he retorted. "Besides, she's not as..." He didn't finish his sentence, but Ally knew what he was going to say. He looked into her beautiful brown eyes. She returned his gaze. He sensed she could read his face and, worse, the intentions of his heart. Until now he thought he had done a pretty good job repressing his feelings for her. Nevertheless, he wondered if it was obvious to her that he was in love with her again.

He fumbled for his next words. "If you need some help finding a place, I have some friends in New York who could help you. I love New York. I could go with you and help get you connected and I could..."

She didn't let him finish.

"I'll be fine, thanks. My contact at McCann Erickson will meet us there and show us around."

"Us?" he replied aloud. It may have been the only word he heard.

"Yes. Ron lives there, remember. He gave me the lead on this job."

Nick felt his world come crashing again. Of course, he knew Ron lived there, and of course he knew Ron could help her, but secretly he had hoped their relationship fizzled. Thus, explaining why she hadn't mentioned him much the last few months.

"Right, Ron. I wasn't thinking, sorry," he pretended. Nick rarely felt so stupid, embarrassed or rejected. Ally looked away. He didn't know how to read her gestures or what to say next, but he needed to know more.

"So, I guess you guys are getting pretty serious?"

"Serious enough," she offered tentatively. If she intended her comment to come off as definitive, it struck him as neutral.

"Serious enough? Just how serious is that?"

"Well," she stalled. "I'm not sure."

"You're not sure?"

"I'm not sure—I want to have this conversation."

"I'm sorry, Ally. I shouldn't ask so many questions."

"Thank you."

"So, I'll just ask one. Do you love him?"

"Nick!" she said, surprised by his abrupt intrusion. "Let's just say, I know he loves me."

"Of course, he loves you. Who wouldn't? The question is, do you love him?"

Ally stalled again, debating whether Nick had a right to ask the question and whether she had any obligation to answer it.

"Yes, I think so."

"You think so?" Nick was clearly off base but he persisted because, as usual, he cared more about himself than he did about Ron.

"Yes, I think so. But..."

"But what?"

"It's complicated. A few things have happened that I didn't plan on..."

"What happened?"

"*You* happened."

"What do you mean, I happened?"

"I didn't plan on you reentering my life, first with the Transitions account, and then with your father. I didn't plan on spending time with you over coffee, over dinner, at the lake house. And I didn't plan on sharing my heart with you again—about my father—about my family. I was content to be over you."

Nick paused to collect his thoughts and decide if he should bare his soul—or leave Ally hanging out there because she exposed her feelings first. She had a right to know how he felt.

"For what it's worth, I was *never* over you, Ally. Oh, I told myself I was, but I lied to myself the same way I lied to you and many other people in my life. And I have struggled to forgive myself for what I did to you. Do you know what it is like to live with relentless regret? I was such a fool."

"You got that right."

"You don't have to rub it in," he said, trying to break the tension that filled the air.

"As I told you before," she continued, "in some ways you are a lot like your father. You have both made bad decisions, hurt people, and had to live with regret." Her words stung but brought clarity to a complicated day.

"What are you going to do then? Are you going to go to New York? Are you sure this job is right for you?"

"It's a great opportunity for me."

"Are you sure Ron is right for you?"

"Nick, I'm conflicted, but I am no longer confused. I think there's a difference."

"How so?"

"I'm conflicted because I see two good options. But I am not confused as to which I should pursue. There's a great career opportunity waiting for me in New York."

"Yes, and I'm sure there's a great guy waiting for you in New York, too, but are you sure he is the right guy?"

"Ron is good *to* me and *for* me. He always has my best interests at heart. He has a good career there, and he wants me to join him. He is the opposite of what you..." She stopped short.

Nick finished the sentence for her. "He's the opposite of what *you are*?"

"That's not what I was going to say!"

"Then what were you going to say?"

Ally looked away then looked in Nick's eyes. "He is the opposite of what *you were.*"

Nick could hear the conviction in which she spoke and suddenly felt his hope of having a relationship with her evaporate.

"I have seen the start of a wonderful change in you, Nick. I think that's great. And, frankly, I am very attracted to you again. But..."

"But?"

"But I know better than to...

"To what?"

"To risk the same thing—twice."

"Ally, I've changed, or at least I'm in the process of changing, and you and Brett are helping me. Can't you see that?"

"Yes, I can see that. And I'm happy for you—and for your father. But I think I need to pursue the great possibilities I have with Ron and a new career in New York."

Nick blinked and looked away. He knew this was a defining moment in his life. He could feel his stomach roll and hear his heart pound as he sensed the finality of the moment. He replayed her sentence back in his mind looking for operative words: "I think I need to..." *She thinks she needs?* Up until now he had always believed in second chances. No matter what you mess up in life, you may, someday, get that second chance to redeem yourself. *Was that moment with Ally now,* he wondered? *Or, did she just close the door?* He waited to see if she would offer more. She remained silent.

His hope for a second shot with Ally must now be over because this moment was hers. She controlled it, and she didn't appear to leave the door ajar. Yet, despite her confident tone about moving to New York to be with Ron, in the inner sanctum of his soul, he doubted her. On the other hand, he wondered if he was simply living in denial again.

As Nick prepared for his account briefing with Sam Morris and Tom Sullivan at work on Monday morning, he wondered how awkward it would be with Ally today based on how their conversation ended on the patio the day before.

He met with Sam and Tom at nine o'clock and reviewed their current strategies and tactics to execute the second phase of the advertising campaign and the new PR initiative they had outlined for Transitions. After the formal review, Sam excused himself and left for another meeting. Nick took the opportunity to talk with Tom about Transitions.

"Tom, it's been a pleasure for me to work with you on the Transitions account the past several months," he started.

"Likewise," Tom responded. "I love what your team developed, and I think it will advance our objectives promoting our addiction recovery services."

"I hope it will, too. But I have a confession to make."

"Really? What do you mean?"

"Well, until now, I have been just going through the motions on this account."

"Really?"

"I shouldn't admit this to a client." He paused. A younger version of Nick would have dropped dead before ever admitting this to a client. "I wasn't sure I believed in your services at Transitions."

"Really? Why not?"

"It had nothing to do with your facility and more to do with alcoholics themselves. I didn't believe alcoholics stood a chance of recovering because, well, I know how hopeless they are to live with. Tom, my father is an alcoholic, and I didn't believe he could ever change."

"I'm sorry to hear that, Nick. About your father, I mean. Is he in recovery or still debating whether to seek treatment?"

"Well, Ally and I spoke to him yesterday about how Transitions can help with recovery. That's what I wanted to talk with you about now. He's been a full-blown alcoholic for almost thirty years. Do you really believe your services can help him? I mean, can you honestly make a significant difference in his life at this advanced stage? I know what your literature says, I wrote it. It's just that, now I have so much at stake."

"Sounds like the moment of truth for you," Tom said with a smile. "Let me ask a few questions. Do you believe in the advertising you created for Transitions?"

"Yes."

"Do you believe what you have learned about us and our approach to addiction recovery? Do you believe in what you have seen happening in our facility?"

"Yes, of course."

"Do you believe the testimonies of the patients you interviewed and the lives you've seen rehabilitated?"

"Not initially, but I do now," he replied, embarrassed by his doubts.

"Are you sure?" Tom asked, testing the depth of Nick's convictions about his own work.

"Let me ask you this. Is your father willing to change, and are you willing to go through the rigors of treatment with him?"

"Yes, I am—and I think he is."

"Then my answer is yes. Yes, Transitions can make a significant difference in his life—and yours—even though he has been an alcoholic for thirty years. Our program, our approach, and our medicine can work—if the patient and his family are willing to work. It's not a guarantee but the probability is in your favor."

"That's all I need to know, Tom."

"It's interesting isn't it, Nick?"

"What's that?"

"How the depth of one's conviction is in direct proportion to how much he has at stake? Maybe there is a lesson in that."

"Yeah. Perhaps we have just reinforced the value of testimonial advertising," Nick offered. "Perhaps we should consider testimonies after the initial campaign runs?"

Tom smiled in agreement as Nick departed.

It was a typical week except for the fact that Ally left for her trip to New York on Tuesday. Although she would be back on Friday, suddenly everything at the office felt different without her. Nevertheless, it was a productive week. Nick completed several creative briefs for new clients whom John brought in, supervised a couple of photo shoots, concepted several ads with three creative teams and, to Sam's delight, approved several dozen invoices for billing.

Nick skipped lunch most of the week except Thursday. He had lunch scheduled with Brett to discuss copy strategy on the two new accounts John had brought into the agency. But he had more to discuss with Brett than ad copy.

It was a beautiful August day, warm and balmy with almost no humidity. For Nick, it was the kind of summer day he dreamed of and a perfect day for a walk down the bustling Chicago streets. Together with Brett, he decided to have a mobile lunch. They stopped at a street vendor and bought Chicago-style chili hot dogs and then walked along the lake shore. Nick could never put enough ketchup on a hot dog. He was careful with every bite, or it would invariably punctuate his shirt.

Brett finished his last bite and poked the end of the hot dog in his mouth before wiping the condiments off his hands. Brett suggested they sit along the shoreline and review the ad copy he had written for the new accounts.

They walked to a nearby bench.

Nick changed the subject as soon as they sat. "Brett, before we get into the copy, can I talk to you about something else?"

"Fire away."

"Last weekend I had a chance to take your advice with my dad."

"Go on."

Nick spent the next twenty minutes explaining how he had forgiven his father, and about how liberating it felt and how Ally reacted to the entire situation. He also felt comfortable enough to tell Brett about Ally going to New York and Ron waiting in the wings.

"You certainly have interesting weekends," Brett said, as a wry smile curled on his face. "In fact, it sounds as though it could be life-changing for all of you. Think about it. Your father could be on the road to recovery. You will re-enter his life permanently and restore your relationship with him. And Ally may start a new career and a new relationship in a new location. That's exciting, but how are you feeling about it?"

"I am both excited and concerned," Nick admitted.

"You're excited about restoring your relationship with your father and concerned about losing your relationship with Ally?"

"Right. Do you think Ally knows how deeply I feel about her?"

"I'm not sure, but I can see it in your eyes."

"Well, if you can see it, then she can see it, too, right?"

"I don't think so."

"Why not?"

"Because I think she hasn't been looking in your eyes."

182

"What do you mean?"

"I don't think she has been looking in your eyes because she may not want you to see what's in her eyes."

"Do you think she cares about me, too?"

"Actually, I think she is trying not to."

"Brett, since we split up three years ago, I have never dated anyone I could love like her. What do you do when you've lost the only woman you ever really loved to another man?"

"Well, it's not easy because, face it, you've made some big mistakes with her. But I suppose there are only two real options. You either go after her or you simply let her go."

"That's it?"

"Well, it's a little more complicated. First, you have to consider the person you love. In this case you have to ask yourself, would she really be happier with you or Ron? That's an act of unselfishness and an act of unconditional love. Can I digress for a moment?"

"Sure."

"Speaking of unconditional love, it sounds like you saw another glimpse of God this weekend."

"In what way?"

"Well, I think you got a glimpse of God's love. Did you recognize it?"

"I don't know. I noticed my father's reaction to my forgiving him."

"And how did he react?"

"He wept."

"Is that love?"

"No. I guess it's sorrow or repentance."

"It's sorrow. It becomes repentance when he acts on his sorrow and attempts to change or he turns from the way he's been living."

"Well, then there's Ally. She wept, too, but she was weeping because of the...?"

"Go on."

"Because of the love and forgiveness she witnessed between a thirty-year alcoholic and his only son."

"And where did the forgiveness come from?"

"From me."

"And the love?"

"From me again, I guess."

"Yes, from you. And the love you extended to your father was from the core of your being. You loved him without him even asking for forgiveness. You loved him without conditions. That is consistent with the character of God."

"Brett, which came first, forgiveness or love?"

"What do you think? You'll have to search your own heart to answer that. I suspect that love came first. Because in the secret place of your heart, your love for your father overcame your resentment of him. In other words, you loved him more than you resented him.

"And that is a beautiful picture of the way Christ loves us. In fact, the Bible tells us that while we were yet sinners, Christ died for us. It was the ultimate act of love before forgiveness. And you got a glimpse of that kind of love this weekend.

"Nick, it may be difficult to comprehend, but God desires a relationship with us. A personal relationship, not just intellectual acknowledgment of his existence. He wants to be a part of our daily lives."

"But what does that look like?"

"You simply ask for it. You invite him into your life. You ask him to change you and help you start living for him, not yourself. Up until now, God has been showing himself to you in glimpses. He wants more than that. He wants to show you all of himself and to play a major role in all aspects of your life so you can, through faith, spend eternity with him."

Nick nodded. Although he didn't fully understand, it made sense, and he marveled at the notion that the God of the universe wanted a personal relationship with the likes of him.

After work Nick went for a long walk along Lake Michigan. He wondered if his father would actually seek treatment at Transitions or if he would renege. And if he did recover, would their relationship? His thoughts quickly shifted to Ally. As he walked along the water's edge, he contemplated her job opportunity in New York and her relationship with Ron. He needed to know if she loved Ron and, if so, how deeply.

When he returned to his high-rise apartment, he turned an armchair and dragged it to the window that overlooked the city far below. He stared into the openness for what seemed like an hour. From this fifteen-story perspective, he watched the people scurry below. He focused on one man who stopped on the sidewalk to greet an acquaintance. He envisioned his life from this vantage point, from God's point of view. From this aerial perspective, he suddenly realized how God saw his life, his every move, his every encounter, his opportunities, his victories, his close calls and his vain attempts to control his life without the advantage of an aerial view. From this chair, high above the street, he contemplated how oblivious he had been to God's presence and purpose in his life.

It dawned on him that nothing escaped God's notice; no idle thought, no random mood, no inappropriate attitude, and no inexcusable action. From this divine view, God saw his life, and his heart, as an open book, the pages laid bare. *Why*, Nick wondered, *would God care about my seemingly insignificant life on this earth when he resides high in the heavens?* Then he remembered what Brett had said during the past several months. God doesn't merely reside in the heavens but in the hearts of those who call upon him. *Why have I never called upon him?*

Staring at a man on the street far below, Nick wondered how he would feel if this anonymous soul suddenly turned, faced him, and waved to him in friendly acknowledgment. The thought warmed him. Conversely, he pondered how startled he would be if that same man turned, faced him, and raised a fist in angry scorn. As his mind wandered, he contemplated how empty he would feel if that man would never turn, never face him, and never acknowledge his existence. *Which man am I? The second? The third? The second and the third? How must God feel that I have never legitimately acknowledged him during the course of what will soon be forty years?* A profound remorse swept over him. As he stared at the anonymous man on the street, he tried something he had done only once before; he prayed.

"God, if you're really there…" He paused at the awkwardness of the attempt. He started again. "If you're really there…" He stopped short again, wrestling with the unfamiliarity of how to address God. He tried once more, "God, if you're really there—make my heart your home. Live there. Forgive me for what I am—and what I've been. Change me. Guide me. Make the balance of my life count."

As he peered down on the people bustling far below, he couldn't possibly comprehend how his life would now be different. But one thing he did know; he somehow felt completely different.

CHAPTER

Early Friday morning Nick stopped by Ally's office to see if she had returned from her final interview in New York. Her computer screen was black so he rode the elevator down to John's office. John gave him a heads-up on a new client's reaction to their creative brief and outlined the next steps so Nick could inform the creative team. He returned to his office in time to answer the phone.

"Nick Conway."

"Hi, Nick. Tom Sullivan."

"Hey, Tom, how can I help you?"

"Well, I've got some good news and some bad news. Which do you want first?"

"It's Friday, and I don't want to jinx the weekend. Start with the good news."

"Well, it's about your father. I called him to explain our addiction recovery services in a little more detail as you asked."

"Go on," Nick said, sensing his father had already backed out of his decision to pursue treatment.

"Your father has agreed to be admitted."

"Outstanding! What's the bad news?"

"He informed me that he does not have medical insurance. Apparently, he also has significant financial issues. Were you aware of this?"

"No, but I guess I'm not surprised. He's lost a few jobs in the past, but he hasn't discussed his current employment, or unemployment, situation with me. What do you suggest?"

"Well, Medicare may take care of some of the cost. Does he have any supplemental insurance or veteran's benefits?"

"No, I don't think so. He wasn't in the military."

"Are there any other benefits he is entitled to?"

"I don't know. I'll have to ask him. I'm leaving work early today and spending the weekend at my home in Lake Geneva. My father lives nearby. I'll stop in and ask him if he has any other benefits. Tom, just how expensive are addiction recovery services?"

"Well, he will be admitted to the facility for detox for almost thirty days. These costs are similar to hospitalization. In addition, he will see several physicians, aides, and a psychiatrist. This adds up, Nick. Rehab is an extra cost. Plus, if he relapses, you may be starting all over."

"What is the probability of a relapse for a thirty-year alcoholic?"

"I don't have a percentage, but the longer someone has been addicted to a substance, the greater the probability of relapse. We are creatures of habit. Without some kind of insurance, paying for services out-of-pocket could become insurmountable for him."

When Nick hung up, he was deeply discouraged and hoped this would not be the order of the day. He wondered if Ally negotiated a deal during her final interview with the McCann Erickson agency, if she officially accepted it, and if she found an apartment in New York.

He stopped by the art department before lunch to see if she was in yet. Her computer was still black so he looked for Michelle and

Lisa, Ally's art directors, and, more importantly, her closest friends. He found them in Lisa's cube reviewing layouts for a new client.

"Hi, guys."

"Hey, Nick," Michelle answered cheerfully as she turned to greet him. Lisa remained focused on her computer screen where she was manipulating a layout and enlarging a corporate logo.

"What's up, Nick?" she finally responded.

"I was wondering if you know when Ally is coming in today, or if she's been delayed in New York."

"She said she'll stop in sometime late today, but I'm not sure when," Michelle offered.

"Do you know if she successfully negotiated her final job offer?"

"She called in this morning," Lisa said, looking up from her monitor. "And they offered her what she wanted."

"So, she accepted the job?"

"No," she stalled. "You know how it is. You think you want something until it's actually offered to you, then you have second thoughts," Lisa explained.

"Ally wanted the weekend to think it over," Michelle added.

"Do you think she will accept it?" he asked, eager for their perspective.

Lisa was emphatic. "Who wouldn't accept a job offer with a big New York agency? Don't we all dream of ending up on Madison Avenue?"

"Did she find an apartment?"

"She didn't say but she did say they looked at some cute lofts," Michelle said.

"They?" Nick asked, turning to Michelle. He knew Ron was with her, but for some reason he reacted to it like he heard it for the first time.

"Yeah, Ron was with her. I guess he was going to help her find a loft or apartment," Michelle explained, before she excused herself to run upstairs with the client layouts.

Lisa turned toward Nick. "You're going to miss her, aren't you?"

"Yeah," he said, trying to mask the sudden despair and disillusionment that gripped him. "But at least I have two weeks to say good-bye after she gives notice."

"Well, not really. More like two days."

"What are you talking about?"

"Didn't she tell you? McCann Erickson needs her right away since they actually made her the formal offer more than two weeks ago. She stalled because she was helping you with your father. Sam is going to be upset, but they want her to start on Monday. She probably didn't get a chance to tell you."

"No, she didn't."

"She said something about you going through a tough time with your dad. Maybe she felt the timing wasn't right. All I know is McCann Erickson tied up the loose ends this week and suggested she look for an apartment. So, this is probably her last weekend in Chicago."

Nick stared at Lisa blankly, pondering what to say. "Would you do me a favor?"

"I'll try."

"I have to be out of town this weekend. Some important issues came up with my dad, so I may not catch her. Would you tell her I'm sorry I can't be here and say goodbye for me? I think she will understand."

"Sure, Nick."

"Oh, by the way, Lisa, I need the layouts for Phase Two of the Transitions campaign. Do you still have them?"

"No, I gave them to Ally for approval just before she left for New York. They should be on her desk or in her back credenza. Bottom left drawer."

"Thanks."

Nick opened the bottom left drawer of Ally's credenza and began to remove the layouts. After he had lifted several layouts out of the drawer, he noticed a handwritten letter tucked in the bottom of the drawer. The letter flapped open at the single fold when he removed the final layout. *Ally, my love,* it began.

He glanced around the room outside of Ally's cubicle then stood over the open drawer pretending to look at the layouts. *I'll read just a couple of sentences, maybe a paragraph, or two.* He held the layouts in his hand and figured he would drop them back in the drawer to cover the letter if someone approached. The letter rested at an angle, and he didn't want to touch it. *That would be going too far,* he rationalized. He cocked his head and began to read...

Ally, my love,

> *I write you tonight with a heavy heart; no, if I am completely honest, a suspicious heart.*
>
> *May I get right to the point? Something is wrong. I feel you slipping away. What troubles me most is, I'm not sure why. Do you feel it? You must feel it. I admit I have been a bit possessive of you. (Okay, more than a bit, but it is only because once a man finds what he really wants in life, he won't let anyone or anything keep him from it.) I know you feel like I'm smothering you. It's just that the more I feel you slipping away, the more I tighten my grip. I realize we agreed at the beginning of our relationship to move slow and keep it open-ended, but I can't help it that my feelings are running ahead of yours.*
>
> *You've been slow to answer my e-mails, and you seldom return my calls, especially on weekends. Where are you? I know you've been busy working overtime, but...*

Nick stopped reading and shifted his weight. He peeked around the corner of her cubicle and stood over the drawer again. He told himself he shouldn't keep reading but he had to know where

Ally stood with Ron, and more importantly, if he had any chance of winning her back. He read on:

> *Suffice it to say, I'm beginning to feel the distance…and the indifference. That's why I decided to send you a handwritten letter. I'm hoping you will feel compelled to answer it.*
>
> *Ally, ever since your car accident you seem… different, distracted, detached and confused. I've tried to explain it, rationalize it, and deny it. But I know it's real. And I think you do, too. What's wrong? What happened? Ever since that night at the hospital when you told me you love me things seemed to have changed. Even when we talk on the phone, I hear the hollowness. Why are you holding back? What are you holding back? Don't I deserve an answer?*
>
> *I've been trying to reach you to tell you I found a new apartment. I think you'll love it. I'll be moving in next month. It will be perfect for us if we… Sorry, there I go again, smothering you by making plans before you agree to them.*
>
> *I think you'll love working for McCann Erickson and living here in New York. There is so much to do and see. It's a marvelous place to be in love.*
>
> *This brings me to the other reason I wrote this letter. Even if our relationship is already in its "sunset," I want you to know it has been worth it to me. I want you to know I love you, Ally. I'm not trying to scare you or control you; I just want to be honest with you, completely honest. And that is all I ask in return.*
>
> *There, that's it. I've put everything on the table…as you always do. In my heart of hearts, I suspect I know what may be going on but I want to believe the best and extend you the courtesy to tell me…in your*

own words...in your own time. We have always been straight with each other so I won't speculate...I'll just wait. However long it takes.

All my love,
Ron

Nick covered the letter up with a few of the layouts he did not need and then gently closed the drawer. He pondered the words that suggested he might be able to rekindle a relationship with her.

As Nick logged off his computer and prepared to leave the office, he let the letter's words play over and over in his head, then he smiled to himself. *I still have a chance with her, a good chance.*

Nick left for Williams Bay early that Friday afternoon. He couldn't concentrate at work for obvious reasons, and he had to visit his father to resolve his insurance issues to ensure admission to Transitions.

It felt like a very long drive despite the beautiful weather. He drove with the windows down, letting the air stream through his hair. He lost himself in thought. *What should I do about Ally? This could be her last weekend in Chicago. If I am going to go after her I need to turn this car around now.* Funny how reality was never quite that simple. There always seemed to be a few minor and major complications. Nick's minor complication was being tied up this weekend solving this urgent insurance issue. His major complication was the X-Factor—Ron.

He let his mind sift through his options. As he pulled up in front of his father's house, he remembered something else Brett had said: "If you decide to pursue Ally, you must ask yourself, will she really be happier with you or Ron?"

Nick spent several hours with his father reviewing his finances, medical insurance issues and pension and considering long-shot options before returning to the lake house late Friday night. As he suspected, his father's insurance situation was bleak and his cash situation was worse. Essentially Chuck was just getting by; too many years of bad decisions, bad debts, bad liquor, and bad jobs—or no job. If he hadn't paid off his house years ago, he could be homeless by now. Nevertheless, Nick trusted Tom Sullivan and the Transitions team. If Nick could find a way to finance this treatment, his father could get his life back.

Nick arose late Saturday morning, showered, dressed and had his coffee and breakfast on the patio overlooking the lake. As he pondered what to do about his father's situation, the deep blue water of Geneva Lake quietly lapped gently against the pier, speedboats skipped along the water, and sailboats glided across the center of the lake beneath the graceful arcs of soaring seagulls. It was another gorgeous day, a great day to be in love—and a particularly terrible day to be alone.

Absorbed in his thoughts, Nick barely heard the voice come from behind him.

"Hey, stranger. I thought I'd find you here."

"Ally! What are you doing here?" he said, stunned to see her.

"A girl has to drive a long way to wish you happy birthday and to say good-bye. You're forty today, right?" she asked with the smile that always made her irresistible.

Her hair was pulled back, and she was wearing denim shorts and a sleeveless coral blouse that made her olive skin look rich and tan. As she stood before him, he was taken aback by her beauty. Nick realized he could be looking at her for the last time, so he committed every detail to memory: her dark, shiny hair, her sleek, well-proportioned figure, slim legs, high cheekbones, and those deep brown alluring eyes.

"Pull up a chair."

"I really can't stay."

"What do you mean you can't stay? You just got here!"

"I know. I was in the mood for a long drive. But I still have to pack, and you know how I hate long good-byes." He wasn't sure if a tear formed in her eye.

Nick rose from his chair to face her. He looked in her eyes and slowly approached her. She returned his gaze.

"I hear your dad may be admitted to Transitions soon," she said, as Nick stood alongside her. They both glanced out over the water.

"Yeah, he has some insurance problems and some serious financial issues so we've hit a snag. But I think I figured out a few options late last night."

"What are you going to do?"

"Well," he said, taking a deep breath. "I need to raise some money for him."

"Raise money? How are you going to do that?"

"I'll sell some stuff."

"Sell stuff? What will Nick Conway do without a BMW or a boat?" she teased, to ease the tension.

"I can live without a BMW and a boat."

"Really?"

"Yeah. But I'm not sure I can live without the lake house."

Ally frowned. "You're going to sell the lake house? Really?"

"Yeah. I can pay a few of his medical bills and solve some of his other financial issues."

She turned and stepped closer to him. "But you *love* this place!"

"I know but..."

"But?"

He looked at her. "But...someone special to me once said that he's my father, and I'm the only family he's got. And, that same someone also said, well, he's the only family I've got."

"You're being wonderful to him. Is there any other way?"

He shook his head. "Not that I can think of."

"I think Transitions could change his life—and yours."

"I think a lot of things are changing my life, Ally."

"Such as?" she asked, as he watched a sailboat glide past his pier.

"Well, I've been thinking through a lot of things. Brett has been telling me more about God and how I've been living my life. I think it's time to make some adjustments. Then, of course, there's...*you.*"

"Me? What do you mean?"

"Let's just say it's very difficult for me to say good-bye to you."

"And why is that?" she asked, challenging him to confront his feelings and reveal his heart.

They looked in each other's eyes, and he sensed that they longed for the same thing. He leaned into her and slid his arms slowly around her waist pausing to sense any resistance. Instead, she placed her hands on his arms lightly running them up to his shoulders and around his neck. She brought her hand to his cheek and gently caressed it with her fingers. He moved closer, pulling her in.

She closed her eyes, parted her lips, and he kissed her. Her lips were soft, moist and tender, and he kissed her again and then again. He felt his passion rise, compensating for all the lost time, for all the stupid mistakes. She kissed his neck and pulled him closer. She rested her head on his shoulder and for a fleeting moment his life was playing out just the way he would script it. He wondered what she was thinking. What she was feeling. He attempted to kiss her again. She hesitated and then gave in to her longing. She kissed him passionately, then just as quickly she gently held him at bay.

Tears welled in her eyes. "I can't do this, Nick."

"Can't do what?"

"I can't love you again. I won't let myself."

"Why not?" he asked, knowing the answer but needing to hear it from her.

"Because of the past—and present."

"What's all of this talk about forgiveness then? I thought you forgave me for the past?"

"I did forgive you, years ago. It's not about forgiveness anymore."

"What's it about?"

"Trust. I could love you again—but I'm not sure I could trust you again."

"You can trust me! I'm changing, or trying to. Can you *see* that?"

"I can see that—but I've been betrayed. Can you *feel* that?" She paused and turned to him. "Everything was just fine, and then you had to ruin it by coming back into my life." Her voice cracked and her words numbed him.

Ally faced the house. Nick faced the lake. They stood nearly shoulder to shoulder, staring in opposite directions. It was a picture of their life directions. He didn't know how to respond to her. He heard the gulls cry overhead. They waited in silence to see who would speak first. He counted the waves as they lapped against the pier giving her time to speak. She remained quiet. Finally, he broke the silence.

"You've got a great opportunity in New York, Ally. Good luck."

He looked out over the water. She paused, and then slowly walked away. He heard her car door click open, then close. The engine turned over. He waited to hear the car click into gear. Instead, it idled. He felt her watching him and wondered if she was waiting for him to turn and come to her. He stood still, his hands buried in his pockets. He watched the sailboats glide across the lake. He hoped she would get out of the car. No, he ached for her to get out of the car—and come to him. His pride swelled.

Go to her. Am I making the biggest mistake of my life by just standing here? At least turn, face her, wave good-bye! Do something! You can win her back from Ron, you know. She wouldn't be here if she didn't have second thoughts about him and New York. You read the letter! Now is your opportunity to take her back. This is your second chance, stupid! Take her from him! Go after her you fool! Even if she rejects you, you will never regret the fact that you went after her. Now go! Before she drives away!

He was conflicted. The car continued to idle. The moment lingered. *What is she waiting for?* he wondered. *Will she really give me another chance? If so, who should make the first move?* He waited. She waited. Suddenly, he couldn't move. He was frozen by a simple truth that would have never stopped him before: Ron loves her. He's good to her. He's faithful to her. He deserves her. And she deserves him.

It was all so clear in Ron's letter, Nick thought, as it raced through his mind: *"Ally, I suspect I know what may be going on but I want to believe the best and extend you the courtesy to tell me...in your own words...in your own time. We have always been straight with each other so I won't speculate...I'll just wait. However long it takes."*

She deserves a man like that, he thought. *And besides, whether she knows it or not, she loves Ron, and she has a great opportunity in New York. Why should I interfere? Haven't I done enough to confuse her? To distract her? To hurt her? And what about trust? She said it herself, how long will it take—if ever—for her fully to trust me again?*

Suddenly, her car clicked into gear. His heart raced. His pulse pounded. And his logic melted. All he felt now was how much he wanted her, how much he needed her, how much he loved her. But if he wanted her, he must go *get* her, now! He felt his heart lunge toward her car, yet his feet remained firmly planted. He still had not even turned to face her. She watched him from the car and his gaze was still locked on the horizon. *She must think I don't care. She will never know the truth. The truth that I not only love her enough to go after her, I love her enough to let her go.*

He heard the gravel crack under her tires as she slowly pulled off of the shoulder. In quiet desperation his inner voice screamed: "Run after her!" He remained frozen.

He wouldn't allow himself to interrupt her life again. He knew he was a major distraction to her, a complication. He could deny it no more. He was her past. Ron was her future. Ron was right for her. New York was right for her. And Nick had no right to alter her life again. He heard the engine gently rev, and she drove out of his life.

Nick never did look back. Instead, he continued to watch the waves gently roll against the shore, and only then was he sure that he was, indeed, a changed man. How that would play out, day by day, he wasn't sure. But he had done right by Ally in freeing her, and now would do right by helping his dad. At last, life was now more than just a focus on himself. And it felt good.

CHAPTER

Driving east on Highway 50 toward Interstate 94 for Chicago, Ally realized she'd never been this confused before. She felt like she'd lost her sense of direction. She knew she was headed east on Highway 50, but where was her life headed? *Am I really going to New York? Do I want the McCann-Erickson job? And where is my relationship with Ron going? Do I love him? Am I being honest with myself?*

Realizing she'd some unfinished business to tend to, she turned left at the stop light in downtown Lake Geneva and left again until she had turned completely around and headed west on Highway 50 toward Williams Bay where she pulled over in front of Chuck Conway's home. Standing at his front door, she paused before ringing the bell. Was this another misguided decision or impractical impulse she would soon regret? She rang the bell and waited. No answer. She pushed it again, waited, then walked around back where Chuck was tilling the soil.

Gus stood nearby, leaning on his shovel. He turned to Ally. "Say, Chuck, looks like we've got a visitor." Gus pointed toward Ally as she stepped around the lilac bush at the edge of the house.

Chuck turned to greet her. "Hey." He smiled, clearly happy to see her again.

"Hey, yourself."

"What brings you to Williams Bay? Chuck asked.

"Well, I was looking for two handsome men to help me with some landscaping," she teased.

Chuck went along with it. "If you're looking to do some landscaping in Williams Bay, I'd say that's a good sign."

"Actually, I need landscaping in New York."

"Landscaping in the Big Apple? Didn't think there was enough green space left between skyscrapers." Gus grinned.

"Honestly, I don't need landscaping," Ally said, "but I am moving to New York. That's why I'm here." She turned toward Chuck. "Just wanted to say goodbye to you and Gus. I've enjoyed my weekends here with you this summer."

Chuck took a rag from his pocket and wiped sweat from his brow. "You really going to New York, honey?"

"Yeah, I'm really going."

Gus looked at her, then at Chuck. She wondered if they could detect her doubt.

"I take it you talked to Nick already," Chuck said.

"Yeah, just left there."

He shrugged. "Hmm, not much of a gift for Nick's fortieth birthday."

"Their relationship is none of our business," Gus said.

"Not trying to interfere. I just hope Nick had something to say about this," Chuck said.

She cleared her throat. "Actually, Nick had *nothing* to say about it."

Chuck took a step back. "You didn't tell Nick about this?"

"I just came from there. I told him I was moving to New York, and, well, he had *nothing* to say. It's no problem. I know he wants me to be happy—and Ron and I *are* happy."

Chuck looked at Gus, then back to Ally. "Well then, whatever makes you happy." His tone was mixed. Ally wasn't sure of his meaning.

"I'm going to have something to drink."

Ally raised her brows.

"Don't worry. I'm just getting water, Ally," he clarified. "Can I get you a bottled water?"

"Sure."

"Something for you, Gus?"

"Nope."

Once Chuck was inside the house, Ally turned away from Gus to collect her thoughts.

"Like I said, it's not any of our business, honey, but I think you're reading a few signals wrong."

"What do you mean?"

"I don't know what's going on between you and Nick. I'm just sayin' that things aren't always what they seem. Men don't always say what they mean or even know how to. I hate to turn against my own kind, but men are sometimes just socially stupid."

Ally cracked a smile and nodded. "I can see that. But don't you mean socially-challenged?"

"No, stupid covers it. The way I see it, the average man just doesn't know how to tell a woman he loves her. We're better off showing 'em, but we can ball that all up, too. I think that's why God made flowers. I expect a dozen roses saved many a marriage."

Ally felt herself relax. She loved Gus's simple country wit and wisdom. Chuck returned and handed Ally a bottle of water. She cracked it open and took a sip.

"Chuck, I stopped by to say goodbye. I'll be leaving for New York Monday. I'd be lying if I didn't admit I've grown fond of you guys this summer."

"You absolutely certain you belong in New York? Chuck asked, probably hoping to change her mind. She could hear compassion in his voice and noticed how much he had softened since she first met him.

"I'm sure," she said.

Chuck took a gulp of his water and looked away. "Well then, you got to do what you got to do. Just don't ever let mistakes I made with Nick affect your relationship with him. I've done enough to ruin his life already."

"On the contrary, in some ways, your life brought us back together. You haven't hurt us, you've helped us connect again. It's just that, well, it's complicated. And then, there's..."

"And then, there's Ron," Chuck said, completing her sentence.

"Yeah, there's that."

Gus smiled. "Funny how everybody's in love with the wrong person. At least, at the wrong time."

"Yes, at least at the wrong time," Ally echoed.

She took another sip. "Well, look, I really have to go. I'm going to stop for a bite at the Oak Fire Grill in Lake Geneva before I drive back to Chicago. There is something else, Chuck. I just want you to know your son is a good man. You should be proud of him. He really cares about you."

Chuck appeared gratified by her sentiments. "Thanks for coming all this way to say that. I appreciate it. I really do. I just had hoped things would be different, that's all."

"It is what it is." She hugged Chuck, then Gus.

"See you down the road, Ally?" Gus asked, breaking the mounting tension.

"See you down the road," she repeated.

Without another word, Chuck turned and began to till the soil.

CHAPTER

Nick was still sitting out on the patio, wondering if he would ever see Ally again or if he just made the second biggest mistake of his life when his cell phone rang.

"Hello."

"Do you love Ally?"

"What?"

"Do you love Ally?"

"Dad?"

"What?"

"What's going on? Why are you asking me this?"

"It's a simple question. Do you love Ally?"

"That's personal."

"Answer the question."

"I don't know? I guess." Nick wondered why he was having this conversation with his father.

"If you love Ally, you have one chance to prevent her from going to New York. That chance is now."

"Where is this coming from?"

"It's coming from me."

"I know that, but why are you suddenly interested in—"

"I just talked to Ally."

"Why were you talking to Ally?"

"I can talk to Ally whenever I want."

"Yes, you can, but why were you talking to her *now*?"

"She came to say goodbye to me after she said goodbye to you. She thinks you don't love her, so she's going to New York with Ray."

"It's Ron."

"Ray, Ron, whatever. The point is, she's going to New York to be with a man she doesn't love."

"Dad, why are you telling me this?"

"I'm telling you this because I don't want you to make a life-changing mistake. We've made enough of those."

"What are you trying to say?"

"I'm trying to say Ally loves you, and if you love her, you will go after her now—right now."

"Dad, look, I appreciate what you're trying to do but . . . it's complicated."

"It's always complicated."

"She's in love with Ron."

"She's confused about Ron, but she's in love with you."

"What makes you think so?"

"I'm your father." For the first time, these words warmed Nick's heart and he realized he was having a significant, penetrating conversation with his father.

"I've been wrong about a lot of things in my life, but even old Gus here agrees with me."

"Dad, I think it's wise if I leave things be. Besides, she's chosen Ron. He's best for her."

"Okay, it's your decision, but if you want a second chance with her, she just left here for the Oak Fire Grill. She's going to grab a bite to eat, then head to Chicago." Chuck seemed to be waiting for Nick to respond. A long silence followed.

"Son?"

"What?"

"She didn't choose Ron. You chose Ron for her. Why not let her choose for herself?"

"What do I tell her?" Nick realized he was being vulnerable for the first time by confiding in his father.

"You're asking me? Gus says to tell her how you feel—stuff like that—but be honest with her."

"You're right, Dad." His heart was contrite. "She deserves that."

"Son?"

"Yeah?"

"You have one shot at this."

"I know."

"Don't mess it up."

CHAPTER

Nick jumped into his BMW and took off for the Oak Fire Grill. It occurred to him to call Ally first to make sure she was still there, but something inside him felt it was better to let things play out naturally. He didn't know what he would say. He would act on impulse and see if it would fly.

When he arrived at the grill, he got lucky and found a place to park on Wrigley Drive in front of the restaurant. He rushed into the restaurant and surveyed the first floor. No Ally. He hustled up the stairs to check out the second floor in the open-air section overlooking the lake. A woman was sitting across the room. Her beautiful silky black hair cascaded over her narrow shoulders. Ally. His heart skipped a beat. She faced the lake with her back to him. The view was spectacular—a cloudless sky, a balmy breeze, and placid water. A serene setting to say what he hoped he had the nerve to say.

As he approached her, he felt as though everything began

to slow down. With each step, he had the same thought. *What can I possibly say to her to reverse her current course—and should I say it?* He stopped beside her.

"Hey, there. Would you like some company?"

Ally pulled back. Her eyes widened and a hint of a smile slowly spread across her face. What are you doing here? I thought you were going to talk to your Dad about his insurance problems."

"Let's just say I talked to my dad but not about his insurance problems. Actually, he talked to me about my problems."

"*Your* problems?"

"Well, *our* problems."

"Now they're *our* problems?"

"Look, Ally, I know we're both a little confused right now. You and this Ron thing, and me and my dad. Can we talk it out?"

"*Now* you want to talk it out? I'm not sure I have much left to say."

"I know, but I do. I have never been one to put myself out there."

"Ya think?" Ally looked out over the lake. Nick wondered if he was too late. Was she already gone? Had she already made up her mind to move on without him? Perhaps he wasn't worth the trouble. If the outcome was already determined he wondered if he should still bare his soul now. It wasn't like him to take risks when the odds weren't in his favor. He swallowed hard and pressed on.

"Just hear me out." He pulled up a chair and sat across from her. "I've made a lot of mistakes in my life. Many of them with you. And for that, I'm sorry. Don't think I don't live with regret every day for my missteps with you—particularly my unfaithfulness. Going forward—"

"Going forward, I'm going to be in New York and—"

"Let me finish. Going forward, I want to rekindle our relationship, unless you're absolutely sure you're in love with Ron."

"I love Ron."

"I don't think you do."

"That's arrogant." Ally shifted her weight in the chair. "What makes you so sure?"

"For one thing, the way you look at me."

Ally folded her arms. "Really? How's that?"

"With a certain tenderness. An undeserved tenderness. You look at me like a person who sees my potential. Like someone who still, somehow, believes in me, and sees the best in me. And I love the way you talk to me."

"Yes, but that's because—"

Nick leaned toward her. "I love the way you encourage me. The way you put me in my place when I have it coming. The way you care about my father and my relationship with him. And, the way you drove ninety miles today to say goodbye to me."

She looked away. "I came to say goodbye to your father and Gus."

"Nice try."

"Well, it is your fortieth birthday."

"Again, nice try. Look, I'm not really here to ask you if you love Ron. You've got to figure that out. I'm here to tell you what I've figured out."

"And what's that? Is this where you tell me I'm making a mistake going to New York and I should stay in Chicago and work for you?"

"No, I'm here to tell you . . ." He paused. He knew he was going to have to put himself out there but he underestimated the cost, the fear, and the risk. The moment was here. "Ally, I'm here to tell you I'm in love with you. Flat out. One-hundred percent. No question. No strings. I'm all in." He looked around the room and noticed other patrons looking at him. He wondered if they heard everything, but he didn't care.

She covered her mouth and leaned back. Nick noticed tears welling in her eyes and he wondered if she was totally unprepared for his honesty. In the past, his candor was carefully choreographed, risk minimized, and a backup plan in place. Not this time. If Ally didn't respond in kind, he was hanging out there flapping in the wind. Alone. Naked. He knew it. She probably did, too. Yet, he was strangely comfortable with it, knowing he had finally shared the truth. He could no longer shrink from it.

Nick felt his passion rise. For once, at least, he was authentic— holding nothing in reserve. He let her off the hook. "You don't have to respond. You just have to know I admit I've made a lot of mistakes, I'm sorry for them, I've paid for them in more ways than you know, and regardless of how you feel about me, I'm in love with you. Period."

The tears that had welled in her eyes escaped now and slide down her cheeks. She quickly wiped them away. Nick continued. He couldn't stop himself, he was on a roll. "I was hoping we could start over. I know it's complicated and you've got some loose ends to tie up, but I'm willing to wait for you to figure it out. In the meantime, if you elect to stay in Chicago, I will clear it with Sam and get your job back. I'll arrange it so you can change accounts so you don't have to work for me. You don't have to say anything now."

"I know, but I *have* something to say now."

He wasn't expecting a response. His heart raced. He took a deep breath.

"I have to sort out how I feel about Ron. And what to do about it. He wasn't the complication in my life—you were. You've been honest with me, so I'll be honest with you."

He gently exhaled. "Go on."

Ally reached across the table and briefly touched his hand. "I think I can love you again. In fact, I think I do love you again, but..." She reached in her purse for a tissue.

Nick helped her along. "But..."

"But as I've said before, I'm not sure I can trust you again." She wiped tears of past pain from her eyes. "We've been here before, Nick. Funny thing about building trust is, it takes time."

"How much time do you need?"

"How much time have you got?"

"However long you need."

"Trust must be earned. It's observable. I believe you've changed—or are changing. And I like what I see. But you have a pattern, and patterns die hard. I need to observe your change over time before I can trust you fully."

He nodded. "Fair enough. I have to earn your trust. I get it."

"Trust is fragile. It's shattered by one event. It's like a jigsaw puzzle."

"How's that?"

Ally looked into his eyes. "It takes forever to put the pieces together and seconds to tear them apart."

"I want to put the pieces back together again, if you'll give me the chance."

"The pieces don't go together any easier or any faster the second time around."

"I know. That's on me. Just give me a shot."

"I leave for New York Monday morning. Perhaps a change of scenery will add clarity and help me figure it out. Let's talk late next week."

"Can I call you?"

"No. I'll call you—when I'm ready."

When Nick left the restaurant, he felt both hope and fear. He hoped by the end of next week she would actually call him. And he feared she wouldn't.

CHAPTER

The next week in the office felt surreal. Ally was gone and there was no telling for how long. Nick was feeling the dry, empty uncertainty of it all. An earlier call from Tom Sullivan helped. Tom had followed up with Nick concerning his father's ability to pay for addiction recovery services and had recommended an extended billing plan that would alleviate some of the immediate financial pressure now that Chuck had agreed to seek treatment in the coming weeks. Chuck wasn't out of the woods yet, but Nick believed a viable financial plan was coming together.

Nick set up a meeting with Brett and Sam Morris in a conference room to discuss a few remaining details to execute the creative work with the Transitions account. At the conclusion of the meeting, he took advantage of an opportunity to pitch the idea that Sam would hire Ally back—if she elected to return. His strategy was to broach the subject with humor since the notion of Ally leaving McCann-Erickson was absurd.

Nick leaned back in his swivel chair. "Sam, have you thought about who you might hire to replace Ally as our art director?"

"Why, you got someone in mind?"

"Actually, I do."

"Really? Who?"

"Well, I was thinking Ally Grant would be a perfect replacement for Ally Grant."

Sam gathered his meeting notes. "What are you saying? You think things won't work out for her at McCann-Erickson?"

"I just think she might realize she would be happier in Chicago than New York." Nick looked at Brett and wondered when he would jump in to give him a hand.

Sam stood to face Nick. "What makes you think so? Isn't her boyfriend there? Didn't he set up her interview?"

"He is, and he did. But she is more of a Midwest girl, not East coast. I'm just saying, sometimes things change and I wondered if you're open to hiring her back if it happens?"

"It's not my custom to give employees their jobs back once they leave. It's bad policy. Once employees are unhappy, there's really no turning back. And if an employee returns, it's typically short-lived. I would need a compelling reason to bring her back. I don't believe in rewarding disloyalty. You follow?"

Nick was surprised Sam took such a hard line when it came to Ally. It made sense with other employees, but Ally? He looked at Brett as if to say, throw me a lifeline here.

Brett returned Nick's gaze and turned toward Sam. "If she can crank out work, what better reason is there to hire her back? And Ally cranks out great work, Sam. She does it on time, on budget, and on strategy. She's arguably your best art director."

"She *was* my best art director." Sam was resolute and paced the room.

"If Ally were to return, why hold it against her? She's simply checking out another agency. I've done it. You've done it. We've all done it. How many agencies did you work for before you started your own?"

"You make a fair point. But I still have my policies and I believe in them. I got this far by trusting my gut. I'll entertain it, but I'll make no promises. Besides, it's a moot point if she loves New York."

Sam changed the subject and walked to the conference room door. "Let's talk about those creative briefs for Kraft by the end of the week and update me on the Transitions account."

When Sam left the room, Brett glanced at Nick. "What's going on? This is Ally's first day on the job at McCann-Erickson and you're trying to get her job back? What gives? Every art director worth his or her salt strives to work in New York."

Nick rocked in his chair. "If she comes back, and I'm not saying she will, she'll come back as a favor to me, not for the job."

"What brought this on?"

"We had a heart to heart and I asked her to consider coming back."

Brett smirked. "You're in love with her again and you're finally getting back together."

"I think so."

"Don't give me that. You know so. Karen and I have seen this coming for months."

"It's not a sure thing, Brett."

"Did you tell Ally you love her?"

"Yeah, that's why she might consider coming back. She needs time to sort out how she feels about me—and Ron."

"Then one of you gets good news and the other . . ." Brett didn't finish his sentence. "So when will you hear from her again?"

"She said she may contact me by the end of the week. The good news is, she said she thinks she's fallen in love with me again."

"And the bad news?"

"What makes you think there's bad news?"

"There's always bad news."

"Then I guess the bad news is, she needs time to sort out how she feels about Ron. I have to wait for her to call me."

"Makes sense."

Brett picked up his creative brief and his notes and approached the door. "Ally wants to be fair with Ron. In the end, when she decides, you can take it to the bank. You know her. When she makes up her mind, she's committed. You have to wait to see who she believes she can be fully committed to for the long haul. Got to give her credit for that. Look, I got to get back. I've got another meeting."

Brett's words were filled with the wisdom of a happily married man and a man of faith. Those were two areas in which Nick deeply desired to emulate him. Yet, as affirming as his words were, there was something disturbing. He had just introduced an element of doubt. While Ally may love him, she was principled enough to do the right thing after thoughtful reflection. Getting Ally back might be likely, but it was not a slam dunk.

CHAPTER 28

By midweek, Ally had met her creative team, got herself reasonably oriented, and had been assigned three marquee accounts. These are the type of accounts she dreamed of working on as a college student.

She gazed out the window from the high-rise office and realized she'd made it. She was an art director in New York, on major brands—household names. She was living her dream. She knew it, and she loved it. Yet, the dry emptiness in her gut confirmed she loved something more in Chicago. A tall, dark, and good-looking guy who was a work in progress—a carefree guy who once made her feel alive and that anything was possible. A guy who was spontaneous, impulsive, fun, and predictably unpredictable. And, yes, a guy who once shattered her trust, but whose heart was changing now. Most importantly, a guy who just professed his love for her. Ally could think of nothing else all week except Nick and what she had to do now.

An old mentor had once told her she should swallow a frog first thing every morning. It was an odd but practical metaphor. "If you swallow the frog first thing in the morning," her mentor said, "everything else you do that day will be easy by comparison."

Ally liked the metaphor. She had a frog to swallow today. Unfortunately, she couldn't swallow it until the end of the day. The good news? This gave her all day to think about it. The bad news? This gave her all day to think about it.

She called Ron and told him where she would like to meet for coffee at six o'clock. She spent the better part of the day rehearsing in her mind what she would say. In the end, she scrapped it and decided to just speak from the heart. She would have to live with what came out of her mouth either way, so what good would rehearsing do. Besides, she didn't want to come across as sounding scripted. Ron deserved better.

Ally arrived fifteen minutes early, ordered herself coffee, and selected a table in the corner to give them some privacy. The table was directly in the line of sight from the front door so Ron could easily spot her when he entered.

He arrived at six o'clock sharp. He always seemed to be mindful of her time. It was one more way he silently demonstrated respect for her.

"Hey," she said as he approached the table.

"Hey." He looked at the coffee she cupped in both hands. "You been here long?"

"Fifteen minutes, maybe. I wanted to get us a private table." She realized how telling the statement sounded. After all, why would they need a private table if she had good news to discuss?

"I'll grab a cup and be right back." He put his backpack on the chair across from her.

Ron returned with his coffee and pulled up a chair. If he was suspicious, he didn't show it. "Well, you're three days into your new job. How do you like it so far? Bet you love it."

"Actually, I do love it. I like my team and my boss is cool. And they gave me some dream accounts."

"Perfect. What's not to like?"

Ally didn't know how to respond and redirect the conversation to what was on her heart, so she found herself repeating his question. "What's not to like?"

"Exactly."

"It's not Chicago," she said.

He took a sip. "Why would you want to be in Chicago? Your job is here. Your apartment is here. Your future is here. And the guy you love is here."

His word choice made it almost impossible for her to steer the dialogue. She had no choice but to abruptly force the conversation.

"Ron, I'm thinking about going back to Chicago."

"What?"

"I'm thinking about going back to Chicago."

"You're thinking—"

She raised her hand. "No. I'm not *thinking*. I'm *going* back to Chicago."

"You're kidding me! Why would you go back there? You just got here?"

"I know—"

He raised his voice. "You don't have a job in Chicago. You don't have an apartment in Chicago. You don't even have family in Chicago."

"I know, but—"

"Ally, are you telling me you're willing to give up all you have here for all you're unsure of there?"

"Yes." The clarity and conviction of her answer shook him.

"Why?"

"Because I am absolutely sure of one thing there."

"What's that?"

Ally knew there was no turning back now. "I'm in love with Nick."

Ron fell back in his chair. Ally stared into her coffee and paused so the full impact of her confession could crash land.

"How did this happen? At what point in our relationship did you start loving Nick again?"

"That's just it. I don't think I started loving him again. I think I never stopped loving him—flaws and all."

"Maybe I never really knew you then."

"What's that supposed to mean?"

"How can you give up on a guy who's been so good to you to love another guy who betrayed you? That's just stupid."

Ally felt a tear form in her eye. She looked away, then into Ron's eyes. "You're right. Love does stupid things sometimes. I can't deny it's stupid but I also can't deny I love him."

Ron pressed her. "It's bad enough to go back to no job and no place to live. But how can you go back to someone you can't trust?"

"I'm working on that—and he's working on that."

Ron rolled his eyes. "How long have you been working on it?"

"I don't know. Since my hospital stay after the accident, I guess."

Ron shook his head. "I knew it. I always knew it. He spent way too much time with you—with us—in the hospital. I should have done something about him then, but I wanted you to choose. And I believed you would choose me."

She heard his tone abruptly shift from anger to anxiety. "What did I do wrong?"

"You didn't do anything wrong. This isn't your fault. If there's any fault, it's my fault. I never meant to lead you on. I've been confused. You're a great guy."

"A great guy? Just not for you, right?"

"Just not for me."

"What do you love so much about this guy that you're willing to risk being betrayed again?"

"I loved him once for who he was. Now I love him for what he's becoming. I like the way he treats me. The way he treats his father. His evolving perspective. He's changing, Ron."

"Famous last words."

She cleared her throat. "Look, there is no need to prolong this. I know we both feel bad enough."

"Trust me, you don't feel as bad as I do. When are you leaving?"

"I'm going to resign tomorrow and fly back to Chicago on Friday afternoon. It's best that way. I never intended to hurt you. I don't know what more I can say. There's another woman out there who's perfect for you."

"There's always the perfect woman out there for the jilted guy. I'm not interested in a consolation prize, Ally. It rarely brings any consolation."

"I'm sorry it ended this way."

"Not nearly as sorry as I am. Well, you've clearly made up your mind. Sounds like I'm wasting my time trying to convince you otherwise." He stood and she followed his lead. He moved in to kiss her goodbye, but she lowered her head. He kissed her forehead, grabbed his backpack. "Look, I really hope things work out for you—and history doesn't repeat itself. Either way, have a nice life, Ally."

When he walked away, she reminded herself that conversations like this never end well. She decided to skip dinner. She wasn't hungry. She had just swallowed the frog.

CHAPTER 29

Ally woke up Thursday morning with an ache in her stomach. It came courtesy of having another frog to swallow. This conversation would not be as difficult as the one last night, since she would be swallowing this frog first thing in the morning.

She scheduled a meeting with Angie, her boss, for 9:00 a.m. and she stated her purpose for the meeting straight up. Angie wasn't happy, so Ally decided to just roll with the punches because it all would be over soon.

"Why did you waste my time with the extended interview process if you had no intention of relocating to New York?" she asked. "Do you know how much it costs recruiting top talent, flying you out here, putting you up, and interviewing other qualified candidates?"

After the initial disappointment, the conversation became academic since they'd only invested minimal time in developing their working relationship. Angie was anything but sympathetic about Ally's reasons for returning to Chicago.

"I suggest you leave today," she snapped. "Two weeks' notice is overkill at this point. We need to reach out to the alternate candidates as soon as possible while they're still available. No point in having a lame duck art director offering her two-cents beyond a three-day career. Please inform your staff and clean out your office by ten o'clock."

After Ally notified her staff, she returned to her apartment to pack and schedule a flight to Chicago on Friday. In the meantime, she would visit a few New York landmarks and some of her favorite restaurants near Times Square. After considerable thought, she decided she would just show up at Nick's office late Friday afternoon rather than call him prior to her return.

Nick felt like he was working at half capacity despite the long hours he was putting in. Too many things were running through his mind at once. Now that his father had agreed to be admitted to Transitions Addiction Recovery Center, would the two of them be able to handle the medical expenses and insurance issues? Would Nick still have to consider selling the lake house to cover these expenses? Would the Transitions program resolve his father's alcohol issues and make a meaningful difference in the quality of his life? Would Ally call him Friday and give him a second chance to work on their relationship or will she walk away and start a new life with Ron? If she happened to return to Chicago, would Sam allow her to return to her job?

He tried to stay focused so he concentrated on the creative brief of a new client John just landed. His phone rang as he read through the conference notes of the last client meeting.

"Hey, Nick, Tom Sullivan. Got a minute? I've got some good news regarding your father's admission to Transitions."

"What gives?"

"I just received an anonymous gift for his account, assuming he actually follows through with his rehab treatment plan."

"An anonymous gift from who?"

Tom laughed. "I can't tell you that. That's why it's called an anonymous gift."

Nick laughed at the absurdity of his question. "Yeah, right. I'm just shocked and I suppose you can't tell me how much the gift is for?"

"I can say this; the amount of the gift will likely get your father through the entire rehab program with no insurance, provided he has no major relapses."

"Isn't it likely that a career alcoholic will have a relapse?"

"Certainly possible. I suppose it depends on the level of emotional support he receives. Either way, there is enough here to get him started. Suffice it to say that finances are no longer a roadblock."

"I don't know what to say? And I certainly don't know who to thank."

"Sounds like a time to simply be thankful then, doesn't it?"

Nick exhaled slowly. "Yes, it does. Thanks for the call. You just lifted one of many burdens off my back today. Thanks."

Nick didn't sleep well Thursday night. He woke Friday morning dragging, still anxious about Ally. He had hoped she would have called before today. A text, email, or call would do—anything to ease his anxiety.

She asked me not to call her. She will call me when she's ready. He hated not being in control. Control made him comfortable. It was one more thing he needed to yield if their relationship was to flourish. *I need to take Tom's advice. I need to be thankful. After all, my dad has agreed to pursue treatment, the finances have been worked out, at least temporarily, and I can keep the lake house. Stay positive.*

It was a typical Friday at the office. Less stress than usual. He didn't have any new accounts to ramp up for, and all of the existing creative work for current clients was on schedule, so Nick could cruise a bit.

By quitting time, Nick had still not heard from Ally. Had she settled into her new job, her new apartment, and worse, a renewed relationship with Ron? He'd been working on his email inbox, trying to clear it out before the weekend. He scanned his inbox again, but Ally still hadn't sent him a message. He checked his phone again in case he missed something. He didn't have any missed calls or texts.

When he returned to his inbox, he noticed an email from Sam Morris. It was strangely vague. Sam asked Nick to "pop in my office for a few minutes at the end of the day." No subject. Nick wondered what was up. Sam was usually more direct. As he stared at Sam's email for a clue, he heard a familiar voice.

"Hey, stranger."

He looked up. Ally stood in the doorway. "Hey, what are you doing here?"

"Do you want me to go back to New York?"

"No, no, I was just expecting a call or text or..."

"I thought I'd surprise you."

"Well, I'm surprised."

"How was your week?" she asked.

"Well, I got some good news. Tom Sullivan called. An anonymous donor came forward to help with my dad's medical expenses. Should be enough to cover the costs at Transitions."

Ally smiled. "That's wonderful. So, you won't have to sell the lake house?"

Nick felt the warmth of her smile and sensed her joy for him and his father. It made him love her more. "Looks like I can keep it."

"Good," Ally said, "because I think I'd like to spend some more time with you there."

"Really? How about this weekend? When do you have to be back in New York?"

"I'm not going back to New York."

Nick got up and moved closer to her. "Why aren't you going back?" He knew he was putting her on the spot but he also knew they needed to define their relationship if it was to move forward.

She threw it right back to him. "Why do you think?"

He wouldn't be denied. "You tell me."

"My turn to be vulnerable?"

"Your turn to be honest."

"Fair enough. It's been a tough week. All I could think about was you."

"Same here. Go on."

She plopped down in one of the guest chairs in his office.

Nick closed his office door and sat across from her.

"I told you last week I wasn't sure I could trust you again and it would take time. Nothing's changed about that. You will have to earn my trust again."

"I understand."

"But I realized the only way you can earn my trust is if we're together. It won't work as a long-distance relationship. I need to observe your heart change, and I'd like to play a role in that change. I don't know if our relationship will work, but I do know I love you. And, at the end of the day, I'm willing to risk potentially being hurt again to discover, once and for all, if we are meant for each other."

"I won't disappoint you."

"In my heart of hearts, I believe our relationship will work and I'm willing to try. A lot depends on you. If we're going to make it, we must not only go slow, but we must go forward. Because for some crazy reason, I really love you."

Nick reached across the table and took her hand. "And I really love you. Ally, let's just agree to go forward and see where this takes us. And, yes, we'll go slow."

Ally nodded, then changed the subject. "So, how was the rest of your week?"

"This might be the best week of my life."

There was a knock on the door and Brett came in. "Hey, Ally, what are you doing here?"

"Long story, but I'm moving back to Chicago. Nick and I are going to give it another shot to see where this thing goes—one day at a time. We don't want people making a big deal about it."

"I got it. Congrats, you guys."

Nick told Brett the good news about the anonymous donor. "You know, it's actually been a great week. I think we should celebrate at the lake house with a cookout tomorrow night. Brett, are you and Karen available?"

"Let me check. She handles the social calendar."

"I'll invite my dad and Gus, too, so that'll make six of us. Once we're all together, I'll share the good news about the anonymous gift and about Ally and me."

"Nice," Brett said.

As Brett turned to leave Nick's office, Sam stopped in.

"Ally? Well, are you back—or just passing through?" Sam asked before anyone could greet him.

"Here to stay, Sam," Ally said.

"Really, what brings you back? Nick said you might return to Chicago."

Nick and Ally looked at each other to see who should field Sam's question. Before Nick could reply, Ally answered.

"Actually, Nick brings me back. I'll spare you the details but we have a relationship we've decided to pursue."

Nick attempted to change the subject by asking an unrelated question. "Sam, got your email. I was just about to pop in your office. What can I do for you?"

"Well, it just so happens that I wanted to talk to you about this very subject. Image that. Since you are all affected by this, I might as well discuss it with all of you."

Brett looked at Nick. "If this doesn't concern me, I'll excuse myself."

"Sit still, Brett. This won't take but a minute." Sam eased his way into Nick's desk chair and put his feet on his desk. "I've given some thought to your request earlier this week, Nick. About Ally's employment. Or should I say unemployment? Anyway, let me get right to the point. Ally, I've never been big on rehiring employees once they leave my employment. The reason for leaving doesn't matter. Your past performance, while stellar, doesn't matter. What matters is loyalty. Make sense? You see, I have a fundamental problem with betrayal."

Ally walked toward him. "I didn't ask for my job back."

"You didn't have to. Your boyfriend already did. You've only been back, what, an hour? By Monday morning, you would make your plea, or Nick would ask me for a favor again. I thought I would nip this in the bud. It's against my policy to rehire people, no matter how talented they are. I think I pay my people well. When they leave, I feel betrayed. Once betrayed, always betrayed. People don't really change. And I'm not one to take chances again once I've been burned. Nothing personal. But it's a good policy, don't you think?"

Nick was furious. "Sam, this isn't Ally's fault. If I would have had my act together, she would've never entertained the opportunity in New York. Don't take this out on her. It's my fault."

Sam stood and paced the room before turning to Nick. "You're right, Nick. It's your fault. But it doesn't really matter whose fault it is. It ends here. Any questions?"

Brett, Ally, and Nick looked at each other as Sam walked to the door.

Before he exited, he turned toward Nick. "Think of it this way. It's for the best. After all, office romances rarely work out."

When Sam left the room, silence followed. Ally gazed out the window. Nick packed his backpack. And Brett slid into one of the three guest chairs.

"There's only one way to look at this," Brett said.

"How's that?" Nick asked.

"It's a bad end to a good week."

"How is that good?" Nick asked.

"You still have a lot to be grateful for. You got your dad in Transitions, you received an anonymous gift and Ally's back for all the right reasons. That's three things to be thankful for right there."

Ally remained silent and continued to gaze out the window.

Nick was still steaming. "You'd think Sam would remember where he came from and how you advance in the advertising business.

Before you start your own agency, you move around—that's all Ally did and—"

"Maybe that's what we should do," Ally said.

"Keep moving around?" Brett asked.

"No. Start our own agency."

Nick looked at her. "Are you serious?"

"Dead serious. We have the talent. In this room, we have a creative director, an art director, and a senior copywriter. All we need is someone to handle accounts."

"That's starting pretty small," Brett said.

Nick jumped in. "Everybody starts small. We would be no different than any other agency startup."

"Except, possibly more talented," Ally said.

"You know, this is something we really should think about," Brett added. "Besides—"

"Think about it," Nick said. "We're young now. We have the experience now. And how long do we want to work for Sam Morris?"

"We need to put a plan together," Ally said. "Besides, I've already made one major decision for our agency. Thought I should get it out of the way up front."

A smile slowly spread across both men's faces.

"We're listening," Brett said. "What decision have you already made?"

Ally's eyes contained a glint of mischief. "I think the name Grant, Stevens & Conway has a nice ring to it."

"Close, but I like Stevens, Grant & Conway," Brett said.

"Look, it's late," Nick said. "We can have this discussion later. For now, let's plan on meeting at the lake house tomorrow night at six for a cookout on my patio. And by the way, you guys got it all wrong. It's going to be Conway, Stevens & Grant."

CHAPTER

Later that night, as Nick drove to the lake house for the weekend, balmy breezes wafted through Ally's hair. During the 90-mile drive, their conversation ran the gamut. They continued to toy with the idea of an agency startup, they discussed what their relationship would look like now, and how they would share the news with his father.

Before arriving at the lake house, they stopped for dinner at Tuscany, Ally's favorite restaurant in Lake Geneva. Ally ordered the Lemon Pepper Whitefish. Nick opted for Mahi Mahi. The ate on the patio, in the quietness of the late summer night. Ally told Nick how she ended her relationship with Ron. Nick uncharacteristically did not ask questions or press for details. Instead, he found solace in the simple fact that he was Ally's choice, and she made that choice without his influence or interference.

Following dinner, they made the short drive to the lake house.

Ally settled into her room and then curled up on the love seat in the living room as Nick grabbed two wine glasses. He poured the wine, handed her the glasses, and opened a window to let in the balmy night air before sitting next to her on the love seat. They discussed his father's rehab, their career direction, and their future together.

"How do you think tomorrow will go when you tell your father about the anonymous gift?" she asked.

"How can he not be happy? Some foundation or wealthy Chicagoan essentially stepped up and said, 'I got your back.'"

"How do you think he'll feel about you and me being back together?"

"Are you kidding? He's the one that told me to go after you. And he said something else."

"What?"

"Don't mess this up."

Ally laughed. "Really? You know, I really like this guy." She slid under his arm so she could snuggle up to him. He pulled her close. She looked into his eyes. He returned her gaze and slowly kissed her, then again and again.

Nick felt his pulse quicken at the thrill of having her so close. He gently nudged her still closer, his arm encircling her now with his chin resting on her head as he held her. He closed his eyes and felt the love he once had for her stir his heart again. Something about this moment felt so right. He knew it was more than his love for her. More than his building passion. He thought for a moment. *Is this what forgiveness feels like?*

She gently withdrew so she could see his face. "When I came here to see you on your birthday last week and we talked on the patio, why didn't you ask me to stay? Why didn't you tell me you loved me then? And why did you let me go?"

"Other than being stupid?"

She smiled. "Other than being stupid."

"I thought I had done enough to confuse you about your feelings for me—and for Ron. I had done enough to complicate your life, to hurt you, to mess things up. I didn't think I deserved you and I thought that maybe Ron was better *to* you and *for* you and you just didn't know it because I was in the way. I let you go so you could see clearly."

"Why did your father get involved?"

"He obviously cares for you. He called me after you stopped to see him. He asked me if I love you."

"And you said?"

"I said I did, and he said then go after her."

"So, you came after me?"

"Yeah, but don't get all mushy about it."

"But it's romantic. Did he say anything else?"

"One more thing."

"What?"

"He said when I let you go, I chose who you should love. He said that I shouldn't choose for you. You should choose for yourself."

"Smart man."

"That's why I came after you. To tell you how I felt, to put myself out there, and to let you choose for yourself."

"I chose you." Her tone was tender. "We have to work through some stuff, but I think we can do it because I believe in you—and I believe in *us*."

"I believe in *us*, too."

"You know, it sounds like you have a pretty good father."

"We've got some tough stuff to work through, too."

"Hey, it's a start. Maybe all relationships that endure start slowly." Ally kissed him on the cheek. "I'm tired. It's been a long emotional week. I'm going to bed."

"Good night."

"Good night," she said with a gentle smile. "Hey, if you think about it, our relationship officially begins again tomorrow."

"Not today?"

"We agreed to move forward together today. We begin again tomorrow."

Nick nodded at the thought. "Should I be writing this down?"

"Not a bad idea." She winked. "Who knows, you might want to remember it someday as an anniversary or something."

Saturday morning was another beautiful August day—sunny, breezy, and near 80 degrees with low humidity. Nick called his father and reminded him about the afternoon cookout. "Be sure to invite Gus, too. We've got a couple of things we want to talk to you about."

"We?" Chuck said.

"Ally is here, and I invited Brett from the office and his wife, Karen. Ally and I have some good news to share with you."

"What time should we be there?"

"Five. We'll eat at six. We'll have steaks on the grill, salad, veggies, and a dessert. See ya at five."

Nick let Ally sleep in while he drove into town. He popped into a grocery store and picked up eight-ounce filets, lettuce, salad dressings, asparagus, yellow squash, and red, yellow, and green peppers, a small cake, and vanilla ice cream.

As he drove, home he reflected on how different his life was from a year ago—no Ally, no sense of purpose in his life, no hope to restore his relationship with his father, no chance of getting him into rehab, and certainly no faith in God. All of that was changing now. And he was connecting the dots between faith and forgiveness and the role it played in restoring his family. In the past, faith was something for everybody else. It never made sense to him. Faith was too impersonal, impractical, and undefinable. Faith defied reason. Now, it was starting to gel. He still needed to figure out how to apply it to everyday life. *Brett can help with that.*

When he arrived back at the lake house, Ally had already showered and had breakfast.

"Want to go for a walk on the shore path?" she asked.

"Sure, I'd like that."

As they strolled, they talked about the precious moments of their former relationship and how to rekindle them. After making their way out to the point, they returned to the lake house, packed a small lunch, and took the boat out for a romantic afternoon on the lake.

Just before five o'clock, Chuck and Gus arrived early for dinner. Nick was cleaning the grill while Ally was cutting veggies and making a salad in the kitchen.

Ally greeted them warmly at the back door. "Hey, Chuck. Hey, Gus. How are you guys?"

"You're back! So good to see you, Ally." Chuck gave her a bear hug.

"Hey, there girl." Gus knew his place and was content to live in the background.

"Nick is out on the patio cleaning the grill," Ally said. "Let's join him."

As they stepped out onto the patio, Ally pointed out the coolers where they could help themselves to bottled water or soft drinks. Nick joined them near the fire pit.

"Hey, Dad. Hey, Gus."

"Hi, Nick," his father said warmly.

"Hi, Nicky," Gus said. "You got a nice place here."

"Thanks. I'll put the steaks on soon. Before Brett and Karen arrive, I want to share some good news with you. First, let me state the obvious. Ally and I are back together."

Chuck nodded and smiled. "I can live with that."

"Thanks, Chuck," Ally said. "I understand you had a lot to do with it."

"I just didn't want him to mess up." Chuck looked at Nick. "Heaven knows you've seen me mess up enough in my life. Don't follow in my footsteps."

"We both made our share of mistakes, Dad. You're not alone in this."

"Welcome to the human race." Gus put things into perspective. "Don't know many folks who haven't made mistakes trying to figure out how to live this life."

Nick motioned for them to sit in the deck chairs that surrounded the fire pit. "There's something else we have to tell you, Dad. Tom Sullivan, my client contact at Transitions, informed me that they received an anonymous gift in your name that will cover your initial treatment, so you won't have any out-of-pocket expenses. Insurance is no longer a problem."

Chuck's bit his lip and looked down. "What? When? Who would do that for me? I don't even know anyone in Chicago?"

"Dad, this could've happened through several channels or foundations in Chicago that donate to hospitals. The point is not how it happened, but that it did happen. Now we can proceed with your rehab on schedule as planned."

Ally was radiant. "Chuck, isn't this wonderful news?" The elder Conway put his face in his hands, probably moved by the thought that someone, anyone, would care enough about his life—his often-wasted life, to give him another shot at redeeming it.

Chuck's voice cracked when he spoke. "Thank God for second chances." He turned to Nick and Ally and extended his right hand. "Thank you for all you've done for me. I don't deserve it—any of it."

Nick pushed Chuck's hand to the side and hugged his father like never before. As he squeezed tighter, he felt his father respond in kind and remembered something Gus said. "When you come to know who your father really is, you'll know he's worth saving." It all fell into place for Nick now. He knew they had a tough journey ahead but he also knew that, for the first time in his life, he loved his father, and he was prepared to go the distance with him, no matter how long the road.

"Hey, save one of those for me," Ally said and hugged Chuck before asking him to help her move the place settings from the kitchen to the patio table. Nick wondered if she was trying to prevent a potentially awkward moment between a father being vulnerable with his son. It would be just like her.

Ally glanced over her shoulder as she walked with Chuck toward the house. "Nick, I think we're ready to preheat the grill."

"Let me fire it up. Say, Gus, you got a minute?"

A speedboat skipped across the lake in front of them as they headed for the grill.

"This is an incredible view of the lake, Nicky."

"Yeah, it is, isn't it? Say, speaking of incredible, isn't it incredible how my dad is so willing to finally get help at Transitions after all these years?"

"It's something."

"You know, Tom Sullivan at Transitions said a number of foundations could have stepped up to provide this anonymous gift to cover Dad's rehab expenses."

"I imagine there's lots of foundations that do nice things for sick people."

Nick opened the grill lid, turned the valve on the propane tank, set the dial on the grill, and pressed the igniter. He heard the burner ignite. He turned on the two remaining dials and heard them crack as he closed the lid. "On the other hand," he continued, "I'm sure there's plenty of wealthy individuals in Chicago who often come forward and make contributions to hospitals and addiction recovery centers like Transitions to help people like my dad—you know, in honor of a loved one who passed."

"I imagine that's true, too."

"You know what impresses me most, Gus?"

"What's that?"

"There are also people who come forward who are not wealthy and yet donate a considerable amount of their personal savings to help a friend in need. You know, life-long friends."

"I imagine there's people like that in the world, too." Gus scratched the back of his neck.

"Do you know any of those kinds of people, Gus?" Nick asked as the grill heated up.

The old man stared out at the horizon and watched a sailboat glide across the water. "Did you say that gift was anonymous?"

"Yeah. Why?"

"I imagine the donor would like to keep it that way then, don't you?"

Nick smiled and nodded. "I suppose you're right."

Gus pointed to the grill. "Say, when you cook those steaks, I like mine well done." He turned and headed back to the house.

When Nick returned to the kitchen, Brett and Karen had arrived and were introducing themselves to Chuck and Gus. He waved a greeting, grabbed the plate of filets, and returned to the grill. Ally and Karen set out the veggies and the hors d'oeuvres and led the group out to the patio table to munch and enjoy the view on a perfect summer day.

The filets began to sizzle on the grill and Nick looked out over the water, then surveyed the five people who graced his patio. As they talked and laughed among themselves, he felt like he had a family again. His relationship with Ally was a work in progress yet headed toward full restoration. His bond with Brett and Karen had transitioned into a deep friendship. His admiration of Gus for his commitment to his father was profound. Yet, most of all, his love for his father, although under construction, was finally genuine.

This all began with two simple acts; an act of faith and an act of forgiveness.

As he flipped the filets and listened to the muted conversation across the patio, he realized that, from the beginning, Brett was right. If you look for God, you can catch a glimpse of him actively at work in your everyday life. A grateful smile slowly formed across his lips as he watched a seagull circle over the lake against a cloudless blue sky.

CPSIA information can be obtained
at www.ICGtesting.com
Printed in the USA
LVHW092350130219
607515LV00001B/14/P